GHOSTS AND PHANTOMS I

A ROLLIE KEMP NOVEL

WILLIAM BYRON HILLMAN

APPRECIATION

Thank all the brave men who work at home, and more so to all the women homemakers who put up with men like me 24/7. Your tolerance goes beyond reason.

I want to thank my friends who work as legitimate lawyers striving to help others, my buddies with the FBI, CIA, Secret Service and Homeland Security and others in law enforcement that opened hearts and minds and shared so much with me. Your time and efforts are appreciated as is your protection and the risks you take in protecting all of us. You are the true sense of what Pay Forward stands for.

Most of all I want to thank and acknowledge and select group of my friends and colleagues, and you know whom you are that have been blessed with financial wealth. The art of giving, sharing and helping those in need is immensely appreciated and you're remaining anonymous makes the gift all the more special. You are the engine that quietly keeps hope alive. May I thank you for those who do not know whom you are?

Always For
My Dianne.

CONTENTS

BEYOND THANK YOU

For the men and women who risk their lives so we can live ours.

Prologue

The computer chirp woke her from a sound sleep. She crawled from beneath a white, down-filled comforter and staggered to the computer desk. She opened the laptop, went to Yahoo, and navigated to her personal account. Her password was entered. Email opened. She found one message, addressed to Watcher. The subject was Engagement. The message read, Terms accepted. Wire transfer done. Viewing today at the Pink Palace. Travel forecast for tomorrow morning is perfect. Please R.S.V.P. She stared at the computer screen for a moment, then typed Will Attend, and clicked the send button. It was confirmed. Payment had been made. All that was left -- check out Louis Baxter in the afternoon, and kill him the following morning.

It felt good to be a blond again. Money couldn't buy a better wig. She parked in a cul-de-sac south of Sunset, across the street from Louis Baxter's house. A map of Los Angeles spread over her dashboard. To anyone passing, she was just another dumb blond who got lost. Baxter lived in a neighborhood of curving roads that bled into canyons leading to God knows where. Pacific Palisades could be confusing to anyone. Without looking up from the map, the Mercedes S65 was spotted in her peripheral vision. The slick AMG model turned east on Sunset Boulevard just as a mail truck pulled up next to her car. Damn! Through the open door, the over-friendly postal carrier was all smiles. Annoyed, she watched the Mercedes disappear.

"You look lost," he said.

The Watcher looked up from the map as bangs from her hairpiece fluttered over her contact-colored green eyes. "I can't seem to find Beverly Hills on this map." She gave him her cutest, most innocent smile. She couldn't blow this guy off. It might stir up concern. "It is around here, isn't it?" Her southern drawl inflated.

"Sort of," he answered. "Where in Beverly Hills are you headed?"

She scrambled, pretending to look on the seat for something. "The invitation said it was being held at The Pink Palace."

"Ah, The Beverly Hills Hotel." He pointed right. "Just follow Sunset, that's the street right there. About ten miles or so up the road you will see the hotel grounds on your left. The whole place is done in pink, so it'll be easy to spot."

"Oh, thank you. I've been driving around for over an hour looking for it."

"It's easy to get lost down here." An awkward moment passed. "Well, have a good time." He drove to the corner and turned left. She watched him disappear into traffic, angrily tossed the map to the floor, turned right and sped after the Mercedes.

Her Audi A8 weaved in and out of traffic and caught up with the Mercedes in front of the UCLA campus. A steady stream of student vehicles poured onto Sunset, snarling traffic in both directions. Baxter's Mercedes was about ten cars in front of her. His wife of thirty years was in the car with him. The woman didn't cause the problem, and wouldn't pay for his indiscretions. Baxter had dirty hands with his own people. Louis Baxter was a Persian cat who ate the Parakeet, and then gloated on a silk cushion in defiance.

Up the driveway of the Beverly Hills Hotel, The Watcher pulled in behind the Mercedes. She couldn't take her eyes off Baxter as he came around and opened the door for his wife. Louis Baxter looked exactly like the photo they emailed to her. He was fifty-four, balding, overweight, and stumpy. The tailored suit couldn't hide his imperfections. The Valet drove the Mercedes off, and another young kid appeared at her Audi door. He opened it, smiled, and couldn't take his eyes off her long, shapely legs. She reached out and extended her hand to him, allowing the dress to slip away. She thought the kid would melt. He eagerly took her hand, and helped slide her from the soft leather interior. She leaned close to the kid and whispered in his ear.

"Park it close, so I won't have to wait very long to retrieve it?" She handed him a fifty.

"Sure," The kid's face went crimson as he pocketed the bill.

"I don't know if I'm going to enjoy this or not."

5

"I'll have your car waiting right up front, just in case." He gave her his best smile. "When you leave, just ask for Kerry."

"I'll do that, Kerry." It was always the same, guys were easy, when they thought with other parts of their body. "You're very sweet." Not really. He would fantasize about her later, but her car would be first in line – ready when she needed it.

She followed a group into the lobby. Among the guests gathering to enter the Crystal Ballroom, were the Baxters, and a dozen or so women dressed like she was -- black, tight fitting décolleté dress, voluptuous figures and spike heeled shoes. She fit right in. A casual stroll took her into the Polo Lounge. The carpets, wall-coverings, and much of the décor were done in various shades of pink, magenta and pinkish purples. She sat at the bar and ordered a Rusty Nail. The bartender gave her a curious look, observed her beauty, and plunging neckline in one quick take.

"Here for the wedding announcement?" He asked while making her drink.

"Yeah. Perhaps that," she glanced at the drink, "will help me get through it."

He nodded. "Know what you mean."

She placed a twenty on the bar. "You won't get upset if I take that with me, will you?"

"Knock yourself out."

He took the twenty and turned to mix other drinks. She picked up the glass, holding the pinkish napkin beneath it, and found her way into the Crystal Garden. There was levitation in the Watcher's steps. The bartender, and most of the men in her immediate area were watching her. She loved to tease. The garden brimmed with exotic flowers, tropical plants and illuminated curving walkways. French doors were open, leading into the Crystal Ballroom. What started as a small group had grown to hundreds. Most milled around aimlessly, killing time until it was possible to slip away unnoticed. Single girls roamed the area, trying to hook up with anyone who looked powerful. It was a typical Hollywood crowd. Appearances and the need to be seen outweighed the boredom of attendance. Women wore expensive gowns. Some covered neck to shoes while others where low cut and revealing. Men dressed any way they felt comfortable, suits, jeans, turtlenecks, and sport coats. Diamonds and Rolex watches were everywhere. Most fringe Hollywood players couldn't afford a genuine Rolex, so they wore the next best thing – a knockoff. Unfortunately, many of the replica watches looked as phony as they were.

A musical group played smooth jazz from the built in stage, and couples danced. Louis Baxter sat at a table facing the dance floor. One of the men sitting at the table looked familiar. She drifted about sipping her drink, and smiled until her cheeks hurt. The guy sitting with Baxter was unmistakably a cop. There was something about all cops movements that gave them away. They moved, watched people, and kept hidden secrets in their eyes that most couldn't hide. This cop was dressed to perfection, threads no cop could afford without some third-party incentives. On his right, sat another man who was clearly there to protect. The suit couldn't hide his bulging muscles and thick neck. She kept her distance, standing off in the corner. She wasn't there to kill him yet. She came to watch. The location had to be perfect, and she'd already discounted his home. Too much security, and too many men willing to die for him. She'd seen enough and set her glass down. The exit was just beyond the rest room, which she needed to visit.

Returning to the ballroom head down, The Watcher hoped to duck out without being seen. She walked swiftly and bumped into Louis Baxter. He was standing right in front of her.

"Have we met?" His voice was smooth and polished. He offered his hand, and she took it.

"Megan Ward," The Watcher slurred without missing a beat. "And no, I don't believe we've had the pleasure." This was the ultimate tease. Adrenaline gushed through her veins. Music from the ballroom drifted, and he held her gaze. His smile was captivating and radiated confidence. If he only knew!

"Dance?" He held out his arms.

"Will you wife care?"

"What she doesn't know won't hurt a bit. C'mon, come to Louie's arms."

The one dance that should never have taken place occurred. Louis Baxter drew her into his arms, pulled her against his fat, chubby body, and glided up the way emulating Fred Astaire. Baxter, however, had no rhythm and couldn't dance. She stumbled, behaving like a drunk. Louis held her tight and looked into her eyes. He didn't recognize her. Had no idea she killed his brother three years earlier, and certainly no inkling he was next. Electricity overwhelmed the impulsive moment. Baxter stopped to catch his breath, and she found her drink right where she left it. He held her too long, and too close. His chubby little fingers started dancing on her back, crawling beneath the fabric covering her breast. His breath was atrocious, so she spilled her drink on his shirt. He backed away.

"You little slut! Look what you've done."

She giggled. "I think I'm drunk." She giggled more and moved closer to him. "Wanna try again?"

"Get away from me." He glared at her, and then stormed off in the direction of a rest room.

Her teacher, Sonny Harris would've been proud. He taught her not to think victims were people. They were simply prey. She was the hunter, and they were the departeds. Sonny taught her discipline. Each job was a covenant, and accepting it was a symbol of one's honor. The job required skill, a life without conscience, and the need to be a perfectionist. He instructed her, and she mastered the profession like a brain surgeon perfected his techniques. Sonny never got caught by the authorities because he remained focused. In twenty, years, Sonny never made a mistake that would come back to haunt him. He had four rules. First, never take time to recognize the contract. Second, locate the target and terminate life quickly. Third, leave nothing behind, and last -- never expose whom you are to a potential witness.

Coming home alone was the best decision of the night. The showerhead manipulated the spray, forcing tiny streams of hot pellets to massage her body. It didn't replace the expertise of Sonny's hands, but it came close. The heat soaked into her pores, and rinsed the anxiety of taking leave of one's senses. The process of cleansing mistakes created a calm, as did watching the bubbles emerge in circular motions before they disappeared down the receptacle of filth. She wrapped her long brown hair in a towel, climbed into the fluffy white robe she had borrowed from the Waldorf Astoria in New York City, and opened a can of ginger ale to settle her stomach. Her condo was bland. Had no personality, no feminine or masculine touches. The pictures on the wall were department store bought. Nowhere in the house were items of a personal basis displayed. The atmosphere was abandoned as if no one lived there at all. She kept it that way in case the need for a sudden move came up.

The Watcher retrieved a silver metal briefcase from a closet in the hallway. Placed on top of the desk next to the computer, she unlocked the combination, snapped open the latches, removed a GSP cell phone, and 9mm Glock from within. Once a decision was made, they never changed their mind. They gave her time to assess the situation, and if she didn't receive a cancellation email – it was a done deal. No one knew her true identity. She was The Watcher. They knew Sonny taught her, nicknamed her The Watcher, and that was good enough. She conquered the art of disguises, moved gracefully around the country, and gained the reputation of being the best female contract player ever. In-between contract obligations, she lived a normal life. She even held a job, albeit part time, and was the life of many parties.

No time for sleep. She dressed in all black, tennis shoes, T-shirt and jeans. She slipped a black baseball cap on backwards and tucked her brown hair beneath it. She called her Swiss bank and confirmed the wire transfer. One hundred thousand dollars had been wired earlier in the day. She deleted the call. The remnants of the crowd were long gone. Like a panther in the forest, electrodes danced throughout the Watcher's body. Feeling energetic and alert, she checked the load in her 9mm Glock and tucked it into her purse. The surge was phenomenal.

She wasn't sure if Baxter knew how to handle the throbbing S65 AMG Mercedes, but she couldn't take the chance he didn't. The two hundred thousand dollar car was remarkably fast. If she were to stick with it, she'd need wheels equal to the task. Seen earlier in the day, an over-powered Ford Mustang would be borrowed for the job. Cars with for-sale signs, parked on vacant lots along Pacific Coast Highway, meant the owners weren't close by. The maroon, pavement eating, machine was perfect.

Chapter 1

It was a rough night. Unable to sleep, Rollie Kemp exercised at 5AM, ate breakfast, showered, got dressed and was ready to walk out the door by 6AM. He wasn't due, however, to check in until noon. His work call was 1PM. To calm his nerves, he took a walk in the dense fog that all but made the beach obscure. At 7AM, he vacuumed the floor, washed dishes, sponged the windows, mopped the kitchen title, and ran out of things to do. Every room in the house was immaculate. Every window had been wiped down. It was ridiculous. He sat out on the patio and watched waves roll through the fog and thunder over the sand. He heard seagulls but couldn't see them. He came back into the house, closed the slider and locked it. In the bedroom, he caught his reflection in the full-length mirror. He looked sloppy in the ill-fitting suit, and decided to change. What the hell was he wearing a suit for? He already had the job, so there was no need to impress anyone, not to mention the suit was perfect for attending a funeral. He climbed out of the tailored material, tucked everything neatly in the closet, and put on black jeans. A cream crew neck T-shirt looked good, as did a pair of well-used dark brown loafers. He finished by donning a multicolored sport coat, and stood before the mirror again. This time, he laughed out loud. He was worse than any women he'd ever met. A glance at his watch created a road map of lines that creased the forehead of his handsome face. It was only 8:30, so he turned the TV on to kill time. It didn't work, so he turned it off, and reread the script with his two lines.

The layer of dense fog continued to hang over the Malibu coastline and curled into the Santa Monica Mountains like a silk blanket. An ambulance siren screeched to a nearby catastrophe and Rollie incessantly felt the muscles in his stomach tremulously ripple. At 9:45 he got up. Normally, at this hour, there would've been plenty of time to drive to Universal Studios. He marveled at the pressure swirling within his head. A frustrated, wannabe actor, he knew one day he'd get a role with actual dialog, and it finally happened. He wanted to be at the studio early, and there was no way he'd be late for his first speaking part. He listened to the weather and traffic reports on KNX radio, discovered there was stop-and-go traffic on the 10 Freeway, and decided to go out of his way. Drive north on PCH, cross over Malibu Canyon Road, and catch the 101 into Burbank. It was longer, but at ten in the morning no one would be going toward the valley. It was miles out of the way, but ironically much faster.

Rollie turned off Pacific Coast Highway and headed east toward the San Fernando Valley. The moment he turned a maroon Mustang, with dark tinted windows, cut lanes right in front of him. Cars slid all over the place trying to avoid an accident. The Mustang darted from the wrong lane back to the right one and slid to a stop on a lot facing PCH. The reckless driver trapped Rollie in a bottleneck mess. Traffic came to a dead stop, and he was boxed in. Vehicles backed up the canyon as far as Rollie could see. Los Angeles was full of road-rage, but this was absurd. Rollie's knuckles tighten. His temper flared its ugly head again. Rollie glanced over his shoulder at the Mustang, and if he had the time or this was any other day but today, he would've gotten out, and punched the Mustang driver's lights out. The guy had to be crazy to do what he did. Rollie watched the speed demon climb out of the Mustang, throw a look in his direction, taunting him, and then hustle off to a dark blue Audi. The guy looked like a typical punk teenager, dressed in all black, baseball cap on backwards and dark sunglasses. The racer took another hard look at Rollie, got in the Audi, and drove off. Rollie's hands formed fists of anger. He jerked his sunglasses off, and watched the Audi disappear in traffic. There was nothing he could do about it. He was in the middle of a traffic jam, and would be late for work if he got into a chase. Instead, his mind went to acting. He took a deep breath. The studio, and a job he'd waited years for were all that mattered.

The fog layer vanished when he passed Mulholland Highway, and the brownish dry hillsides came into view. The air thickened as he left behind the crisp illusion the ocean offered. Yellowish smog replaced the overcast. Vehicle exhaust fumes raked an already putrid environment, casting off air as thick as mud. Traffic thinned out, and Rollie forgot about the road-rage episode. He drove without incident through the canyon. The morning rush hour on the 101-Freeway was over. He ambled into Burbank, took the Lankershim exit, and drove to the guardrail at Universal Studios back gate. The guard inside the booth was all business. He was a short, thinly built black man in his late fifties. His gray hair was closely cropped, his uniform dark blue, starched crisply, and fit to perfection. He wore square-rimmed glasses. The name tag above his breast pocket said Jackson. A clipboard jumped into his hands when he looked down at Rollie. Rollie loved the professional look, and hoped if he ever played a guard in a film or TV show – he'd look as good as Jackson did.

"Name?"

"Rollie Kemp."

The guard adjusted his glasses, scanned the list on the clipboard and nodded. "You know where you're going?"

"No, Mister Jackson, it's my first time here."

The guard nodded again. He gestured with his head, "Park over there on the left side. I'll have a production assistant pick you up. Wait by your car, and don't wander."

The guard lifted the electronic rail and Rollie drove over the gravel-covered parking lot where hundreds of cars had arrived before him. He found a space at the farthest end of the lot, and before he could lock the car an electric golf cart pulled up.

The driver was a young blond-haired girl with perfect teeth. "I'm a PA. My name's Tiler Adams and you must be, ah," fidgeting, she scanned her clipboard and found his name, "Rollie Kemp?"

He was already a wreck, too frazzled to notice her beauty. "That's me."

"Hop in." She smiled, but he didn't see that either. "You're early, but that's a good thing. Let's get you to wardrobe, and then I'll take you over to the stage." The shapely twenty-something, Tiler was pretty, in the-girl-next-door kind of way. The moment his butt hit the bench seat, she roared off toward the studio soundstages. Rollie hung on for dear life.

Rollie Kemp held his arms out for Maggie, the wardrobe lady, to slip on a worn leather jacket. It was too tight, so she handed him another. The second was a perfect fit. Maggie straightened Rollie's collar and stood back to give him the head-to-toe look. She carefully ran her hands over his back and brushed his buttocks. Rollie looked at his reflection in the full-length mirror. He looked good, and then he caught the older woman eyeing him like a hungry cat. She probably thought any man was drop-dead gorgeous if he paid a little attention to her. "So you do this all the time, whaddya think?" Yeah, the ladies loved a big tall guy, but the look Maggie was giving Rollie was new. She was ready to strip his clothes off and pounce.

She stepped back, flushing. "You're tall, lean, masculine in a Richard Burton, Russell Crowe sort of way. I say, Rollie Kemp, you not only look good, you look great. What are you, about six two – and, ah, twenty-six?"

"Close. I'm six-three and thirty-two."

"Late start but it won't matter. You're very different from anyone I've ever laid my eyes on. You have it all." Maggie was all but drooling at him.

"I bet you say that to all the guys, right?"

She blushed. "Get out of here before you're late."

Rollie felt ten feet tall. After attempts at college, the police academy, and months of mundane jobs delivering pizza, loading trucks, driving cabs, and even working in several bars -- he maintained patience while waiting for his agent to call. And call he did. He landed Rollie a speaking role in a major TV show, Over the Clouds. He had two lines. Two! Hallelujah! He gave

Maggie a nod and a hint of a Rollie Kemp smile. He knew she loved to touch men and had a hard time keeping her hands off his body. Harmless, Maggie was one of those love-gone-bad divorcees who, in her mid-forties, felt old age roaring toward her. Her short-cropped blond hair, the tight fitting jeans, and low-cut blouse didn't hide the retread look on her face. The makeup was caked and couldn't cover the inevitable crow's feet around the eyes, or the double chin that was starting to sag. Yep, all in all, she was harmless.

"Thanks, Maggie."

Outside, the same production assistant that picked him up in the parking lot waited in the golf cart. She whisked him off toward stage twelve. As they pulled up outside the massive soundproof doors, a few extras and day players scrambled inside ahead of them.

"Thanks for the lift." Rollie was still too nervous to give her a second look.

"Don't mention it. C'mon, I'll show you where to go."

The moment Rollie and the production assistant entered, the red light started turning. Not just at Universal Studios -- everywhere in Hollywood the spinning red light meant you stayed outside or shut up until it was turned off. They were either filming or ready to film, and if someone opened the door it probably ruined the shot. A wasted shot cost many their jobs. Inside, Tiler pointed to a man standing right in front of the camera, looking over script notes.

Rollie nodded at Tiler and then strolled over. The director was much smaller than Rollie, with blond shaggy hair, a cocky attitude, very skinny, and well dressed in typical Hollywood fashion. Three hundred dollar shoes, no socks, a silk shirt, and worn jeans that looked expensive and fit like tailor-made goods. From a distance, the guy looked like a twenty-year-old kid, but up close Rollie discovered he was late forties.

He looked up as Rollie approached, "You Rollie Kemp?"

"Yeah, I am."

"I'm Diz O'Lare, your director." They shook hands while he looked Rollie over, nodding. "Yeah, Maggie's done it again. You look great."

"Thanks"

"I need for you to be cool, Rollie. There are no small roles, understand?"

"No small roles, of course, I knew that." Small roles were for star-struck dopes like him, and leading roles with lots of lines were for name players and stars. "I'm your guy," Rollie said.

"Good. What's your first line?"

Rollie spit it out, "I came as fast as I could get here, doctor,"

The director nodded. "You do know how to hit a guy and make it look like you really belted him, right?"

"Sure," Rollie lied. The people he threw punches at, remembered getting hit.

"Have you thrown punches before?" Diz sat in his director's chair and waited. He raised an eyebrow that sent jagged lines throughout his face -- deep crevices that exposed the age on his ageless face. The luminosity in his gray eyes sparkled. "Screen punches?"

"I trained in New York." Rollie answered. He knew how to throw a punch with the best of them. On the streets in Brooklyn, Rollie learned to punch first, and ask questions later.

O'Lare lifted his chin. "Show me?"

18

Standing back, Diz O'Lare held out his well-manicured hands, taunting. Rollie shrugged, snapped a quick left jab, avoided Diz's outstretched hands, and nailed the director right in the nose. The punch dropped O'Lare to the floor as though his legs had been chopped off. An instant hush descended over the cast and crew members. Rollie wanted to say whoops.

"What the hell did you do that for?" O'Lare grabbed at his bloody nose and shot to his feet. Blood dripped all over his deerskin Bally shoes and his hands waved in frantic motions, flailing wildly. He calmed his head jerked to an unasked question, and then his hands stilled at his side. Al asked you to show me, not hit me, asshole." His voice was calm, his pronunciation slow and precise. "What is this, your first job on a film?"

"No," Rollie answered, stepping back in a threatening stance. He thought the guy would punch back, but he didn't. He couldn't volunteer it was his second acting job. The first was as an extra when he got to join SAG, so he kept quiet, and waited for the director to vent.

O'Lare caught a reflection of himself in a mirror the makeup guy was holding, and started laughing. His smashed nose looked as though a hefty fat beetle had been squashed on the tip. "Damn!" He stared at his nose, and then to the cast and crew, he said, "Will you look at this?"

They all did, and some smiled while others nodded. No one said anything.

"It doesn't look that bad." Rollie didn't know what else to say.

The guy's nose looked awful and was probably broken.

"The cast will love this," O'Lare said. He turned to Rollie. "See you on the set, slugger."

Diz was one strange dude. He walked to the dressing rooms with his staff, and Tiler led Rollie off to wonderland. He entered the hospital set where he met Luke Waters, the actor playing opposite him. Luke, a famous movie star, had fallen from grace until the television show resuscitated his career. Even though, Luke was a complete jerk to everyone, Rollie was still in awe standing next to him. The star always played a tough guy, but Rollie knew right off the body language spelled wimp with a capital W. In New York, a guy stood with a stiff back, rigid arms, strong handshake, and stared a man down. A tough guy didn't blink, look down, or deliberately avoid eye contact, but screen-legend bad boy Luke Waters was doing all that and more. When his gaze built enough courage to look at Rollie, a flicker of fear filled his eyes. Rollie swallowed his laughter while the rest of the cast and crew smiled. Even Rollie knew Waters had a reputation throughout the industry of being a complete dick. The star was handsome, almost as tall as Rollie, and firmly built. Luke Waters was rude to everyone, and had a reputation of playing the tough guy. Obviously word got out, behind his back that Rollie was a loose cannon. Rollie relished the thought their scene included a punch.

When Rollie stood toe to toe to rehearse, Luke backed away. "You do know how to throw a stage punch, don't you?" Luke's voice had nervous written on the words.

"Sure, you move left, I throw to my left, and just miss you." For everyone's satisfaction, Rollie faked a punch. He'd watched enough TV shows and knew how it was done.

The other cast members gathered behind the crew.

"I move left," Luke repeated, "and you throw left, good. That's good. Okay, let's shoot this scene," Luke Waters said in his phony screen voice. He cleared his throat, loudly, deliberately close to the microphone.

The sound man sat up and pulled off his earphones. "What the hell was that for?"

Luke didn't bother looking in his direction. "Just wanted to make sure you're awake. Don't want you to miss anything." He grinned at the crew, and O'Lare. "I'm ready now."

O'Lare couldn't repress his excitement. "Roll the camera."

"We have speed!" the sound man shouted.

O'Lare quietly said, "Action."

Rollie dashed in and spit out his line. "I came as fast as I could get here, doctor. How is she?"

Luke Waters lowered his gaze to the floor, shifted his weight, and said his line with great passion, "She passed on about an hour ago." His sorrowful eyes looked up at Rollie with great sympathy. He raised and lowered his shoulders sympathetically.

Then came Rollie's big moment. He belted out his second line, a gut-wrenching scream. "No!" He glared at Luke Waters with all the hatred he could muster. "You killed her!" He ad-libbed a line and watched the surprise in Luke's face. Damn it felt good. Then, without warming, he threw a punch to his left. Luke Waters ducked right and walked right into it. Bam! Square in the eye. The crushing blow sounded like a watermelon splattering. Luke Waters dropped to the floor faster than the director had, and his eyes welled up with instant tears. He scrambled to his feet and ran off to the makeup guy for touch up. Both the cast and crew laughed. They turned and gave Rollie a hand. Rollie thought it was good, and bowed.

O'Lare shook Rollie's hand, but the director had a mischievous gleam in his eye. "That was great, Rollie, but I'm afraid we'll have to shoot it again."

They shot the scene ten times just to make sure they got one good take. Luke Waters only got hit two more times before he learned to duck left. He seemed to be a good sport about the whole thing, and makeup hid his swollen eye and puffed nose. The director called it a wrap, Luke walked off, and Rollie headed to the dressing rooms to change into his clothes.

On the way, a huge guy dressed in all black joined him. They walked out together, and the big guy followed Rollie all the way to the honey wagon.

"You got a problem?" Rollie asked. Rollie didn't like getting cornered, even though the guy towered over him.

"Name's Drake Fargo."

The big guy had to be six feet six or taller. He extended his beefy hand, and cautiously, Rollie shook it. Fargo was huge, no waist, a barrel chest, handsome worn face, and a head full of black bushy hair. Probably mid-forties.

"Rollie Kemp."

"He's gonna make it hard for you to work on the lot again."

"Who?" Rollie looked around.

"Luke Waters. He doesn't have a sense of humor to match yours, and Diz just pulled your chain. He got a laugh at your expense."

Rollie stared in disbelief. "It was a joke. No, it was an accident. I can't help it if the guy's stupid."

"What else do you work at to make a living?" Fargo asked.

"I'm working on my acting career. It takes time."

Fargo handed Rollie his card. "Keep it in the safe place. In between jobs, if you're looking for something that pays well, and is fun, give me a call."

Rollie read over the card, turned it over to a blank backside, and then looked at the front again. The hair on his arm stood at attention. "You're a private dick?"

"If that's what the card says."

"You want me to work for you?"

"Why not?" Fargo's gaze roamed over the studio lot then came back to Rollie. He was a strange duck with a father-like smile. "This might be exciting, kid, but makin' a living at it sucks you down an endless gutter."

"You sayin' I'm not very good?" Rollie stood rigid.

"I'm sayin' it's a flesh-eatin' business, and it might be fun to complement it with something else you can enjoy. You throw a good punch. Call me if you're interested."

Before Rollie could respond, Fargo walked away. Rollie watched him, shrugged it off, and turned right into Tiler Adams. This time, Rollie took a good look as if he'd never seen her before that moment. Wow, he was stunned he hadn't noticed her before. She had soft blond hair, the bluest of blue eyes, and a smile that could melt steel. On top of that, she carried the innocence of a Southern belle. A look he loved. He had heard from others on the set that she was married or was about to get married, and that put her off limits to everyone.

"Hi," she whispered, blushing in various shades of pinks. "I've been working on the horror film shooting on the next stage, and lost my voice screaming at extras all day. I sound terrible don't I?"

"No, actually it's sexy."

"You think?"

"Yeah." An awkward moment of silence passed. "So, your name is Tiler, right?"

"I'm impressed you remembered my name."

"It's a great name, one that's hard to forget. So, how's married life?"

"Married?" Tiler blushed. "I'm not married. I have yet to find a guy I'd want to date more than once. Who said I was married?"

Rollie shrugged. "I don't remember. I just figured you were with someone, and I'd never interfere with, well, you know?"

"Is that why you haven't called me?" She sounded upset.

"I don't remember getting your number."

Tiler dug into her purse and pulled out a pen and notepad. She jotted down her number and handed it to him. "You do now. Call me sometime. You seem like a nice guy." Her face flushed again. "I gotta go."

Rollie watched her run off, looked at the paper she had given him, noticed she spelled her name T-i-l-e-r, and smiled. He turned to enter the dressing room as Luke Waters drove by in a Porsche 911 Carrera 4S Cabriolet. Luke stopped. His lip was puffy and his eye swollen. He looked dreadful. Damn, Rollie thought, that must hurt like hell.

"You'll regret today." Luke had a hard time talking.

Rollie stared at him. "What's that supposed to mean?"

Luke's upper lip curled back. "You'll see." Tears flushed over the star's eyes. He covered them with a pair of dark sunglasses.

"Luke, listen ..."

"You got nothing to say to me. Nobody humiliates me as you did and gets away with it." He revved the engine, and slowly rolled off, singing over his shoulder, "You'll see."

Chapter 2

The one thing she didn't anticipate was a traffic jam.   Damn fog! It wasn't thick enough to obscure visibility. The guy driving the Infiniti FX saw her. No doubt. Damn him to hell!   She was the Watcher, not the watched.   She had never been made, never! When the catastrophe hit the papers, he'd come forward. They'd have a witness. She stood in the bathroom of her condo, staring in disbelief at her disguised reflection. Of course, no one would know what the Watcher actually looked like, so what the hell was running through her mind?   In the past ten years, she had never deceived herself. The one time she strays from the plan she ends up making a colossal blunder. Why didn't she just shoot his ass?   No, she had to hot-dog it, had to feel the rush. Stupid! They didn't know, but she did. And who was the guy driving the Infiniti? Why did he look familiar?   A gut-feeling rose -- she'd seen him before.

Until she cleaned this up, changes had to be made. A new slate might create a temporary tourniquet, to slow the bleeding. Everything about her demeanor had to change. She'd give herself a makeover, and go back to the bland look. The Audi had to go in storage. She'd activate the office in West Hollywood, and go back to work. Her skin felt cold. She touched her arm, adjusting to the sensation of hungry insects scattering beneath the skin. She knew there were no insects, and yes, she could still rationalize with reality. Yet, the sense of creepy-crawlies beneath her skin felt so real it could drive the mind nuts. Her body felt as though it was being eaten from the inside. It was his fault, but she wouldn't let dad's name to seep into her brain. She was the Watcher, and he was dead! Damn him to an infernal hell.

The Watcher changed into a soft pink strapless dress, donned the black wig with bangs, and drove to the storage lot in Torrance. Traffic was thick as syrup, but the miraculousness of moving parts kept her alive. The only reason she stayed in California was the population. Regardless of the time of the day, there were people. Traffic filled the freeways, bodies moved everywhere you went, expensive cars were plentiful, and the surroundings offered lots of protection when you were on the run. People had no time to examine what others did. They were too busy with themselves.

The storage lot was in the industrial section, west of the 405 Freeway. No one was ever around in the middle of the day, especially at lunchtime. Sprawling factories and office buildings dotted the surrounding landscape. The cement block containers spread over the lot, were large enough to accommodate motor homes, small yachts and automobiles within. They were secure buildings with roll doors, heavy locks, and out of harm's way. She kept all her cars here and rotated them frequently. She decided to leave the Audi A8 behind the smoke-silver Mercedes SL 600 and take the silver Lexus SC. She drove around the storage buildings. The office had a sign on the door, Out to Lunch. No life anywhere. Unseen, she drove out of the storage lot.

Back in the safety of her Hollywood condo, she showered again, changed clothes and checked the computer for emails. She logged into Yahoo email and found one addressed to Watcher. Subject: A Marvelous Day. Message: A good airdrop. Well done. She deleted the message and logged off. She sat at the desk, in the dark, and reviewed her options. Until she received the next contract, there was only one thing to do. The guy driving the Infinity FX could be an eventual problem. The only way to make sure that didn't happen was to dispose of him. Driving on PCH at 10 in the morning meant he lived nearby. If not, he knows someone who does. She didn't get that good a look at him, but still the familiarity sent a chill through her. He was a handsome man in his early thirties with that stupid movie-star look. She remembered his anger. He was smoking rage. Obviously he had lots of violence built up that he wanted to unload on someone. The impression he tossed at her said he wanted to rip her heart out with his bare hands. She wished she could have seen his eyes. Why would a guy wear sunglasses in the fog? She laughed when she realized she too was wearing sunglasses. The merriment faded. First, she'd find out whom he was, watch from a distance, get to know more about him to avoid another mistake, and then -- she'd kill him.

Chapter 3

Rollie stepped from the air-conditioned dressing room, and the late afternoon heat smacked him with a wake up call. Smog, and fumes from L.A.'s overcrowded automotive populace burned his lungs. A constant roar from the nearby freeway, traffic in general, and all the humans that migrated to the coast helped saturate the oxygenation with a putrid yellowish haze. Looking back at the studio, life would continue without his presence. Gone were the golf-cart rides and helpful assistants that greeted his arrival. The job was finished, and he was left to trudge over the steamy asphalt to the gravel parking lot where he left his car. Stars parked underground in a cool setting, but day-players and extras were left to the environment.

In the parking lot, Rollie was about to climb into his car when he saw the reflection of a man behind him. The man was short and stocky. His arms and legs bulged like tree trunks. There was no apparent neck, and a shaved head as round as a bowling ball made him all the uglier. When Rollie turned to face him, the guy curled his upper lip in an attempt to warn of his evil intent. Rollie almost laughed. He grew up with clumsy goofballs like this one, and easily ducked when the man threw a punch. Big Boy staggered from the missed roundhouse and Rollie punched him under his rib cage. He followed that punch up by smacking him in the face with two swift jabs. Something broke, and blood splattered. The man dropped to his knees, grasping his nose.

"Aw jeez," Rollie blurted out. "Look what ya made me do?"

The guy tried to get up, but his legs were noodles. What little balance he had left allowed him to sink into a sitting position. He stared up at Rollie with sad eyes and blood dripping from every orifice on his head.

"Who the hell are you?" Rollie asked while unconsciously clenching his fists. It took everything he had not to hit the rugged lug a few more times, but he looked so pathetic all crumpled on the ground.

"Jake Lintero."

"Why were you tryin' to punch me?"

"I'm Luke Water's bodyguard." Jake was whispering, trying to catch his breath.

"Oh, that explains everything. So you took it upon yourself to punch me?"

"Luke thought it would be a good idea." He winced, holding the side of his head.

"Well that was bright of him. Next time you see him, tell him thanks."

"I think I should go to the hospital," Jake whimpered, "my eye's hurtin' big time."

Rollie took in Jake's face. The swelling had closed one eye, and the other was catching up. "You can't see, Jake. How ya gonna drive?"

"I can make it."

Rollie shook his head as he helped the hefty man to his feet. "Get in my car. I'll take you." Why the hell did he care? He just beat the stuffing out of the guy and now he was helping him, a gesture even his confused mind couldn't comprehend the logic with.

"Thank you." Jake almost started crying. "You're a standup guy, Rollie"

"Yeah, I'll remember that. Just don't get blood on my seat."

While Rollie hung out in the emergency room, he ran into Drake Fargo again. He didn't want conversation, just a bed and some sleep. The all-nighter without sleep was catching up, and coffee played with his nerves. Fargo sat next to him. Neither said a word for an exceedingly long time, and then Rollie spoke without looking at him.

"What are you doing here?"

"I came to see how bad Big Jake was." Fargo sounded distant.

"So how is he?" Rollie asked.

"He's got a concussion."

Rollie turned facing the burly man. "That's all?" He was sure he'd hurt him more than just giving him a concussion. Aw gee, too bad.

Fargo slanted his head, "And a broken nose."

"Then he's okay?" Rollie mysteriously felt relieved. While the eye socket looked grim, it obviously would heal. Every kid he knew growing up had broken their nose at one time or another, so the guy's busted nose was no earth shaking moment. What was everyone so worried about?

"Well, he also got his feelings hurt." Fargo said, toying with his hands.

"Well, golly, ain't that too bad? Maybe next time he'll get his legs broken."

"Have you ever considered attending some anger management?"

Rollie shot to his feet, and Fargo joined him. They stood toe-to-toe, neither giving an inch. Rollie looked into the burly man's eyes, "I don't want to hurt you." He rolled his fists.

Fargo stared down into Rollie's eyes, "Nor do I need to hurt you, kid." He buried both hands into jacket pockets. "You need to get a handle on this before you kill someone."

What am I missing here? Why all the concern about Jake's condition, and my temper?"

"Jake's a friend and your temper got in his way."

"He swung first. What was I supposed to do?"

A smirk cut into Fargo's lips. "You shoulda let him hit you."

"What?" Rollie saw the smirk, and had the urge to go crazy. He caught it. "Okay, I'll play your game. Why should I let some moose hit me?"

"'Cause you deserved it. You hit Luke Waters, didn't ya? Fact is you hit the poor guy several times much to everyone's amusement — including yours." Fargo looked off down the hallway. "If you're gonna come to work for me, kid, ya can't go around punchin' people."

Rollie laughed. "Who said I wanted to work for you?"

"You got a bunch of money stashed?"

"Some, yeah. I got money from an accident and some solid investments to fall back on." He regretted sharing this information the moment it slipped from his mouth. The man was a total stranger, even though it felt as if they'd known each other for a long time.

"That's good you have funds set aside because that means you'll function cheaply."

"Let's get back to why someone would have said I wanted to work for you?"

"You will." Fargo paused, and then explained. "Luke had the casting director who hired you fired. You'll have to wait for Luke to leave the studio before you'll ever work there again. I'm the best option you have. Although your style needs some polish, I rather like you. I'll be seein' ya around. Call me. My cell numbers on the card."

Rollie watched Fargo walk down the hall and enter Big Jake's room. The guy was right. He had to get a grip on his temper. The punch first, and ask questions later crap wouldn't work in Hollywood.

When Rollie got home, he found four messages on his answering machine. The first was from his agent.

"What the hell's a matter with you? Don't ever call Harvey Goldman again, Rollie. Hear me? You're a loose cannon. No, wait! You're a total and complete idiot. You're fired! No client of mine is gonna go around town bustin' balls! A stupid moron! Don't ever call me."

The second was from the production manager on the set.

"Rollie? This is Sam Colt, the production manager on the set you just ruined. Stay off the Universal lot, and consider how lucky it will be not to have been arrested or sued by the studio or Luke Waters."

The third call was his accountant, Shelly Bufko. Her voice was soft, sultry, and an inch short of hilarious. "Rollie pick up! Rollie! You have to call me back, Rollie Kemp. Your taxes are done, and you owe eighteen thousand dollars to the Feds, and six thousand five hundred twelve to the state." She hesitated, her long nails tapping on the receiver. "I don't know why you didn't show up for our drink. And just so you know, my fee for doing the taxes is fifteen hundred 'cause I saved your cute ass a little over five thousand and change. I'd appreciate a call back and a check when you pick up your files. Don't wait too long or you'll have to file an extension, and in a few weeks you'll go into penalty. Oh, and Rollie? You're a jerk!"

Rollie heard the receiver slam down, followed by a loud dial tone.

The fourth call was from Millie Jackson. "Rollie? This is your grandmother, now pick up the phone!" There was a long, silent hesitation. "Okay big shot, you must be working, and if you are you owe me an explanation. If you're out goofing around, don't bother calling me back, I'm not that important." The call ended with a beep.

Rollie glanced at his watch, an vintage Omega Constellation fourteen-caret gold automatic chronometer officially certified, a timepiece given to him by Millie Jefferson, the love of his life. She saved him from going in the wrong direction.

On the table, next to the answering machine, was a videophone. When he moved to California, Millie cried, saying she would never see him again. Before he left Charleston, he bought two videophones -- one for her and the other came with him. He should have called her a couple days earlier but, in all the excitement of his first acting role, he forgot. Now, crushed with guilt, he dialed her number. It rang six times before she finally answered. The video screen, however, remained black.

Millie sounded testy right off, "You're late."

"Hello to you too." He loved their little games. "Turn on the video."

"No! No need to see the face of someone who has little time for an old woman like me."

"Grandma?" There was a note in Rollie's voice, and she picked up on it.

"What?"

"Turn on your video. My hearts aching to see your pretty face."

Suddenly the screen lit up, and there was Millie Jefferson in vivid color. She was an African American, sixties, thin, and ferociously full of vitality and sparkle. Her gray hair was pulled back in a bun, and she wore looped gold earrings. Millie was the first black person Rollie had ever known personally. He witnessed her husband, Clarence, fighting off two guys who were trying to rob him. As they beat on him, Rollie came along, and not only stopped the holdup, but beat the hell out of the two-wannabe crooks. He was fourteen and the two guys he thoroughly blistered and disarmed were in their early twenties. Both ran off to get away from the windmill punches Rollie threw. He and the Jefferson's became friends. Millie would cook for Rollie after his mother passed, and became the grandmother he never had. When Clarence died from a heart attack, Millie gave Rollie the wristwatch. They had no children, and she said Clarence would have wanted Rollie to have it. He promised Millie he would never part with the watch, and, of course, he never would. Every time they talked he offered to bring her to California, and she refused. When his penny stocks turned to pure gold, he found her a little condo in a retirement village along the coast in South Carolina where she still lived. She insisted he keep the condo in his name, so he did, and said it was hers for as long as she lived.

"I almost gave up on you." Millie spouted angrily.

Rollie stared at her image, seeing the warmth and love in her eyes. He marveled at the feeling that washed through him. He thought about love every time he saw her, and realized deep down how much he adored her. "Let's try hi, and how are you first."

She frowned. "Oh, you wanna play that game?"

"Yep."

"Hi, Rollie. Where in the world did you go? Have you become a working actor yet? "

"Hi, grandma. I was out for a little while, and no, I'm not a working actor yet." He couldn't tell her about his day. "So, is my favorite girl taking good care of things?"

"Just fine, sittin' here all day waitin' for a grandson who doesn't care to call me. He must be too busy for an old lady like the one on the other end of your phone."

"Hey, Grandma?"

"You must have the wrong number."

"I love you." Rollie got serious when he touched her face on the screen. "I was sitting here looking at the ocean, and the first thing I thought about was you. It's amazing how much I miss you." He sat back. "You sure look pretty. You get your hair done just for me?"

Millie teared up and sniffled. "Oh, Rollie. You always know the exact right words to say when I scold you." She brushed her hair back.

"You need to come out here to California." Rollie perked up.

"You know I can't fly. I'm afraid of those big things. No, you will have to come here, and you better do it soon."

A concern gushed into his chest. "You okay?"

"I am now. You made my day, Rollie." She blew her nose. "Are you taking good care of yourself?"

"Yes ma'am, just like you taught me."

"I love you too, Rollie. So, big shot, if you missed me enough you would get on one of those big birds and fly here to see me, right?"

"I think I'd like to do that, Grandma. Give me a couple of weeks to get things in order, and promise you'll cook some fried chicken and biscuits?"

"I'd love to cook for you. You comin' alone?"

"Don't know." He realized how good it felt talking to her. "You take care, and I'll call you in a few days, okay?"

"Yep," Millie answered. "By the way, do you have the time?"

"Yes, ma'am, I do." He held the watch up so she could see it. "It runs as good as always."

Her smile lit up the whole screen. "God blesses you, Rollie. I can't wait to see you."

She hung up like she always did. She didn't want to hear anyone say goodbye. She told Rollie saying goodbye was like kicking someone out of your life for good. He glanced at the watch and smiled. A terrible day just turned around. His childhood sucked until Millie came along. His old man beat him and his mother good. He felt guilty not being strong enough to stand up to the old man, and protect his mom. After his pop's life was snuffed out for cheating the people he worked for, his mother moved them to the South, and then grew weaker from the cancer eating her insides. As the disease swallowed the life, she never enjoyed, she had nothing more to offer Rollie. She loathed the life she passed on to him and was sorry not to be able to stick around and help him grow up. When his mother left the earth that caused her such grief, Millie and Clarence came into his life. Millie loved to fuss over him, make sure he had clean clothes and enough food to eat at school so the other kids wouldn't make fun of him being poor. It wasn't that Millie or Clarence were rich -- they were a far cry from having much more than just enough to get by, but had no problem sharing what they had with Rollie.

Thinking about his old man caused the involuntarily clenching of Rollie's fists. His old man deserved a beating Rollie couldn't give him. He could still see him slapping his mother's face. Rollie slammed a fist into his palm. Yeah, he still carried lots of anger around.

Chapter 4

Detective John Rader, a ten year vet in robbery homicide sat with a fresh cup of coffee. His desktop was cluttered with files on one side, and family pictures on the other. There were several shots in single frames of his wife, and three more of his two daughters. One picture had the wife wearing a bikini, coming out of the ocean, offering a million dollar smile. In the second photo, she was pregnant, standing with two little girls. The wife was pretty with an exotic flair. The girls in the photo obviously had their mother's genes. They'd known each other since grade school. She was the only woman he ever dated. She was the love of his life, even though she'd been up all night with morning sickness. Her pregnancy was weird, and off kilter. Her so called morning illness started at midnight, and sometimes lasted the night. She'd eat ice cream or have a Pepsi, and then spend hours tossing it. He was exhausted, and the baby wasn't even born yet. Sleep depraved, the hint of taking a nap seeped into his conscious thoughts. The morning was quiet. The conference room upstairs was empty, and the cot was calling him. He sipped the coffee, and decided to put the lid back on. He would nuke it after his nap. As he rose from the most uncomfortable metal chair on earth, the phone rang. Damn! He snatched angrily at the receiver.

"This is Rader."

"John?"

Rader didn't recognize the voice at first. "Yeah, who's this?"

"Sheriff O'Hara at the sub-station in Malibu."

Now Rader remembered. "How ya been Mike?" It had been a year or two, but Mike O'Hara helped Rader on a case that got his partner killed. Organized crime figures tried to outrun them, and got chased into Rader's Santa Monica domain. They were cornered, and behaving like the crazed animals they were, jumped out of their car shooting. Mike's partner stepped in front of a bullet. O'Hara botched his entrance and faced an inescapable predicament. Rader's timely intervention saved his life. They continued to stay in touch, and on occasion would go out to dinner or barbecue with the family.

"I still miss Bobby, but life goes on." There was a hesitation in Mike's voice. "The reason I called is we're investigating a hit and run up here on Malibu Canyon Road, and I think you guys should come up and take a look."

Rader, with his partner, Frank Mustio, watched the gigantic yellow crane with black spider legs haul wreckage from a narrow fissure off the side of Malibu Canyon Road. The cables laboriously screamed from the weight. The surrounding hillsides splashed smog-damaged chaparral every which way. The once green vegetation was brown and leafless, matching most of the hillsides throughout southern California. Mustio, the shorter of the two walked back to their unmarked sedan and got on the radio.

Rader knew the road was one of the most treacherous around. The constant weaving blacktop was a multiple regeneration of wagon trails cut through the mountains. At various stretches along the journey between the San Fernando Valley and Malibu, the canyon was notorious for accidents. In certain areas, the abrupt drop-off could plunge hundreds of feet. Some of the cliff edges were unguarded, and too often autos flew off into sheer oblivion. He was standing at a particular area referred to by locals as the dead man's curve. The roadway widened into three lanes, chiseled granite on one side, and a sheer drop-off on the other. Unfortunately, the nickname was apropos -- the scene of many previous fatal accidents.

Behind the crane was an array of law enforcement and emergency vehicles. Several black and white's, fire trucks, an ambulance, the coroner's wagon and three unmarked cop cars. Overhead, a police helicopter shared airspace with several local TV news choppers. People swarmed the area, waiting for the ME to complete examination of the body while others searched every nook and cranny for evidence from the accident. Traffic was backed up in both directions, Mulholland Drive to the north, and south all the way down to Pacific Coast Highway.

Sheriff Mike O'Hara, a tall, strapping redhead with lots of freckles greeted Rader. They shook hands as the enormous crane set what was left of the black Mercedes S65 sedan to the side of the roadway. The car has obviously rolled several times, flattening the top.

"The ME wanted you to see this." O'Hara said, glancing over his shoulder.

"Chow asked you to call me?"

O'Hara nodded. "It looked fishy, he said, and that you'd understand."

"Was Baxter alone?" Rader asked.

"Yeah," O'Hara answered, "the same prick who got off last time."

Rader surveyed the accident scene. He could imagine and almost hear the screech of the Mercedes brakes, trying to stop before plunging over the side. "I guess he couldn't get away with it this time."

"Justice in slow-motion." O'Hara mumbled.

Rader had pulled the file on Baxter before he left the station house. Last address they had on him was in Pacific Palisades. Rader guessed he was on his way home. The last investigation into Baxter's participation in murder got all messed up. Their entire evidence bag disappeared, and his only witness vanished. Rader couldn't make the case stick, and Baxter walked. It left a bitter taste. Everyone in the department knew Louis Baxter was connected to organized crime, was a known union negotiator who used force, and got away with murder. He was a scumbag who did business with unscrupulous people, and it finally caught up with him.

The ME finished examining the body while other detectives scoured the wreckage.

Rader sank both hands deep into his slack pockets, watching Dr. Fong Chow, the medical examiner, walk toward him. Chow was a small compact man in his forties. His white hair was cut short, and he kept his mustache trimmed to a thin line above pale lips. His light brown suit looked as though he'd slept in it for a week. "Retribution is great, doc, but you didn't call me out here to look at a traffic accident."

Chow glanced back at the wreckage. "He wasn't wearing a seatbelt. It had been cut. Got tossed out halfway down the ravine before car settled in riverbed at bottom. The body very loose. Been dead two, maybe three days." He tugged at a shirt collar that was too tight. "Hiker man, walking two dogs, discovered the body and called in on his cell phone."

Rader took in the wrecked Mercedes. "Accidents happen, Dr. Chow."

"Yes, accidents do – ah, but this car was – how do you say, pushed, yes that's it. A good word of which might explain everything. Pushed."

Rader glanced over Chow's shoulder to a vehicle that was reduced to a pile of crushed metal. "How do you know it was pushed when it has dents everywhere?" His twisted neck indicated he was teasing, but Chow missed it.

"Ah, detective observant. That good."

Rader wasn't amused. He removed one hand from the slacks pocket, and ran it through is curly black hair. It was an awful habit he acquired years ago, whenever he got nervous. "You're enjoying this, right?"

Chow unfolded a tiny pair of reading glasses, adjusted them to the tip of his nose, took a small notebook from his pocket, thumbed through a few pages, and then browsed over Rader's face. "It says here, after examination that the victim's car show signs of push." He turned a page in the notebook and used a finger to scroll down the page. "Ah, yes. Paint of unknown origin on bumper match paint on passenger door, two places – ah, and one more time front fender." He closed the notebook and observed Rader's reaction. "You want know cause of an accident or cause of death?"

43

"Cause of death is obvious." Behind Chow, Rader saw his partner, Frank Mustio, climb from their Crown Vic and slam the door. Mustio and Rader were known as the Mutt and Jeff of the department. Rader was six four and Mustio five six. They were athletic, in their early thirties, and together since passing the detective exam years ago. They were like an old married couple. Mustio avoided Rader's obvious frustration, lowered his head, and kicked up gravel as he strolled towards them. Rader didn't take his eyes off his partner.

"Not so." Chow continued.

"Okay," Rader replaced his hand into the slacks pocket, "cause of death?"

"Crime man shot in the shoulder. Come, I show."

Chow turned, bumping into Mustio as he walked back to the coroner's wagon.

Mustio read from his notebook. "Baxter's prints check, and address on his DL is the same as the one in our file."

Rader's jaw tightened, "We'll need a search warrant for the house."

Mustio nodded, made a note in his book, and fell in step with them. "I'll phone it in. The rescue guys recovered a briefcase."

Rader almost didn't want to ask. "What's in it?"

Mustio read from his little book. "Two hundred grand, a 9mm Glock eighteen, thirty-three rounds of nine-millimeter pops and two extra mags."

Rader remembered Louis Baxter. He was a pompous ass who had an answer or excuse for everything. Not this time. Live by the sword, and die with your own greed slitting your throat. Rader enjoyed the judicature.

They stood together at the back of the coroner's wagon. Chow pulled the body tray out, and unzipped the black bag. Louis Baxter had abrasions everywhere. Eyes were opaque and glossed over, face badly bruised and chalky. He wore a Rolex, gold chain around the neck, and diamond wedding ring. The clothes were expensive, dark navy silk suit, shirt and matching tie. Chow rolled the body just enough to expose a small hole in the shoulder of the suit. The surrounding area was covered with dried blood. "Heavy blood loss, indicate shot before accident occurred."

Rader looked closer, and then ran his eyes over the rest of the body. Baxter had only one bullet wound. "Why shoot the guy first, and then run him off the road?"

Mustio tried to look between Rader's arms. "Maybe they shot him earlier, didn't complete the job, and had to chase him down?"

Chow shook his head. "No, chase first, shoot second, run dead man off road third."

Rader was frustrated and ran his hand back through his hair. "You just said he was shot before the accident because of blood loss, right?"

"You good but slow. Blood loss mean he bleeding before death take him, but not much before accident finish job. Bad guy follows. Try to push over fail. Good guy outruns bad guy. Bad guy catch up, angry now. Try again. Bad guy car not strong enough. More anger, now he embarrassed." Chow took a deep breath, slowly exhaling. "Good guy tried push bad guy over."

"Who's the good guy, and who's bad?" Mustio wanted to know.

Rader ignored his partner's question and walked up the canyon road. He saw the fading tire marks. A few days' earlier two cars obviously hit each other. Further on, a brake slide followed another set of skidding tire marks. Tiny pieces of glass from broken taillights still cluttered the side of the roadway. Crime Scene Techs were picking pieces up with little tweezers, using lots of evidence bags, and small plastic bottles. Rader's pulse increased as he walked to the wreckage, and examined the car. Mustio came up behind him with Chow trailing.

"This was a hit." Rader was mumbling, talking to himself.

Mustio walked around the car, saw mismatched maroon paint on the Mercedes bumper. "I don't get it."

Rader glanced at Chow. "The wreck didn't kill him, did it?"

"Ah, detective most observant. No. Accident not cause."

Mustio glanced over the entire car again. "If the accident didn't kill the guy, what did?"

"The bullet," Rader answered. Deep in his gut came the growing excitement of a new case. "The damn bullet went through the shoulder and penetrated what — a vital organ? Had to be, but the bad guy doesn't know this and continues to bash a dying man's car, leaving us a trail of the vehicle body parts as he goes. By the time he gets to the side of the Vic's car, the guy has bled out, is already dead, but his car is slowing down, and bam!" His head shook. "The bad guy was too stupid to know. Whoever did this shot Baxter out of fear. He was about to get outrun by a faster car, so he shoots first and continues to hit his car until it slows down. Then, bingo!"

Mustio finished for him. "He pushed a dead man over the cliff."

Rader's eyes adjusted over the canyon walls. The morning sun almost made the dead, burned out brush look attractive. "We need to find out whom Baxter pissed

46

off." He looked at the crushed Mercedes. "I want to know where he was going, what he's been working on, where the two hundred grand came from, when he took his last piss, and who benefits from his execution."

Chapter 5

Rollie couldn't get a decent night's sleep for days after the studio incident. He ran on the beach, got into a routine at the gym and called everyone he knew. There was no help coming. The temper thing had finally caught up with him.

He called all the key agencies in town and couldn't get one agent on the phone. It was worse than face-to-face rejections. He found Tiler Adams phone number and called her.

"Whom ever this is, am I to be expecting a call from you?" She asked when answering the phone.

"I don't think so," Rollie said.

"Is it important?" Tiler quizzed.

"Are you talking about my phone call?"

"Uh huh."

"It is to me." Rollie answered.

"Okay."

The silence was golden. She said nothing more, and Rollie was tongue-tied. He wasn't sure if she knew whom it was, or she joked with everyone that called her.

"This is Rollie. You remember me?"

"Ah, no, I don't think so. How 'bout a little reminder?"

Was she making fun of him, or did she have a weird sense of humor? "We met." How ridiculous was this? Reminding a girl where they met was a first for Rollie. "At the studio."

"I meet lots of people at the studio."

"This isn't going very well, is it?" Rollie had disappointment in his voice.

"Not so far."

He tried to imagine her face, but instead saw blond hair, blue eyes and delicate lips. He remembered she had a dazzling smile. "Can we start over?"

"Do you do this all the time?" Tiler teased.

Rollie's mouth got dry. "What? Do what all the time?"

"Stumble over your tongue." She was almost giggling.

"Maybe you make me nervous."

"Do all girls make you nervous," she asked

"No!" He was getting crazy, about to hang up.

"Just me?" She said it softly.

He hesitated. "Maybe I should call some other time?"

"What's wrong with right now, Rollie Kemp?"

He sat back and nearly tumbled out of the chair. She was putting him on, and got him good. Embarrassed, he started laughing. She joined him.

"You had me. How did you know it was me?"

"Cause you're the only guy I've given my number to since I moved six months ago."

"Dinner," he blurted out. "How would dinner sound?"

"I haven't heard the sound of dinner. How does it go?"

"Tiler!" Rollie was exasperated.

"Depends on if I'm hungry,"

"You're not making this easy."

"I'm not easy, Rollie. If you're looking for easy..."

"I'm not. Let's go back to dinner. Some night when you think you might be hungry."

"A girl does have to eat, doesn't she?"

"She does." Rollie felt alive for the first time in a remarkably long time. She had his sense of humor, and she got under his skin.

"I'll meet you at Something's Fishy tomorrow, at seven?"

"Seven's good." Rollie said.

"You know where it is?"

"I do, but do you?" He smiled and thought she might be doing the same.

"I guess you'll find out tomorrow." She was still laughing when she hung up.

Rollie arrived early, reserved a widow table, and ordered an expensive bottle of Merlot. Something Fishy was a small restaurant overlooking the Pacific on PCH. The floor of the restaurant was dotted with straw. The tables were covered with elegant linen, fine silver, and buckets of peanuts. Each table had a silver candelabra with small scented candles, and a tray filled with lavish hors d' oeuvres. It was romantic and down to earth all rolled into one. Outside the view was captivating with rolling ocean waters, capping waves, the distant glimmer of Catalina Island, and seagulls. Every once in a while a group of brown Pelicans flew by. The sunset burned the sky, captured drifting clouds, and painted them various shades of magenta.

Tiler walked into the restaurant and caught the attention of every man in the place. She looked stunning in black slacks, and a pink cowl-neck sweater. She spotted Rollie, paid categorically no attention to anyone else, and walked to his table. Rollie stood up, and she greeted him with a peck on the cheek. He couldn't remember the last time he was a nervous little boy.

"Hi." It was about all he could get out at one time.

"A man of few words?"

"Sometimes."

He pulled her chair out, and she slid onto it. He adjusted her chair and then sat at her side. They both faced the ocean.

"I owe you an apology," she said.

"For?"

"I take care of my grandmother. Usually I have someone in to watch her, but the nurse we have couldn't make it tonight."

Rollie stomach rolled. He hoped she wasn't blowing him off. She said it with such sincerity. He nodded as a gentleman was expected to do while his insides burned with disappointment.

"How much time do you have?"

She frowned. "An hour?"

"Not to worry. We'll have a glass of wine, eat diner, and get you home right on time."

She sparkled. Her cheeks blushed a glowing rose-hue. "You're very sweet. We'll do this again, I promise."

The hour dashed by so quickly, only one half bottle of wine had been consumed. They talked, giggled about the studio, his famous punch, and never got around to personal things. The conversation was typical, first-date garble. Both were careful not to give too much away, and yet Rollie wanted more. He walked her out to her car, a silver Infiniti G35, and started laughing.

"What's so funny?" She asked.

"Our taste in cars is similar." He pointed to his Infiniti FX, and she got the joke.

He opened her car door, and they stood inches apart. Her eyes glassed over, and one lone tear ran down her cheek. She quickly brushed it aside. "Call me?"

"I will." He promised.

She leaned forward and pecked his lips ever so slightly. She climbed into her car, and drove out of the lot without looking back. Rollie watched the car disappear into traffic. As he walked to his car, the parking lot attendant ran towards him.

"Look out!" The attendant shouted.

Rollie turned just as the attendant tackled him. A speeding car was careening out of control down PCH, coming right at them. The headlights were blinding. Rollie, with the attendant's assistance, rolled out of the way as the sports coupe fishtailed, just missed them, bounced off a nearby curb, and sailed on its way without hitting anything. Rollie jumped up, helped the attendant to his feet, and both men brushed the dust from their clothes. The little sports car didn't even slow down.

"That was close," the attendant said.

"Yeah, it was." His eyes traveled down PCH after the sports coupe, watching the taillights disappear. He didn't have time to get a good look at the car. Turning to the attendant, he took a hundred dollar bill from his wallet and handed it to the kid. "Thanks."

The kid looked at the hundred and beamed. "You're welcome."

The kid walked off, but Rollie's eyes stayed on PCH. It happened too fast, he wasn't sure if what he just witnessed was an accident or done deliberately? Either way, he was happy to be alive.

Chapter 6

The phone call was four hours late. Fabrio expected it before 11PM. He told Ronnie to call regardless of the hour. The call was urgent. Fabrio had dozed off and when he woke he was soaking wet. Fabrio Tallagi hadn't slept through an entire night in years. Demons and childhood memories deceitfully pervaded the brain matter of his conscious mind. Images came when they damned well pleased. Admittedly he had his share of dark moments, but never a day went by he didn't seek refuge from self-incrimination. He blamed himself for every mishap. He accepted the fact he needed discipline to avoid losing it, and to control the rage that brewed from within. He'd been angry a long time. The nightmare came and played over and over. He was just a kid, in the wrong place at the wrong time. He was fifteen, full of innocence, and naïve, as the day is long. He was still a virgin, so he tagged along with the older guys to learn about girls. He didn't see the fight coming, nor did he see the guy with the gun. Shots rang out. Punches were thrown. He ducked down, thinking he was safe. Then he saw the blood between his legs, and knew it was useless. Doctors said Fabrio would never have kids, but he'd live. Yeah, he'd lived through adolescence watching all his buddies date, get married and have kids – and do things he would never experience. He had nightmares instead.

Fabrio worked for the Pataglia brothers for over twenty years. His assignments kept him sane. In a strange way, the violent action kept life compelling enough ti stick around. He'd forgotten how long ago it was, how many years back he'd have to go, to remember Anthony Pataglia telling everyone he was their number one enforcer. He was proud to protect the family who took him in when no one gave a damn about him. He was skilled, protective and invisible. The Feds considered Fabrio a ghost and never got a full identification on what he looked like. He had never been arrested or thought of as a suspect.

Fabrio was tired of tossing and turning. He crawled from the king-sized bed and turned on a table lamp. The nebulous light cast a ghostly illumination throughout the expansive living quarters. His lavishly furnished Manhattan condo was more than he deserved, but the Pataglia brothers owned the building and gave him the place. They wanted him to be comfortable, and close by. They even brought in a decorator, and when she left the placed wreaked of masculinity. Leather couch, recliners, big-screen television, movie posters, electronic games, and adventurous toys Fabrio didn't know existed.

He got up, wearing boxer shorts, and meandered into the bathroom. The mirror over the sink caught his reflection. He washed the sweat from his face with cold water, eyeing the impression with a frown. He hated mirrors and loathed the reflected portrait. He stood average height, average weight, and wore normal facial features that weren't offensive or scared. He was essentially unremarkable, a guy on the street that no one remembered. Fabrio could fit in everywhere. Eyeing his physique, it looked normal. But to the unsuspecting, he was a killing machine. He could take most men down within a second or two. Like a tiger in wait, he kept his body toned.

There was neither joy nor sorrow when Fabrio was told to straighten something out. When the time came for him to get involved, there was only one way to resolve matters. He had never taken the life of someone innocent, and he never brought harm to a woman. His assignments were always someone connected to family, someone who had significantly screwed up. He dried his face with a soft pale blue towel and took a deep breath. He was getting angry. The absence of the call was excruciating. He wiped a few spots off the mirror and studied his reflection. Why couldn't he have been handsome, and normal? Why had he been soiled so early?

Fabrio roamed through the spacious apartment in the semidarkness, pacing like a caged hamster. The phone call was late, and he started to wonder why? He picked up the Rolex watch Anthony Pataglia had given him, and stared at the dial. It was 3:20 AM, and that meant it was after midnight in California. He snapped the watch around his wrist when the phone rang. The ring startled him. He answered on the second chime.

"Fabby, it's Ronnie."

"You're late!"

"I know, sorry." Ronnie sounded apologetic.

"Did she go to the interview?" Fabrio asked.

Ronnie hesitated answering. "No, she wants nothing to do with him, man."

"Who told said it was her old man trying to help?" Fabrio sounded accusative.

"She knew." Ronnie was defensive. "Tawny hates him. You know what she told me?"

Fabrio closed his eyes. "What?"

"She told me to fuck off, and to tell her old man to leave her the hell alone."

"Are you saying she turned Arnie's offer of co-starring in his film down too?"

"Fabby, she knows Arnie gets his financing from Anthony. The girl's not stupid. When Pataglia made her break up with Nick, and the kid ran and joined the army…" His voice trailed off. "The day Nick died in Iraq was the day Tawny died. She said she'd never forgive her father, and would do everything in her power to embarrass and degrade him."

"You think she means it?"

"Of course she means it. Hell, the girl screws everything in sight. She flaunts herself, runs around half naked, and tries any drug she can find. Don't say I said this, but Tawny is an all-out tramp. The only thing she doesn't do is take money for doing it. She just gives it away without a care in the world."

Fabrio felt his heart skip a beat or two. He ran his hand over his face. Maybe it was a good thing he didn't have kids. "Okay, I'll deal with this. What have you learned about Baxter?"

"He's dead."

"What?" Fabrio shot to his feet, and started pacing. Ronnie Mauten, like Fabrio, worked for the Pataglia brothers. He was an east coast lawyer, turned west coast film producer. He worked tirelessly with Louis

57

Baxter, investing pension funds and building union ties with the film community. He had a team of lawyers. The Teamsters stood behind them, as did many producers, and independent filmmakers. The studios and guilds were their enemy, but why would anyone kill a man trying to work things out? Fabrio knew most union and guild workers were against low budget employment, but for the unemployed crew people, actors or anyone else who worked in the industry – it made sense. For years, they vowed to fight a new contract to the bitter end. Behind the scenes, Anthony Pataglia, and his brother, Vincent, controlled or manipulated union and guild management. The Moe Brayden family in Philly wanted to move in. Mark Lipesky and his son Drew had used force in the past -- but it hadn't helped them. Obviously they were back to try again.

"They made it look like an accident," Ronnie said, "but word with my LAPD connection is -- Louie was murdered. They suspect it was a professional hit."

Fabrio sat on the leather couch. He ignored the chill from the rawhide on his bare legs. "How the hell do they know that, Ronnie?"

"Because he was shot with a hollow-point bullet under the armpit. He was dead before they ran him off the road."

Fabrio got up and looked out his sixteenth floor window, watching cabs roll over the steam pouring up from the manholes in the center of the street below. A siren could be heard, breaking the silence of the night. "What did Baxter do to get himself killed?" Fabrio could hear Ronnie breathing when he hesitated to answer. Labor negotiations weren't supposed to get turbulent. "You there, Ronnie?"

"Yeah, I'm here. Baxter talked about pension funds and the low budget deal Mr. Pataglia wants to replace the old one with. The meeting seemed to go okay, you know, ah, no flags or shouting at us."

"What did they do?" Fabrio asked again. The annoyance in his voice was unmistakable.

"The only comment they made was that it would never happen."

"That's it?"

"Well, no, not exactly." Ronnie was hyperventilating.

"Ronnie!" He snapped the name, like a warning.

"Sorry, Fabrio. We were told to come back with a different proposal, or not come back at all. It sounded like, you know, an ultimatum."

"Who was in the room?"

"A bunch of guys I don't know. The short guy from Philly, Lipesky, was there with his son. I think the kids name was Drew."

"Mark Lipesky was there in person?" Fabrio asked.

"Yeah, yeah, he was. His kid looks like real trouble."

"They don't know what trouble is! Who else was there?" Fabrio pressed, trying to get passed bullshit dialog.

"Well, William Drone, our attorney, Elliot Titlebaum, a couple of guys from Vegas, and the labor boss, Harold Fine." Ronnie reluctantly answered.

"Vegas?" Fabrio mumbled angrily.

"Yeah, two guys I don't know. They never said a word."

"Give me your take?" Fabrio said.

"I think it's bogus and has nothing to do with current negotiations. Lipesky is still mad about what Louis Baxter and his brother did to him a few years back. You remember," Ronnie stated. "It all changed when they stopped Lipesky from bringing his kid in to run things out here." Ronnie's voice relaxed. "I forgot about all that until you brought up his name. We're okay. I'll sit down with William and Elliot and we'll draw up a new proposal. Their hands are tied without us."

"I'll bring the Pataglia's up to speed. You'll call him in the morning?"

"I'll do that Fabrio. Sorry for the late call."

When the phone line disconnected, Fabrio heard nothing. He punched in a new number. The call was answered on the second ring.

"It must be important?" The voice has sleep mixed with anger.

"Can we meet?" Fabrio asked.

"How long will it take you to get here?"

"Half hour."

"Come in the back way."

It took Fabrio the full thirty-minutes to dress, catch a cab, and arrive at Anthony Pataglia's waterfront villa. He walked down the driveway. When he circled the four-car garage, Anthony Pataglia was standing in the dark waiting for him. Two bodyguards stood off in the shadows. Pataglia, in his fifties, stood over six-feet, thin framed, shaggy black hair and dressed casually in tan slacks and a dark blue turtleneck sweater. He was a handsome man with strong features, square jaw lines, well-tanned skin, seriously inquisitive brown eyes, and the overall look of a well-heeled businessman. They shook hands.

"What did Ronnie have to say?" Pataglia asked.

Fabrio knew questions about his daughter came first. "She's refused all help from us."

Pataglia's eyes traveled off into the dark of night. "I want you to find a young producer or director. Someone both she and I can trust."

"I'll have either Ronnie or Arnold hand pick someone."

"Good. Do it soon. I had hoped she'd forgive me by now."

"Time has a habit of healing things." Fabrio said without much conviction.

"I hope you're right. Now tell me about Louis?"

"He was deliberately taken out."

The signal Pataglia shared with his head gave Fabrio the impression of an unstated acknowledgement. "Lipesky wants to take the unions in a different direction."

Fabrio was surprised. "You knew he'd be there?"

Pataglia turned his eyes to Fabrio. His expression changed. It wasn't a smile. It was perception of things to come. "I expected him to be there." His eyes traveled to his bodyguards. "It's going to start soon, Fabby."

"Ronnie Mauten thinks Lipesky is still angry over the Baxter's nudging him out of Hollywood. Ronnie believes it's over now."

Jaw muscles tighten Pataglia's facial expression. "No, it's just beginning. The union contracts are outdated, but this is something else. Hollywood has notoriously fought change."

"What would you like me to do?"

"Louis Baxter started out good, but I haven't trusted him for years."

"Me either." Fabrio, answered, "He was as strange as his brother."

"Lipesky needs to be shut out completely. His tired, outdated use of muscle to threaten us is an old story. I want you to talk with William Drone and Arnie Aronjelovich tomorrow. After I speak with Ronnie, you will help me get everyone on the same page. If we catch it early, things might still be manageable."

Fabrio fought the heat rising from within. "Lipesky will fight."

Pataglia nodded, "Yes, I suspect he will."

"It's been peaceful a long time,"

"It has," Pataglia said. "At the same time there is no way for us to forget that grudges create hostility, and at the end of the day, an eye for an eye settles matters. Old school my friend. We need to be ready."

Chapter 7

Rollie had a hard time finding another agent. Word spread that he was fluttery, had problems with conformity, and consistently infected with alienation. That said, Rollie Kemp had other issues like being abruptly dispositional and in desperate need of vehemence counseling. In short, Rollie was a time bomb waiting to detonate. He lowered his sights and found Mildred Wanamaker. Old school Hollywood, Mildred was in her seventies and managed her own agency. She agreed to meet with Rollie, and told him straight up not to expect much. Her office on Hollywood Boulevard, a third-floor walk-up, would be classified a dump by anyone with eyesight. Rollie sucked it in and lumbered up the stairway. The floors were polished linoleum, circa 1950. Fourth door on the left came tinted glass with gold letters -- The Wanamaker Agency. Rollie had nowhere else to go. "What the hell," he mumbled. It could be worse. Reluctantly he entered.

WILLIAM BYRON HILLMAN

Inside, the office was decorated like a 1940 Bogart film. The place was spotless. Movie posters and autographed celebrity pictures hung everywhere. The furniture was antique, and probably worth a fortune. This was not what Rollie expected. The reception desk was void of personal touches, and looked as though it had been that way for some time.

"In here," came a too-many-years-of-smoking, throaty voice.

Rollie approached the door marked private and stepped into a remarkable office. The walls were clustered with more pictures, autographed items, and several posters from famous films. The autographs were all addressed to Mildred, or Miss Wanamaker.

"Sit." The raspy voice belonged to Mildred Wanamaker. Her snow-white hair was hidden beneath an giant colorful hat with a purple feather rising from it like a bird's broken wing. Her face was a roadmap of traveled wrinkles, and yet she carried a hint of glamour that boldly told everyone she was once a heart-stopper. Her eyes were emerald green, and what little makeup she wore was done tastefully.

Rollie dropped into the leather chair in front of her desk while Mildred watched in silence. Her gaze traveled over his body, not with desire but interest.

"I'm Rollie Kemp."

"I know who you are hot shot. I'll say one thing. You got the look. Word around town is you're light in the talent department, and have a temper like no sane guy they've ever seen."

"I can sit on it."

"Good, and I hope you have lots of patience. Time heals everything in this town. Next month, for example, the production manager who fired you will be out looking for a job. In a couple of months, they'll forget you're a complete jerk, and a few months after that they'll try to remember what people said about you. If you behave, and stay out of trouble, I'll get you some work. You ready to wait a few months?"

"Whatever it takes."

"Good. So in the meantime, find some kind of work away from the business. Stay out of the way, and let Father Time do the healing. That's it." He was dismissed. "Call me in a couple of weeks."

Rollie stayed in the chair a beat too long.

"You might want to take some acting lessons."

"I thought —"

"Don't think, Rollie Kemp. There are more important things happening than having you going around thinking. Get a job, stay out of the way, and call me. Now get out of here. I have work to do."

On his way home, Rollie started laughing. He always referred to his old man as a loser. A wise guy who worked the streets of New York, and worked them so good it got him killed. Now here was the old man's son, and he wasn't doing any better. At thirty-two, he'd tried just about everything -- studied law for two years, got married, and then divorced. He breezed through the police academy only to be nearly killed in a freeway mishap. The accident left him unable to pass the physical, but the settlement gave him enough money to make things easier. As his body healed, he invested in Penny Stocks. He bought several million shares in two unheard of companies. It cost him less than five hundred dollars, and they both went through the roof. His investments were better than winning the lottery. He spread his profits, kept some in place, and did well enough to take care of what was most salient in him. He bought a condo for Millie, picked up a beachfront fixer-upper in Malibu, and went back to college. A year of lackluster journalism ended when he met Ashley Moreland. Ashley talked him into joining the cast of a play, and he got the bug. People kept telling Rollie the star look was right there, and it didn't take long to believe them. He had a fling with Ashley, but that ended when she married a stuntman. Rollie felt betrayed, but this new feature called acting was fun. He continued the endless journey in search of the real Rollie Kemp. Most of the time he felt like a drifter as the direction in which he traveled was blurred.

The acting career became a significant challenge. Rollie performed in plays, received mediocre reviews, and waited for the phone to ring. He worked odd jobs he'd mastered earlier in life. He felt compelled to earn a steady income so his nest egg would increase rather than slowly be eaten away. He played a dog in a small low-budget film, and the film received excellent reviews. His co-star, a fellow out-of-work actor, Lance Straight took him aside when the film wrapped. They walked the lot in their dog costumes, and Lance asked Rollie if he would like to be a reporter for a day or two. Lance had read some unpurchased screenplays Rollie had written, and thought he might be missing a career. The writing was for an entertainment-oriented tabloid. Rollie was assured there'd be no pressure. Lance was one of those chubby guys who did extra work when he got a chance. He stood five feet four inches, and weighed in somewhere around three hundred pounds – give or take a few. Lance didn't work much as an actor, and found a second career writing cheap-thrill stories for the tabloids.

"Now listen, Rollie, the jobs only for a few days. One of the writers got sick, and may or may not come back. It'll be a piece of cake. You'll get leads, and all you have to do is write stories around them. You will learn to create entertaining fiction from each lead. A little lie will not only grow but also force you to master fudging a lot. You not only want people to read it, you'll want them to believe it. The naked truth is the more you lie, and more people believe it. It's a nation of idiots who will believe anything if it's in print.""

"I'm just learning how to write a script, Lance. I don't know about this gossip stuff."

"No problem!" Lance answered too quickly.

"I'm also an actor, Lance. What if I need to take off for an interview?"

"No problem. You 'll need to create a pseudonym."

Rollie didn't like doing anything under someone else's name. "Why?"

"Because no scribbler in this building writes under our real names. You piss people off, and someone might come looking for you. Fictitious characters can mingle or disappear." Lance put his hands over his ample hips. "Pick a handle."

"How does Robin May sound?"

Lance laughed when he heard the name. "You'll be working with stars, and stuff. It's perfect. With a name like that, the readers won't know if you're a man or a woman? If the readers think you're a woman, the ugly fact might be you get more work out of it."

"OK," Rollie said, Abut only for a few days." He needed a job. When he got around to paying his taxes, his cash reserves would be minuscule. Tapping into his investments wasn't an option he'd consider. He took the job. The days became weeks, and the weeks became a month. Rollie worked from a tiny corner desk on the second floor of a shopping mall. The mall was on the corner of Sunset and La Brea, in the heart of Hollywood. The Tabloid was printed elsewhere, and the owners spared no limit to an expense account. As long as it didn't exceed a hundred bucks, you could do whatever. Anything above that needed approval.

Rollie actually enjoyed working a regular job. Most of the time he was alone in the tiny office. In the middle of writing a story, his cell phone rang. The ring surprised him. He couldn't remember giving the number to anyone, so he answered it carefully. "Yeah?"

"Is that how you answer all your calls, hot shot?" Mildred Wanamaker's voice couldn't be mistaken. "You still there?"

"Sure. How are ya, Mildred?"

"I heard you slapped a girl around. Is that true?"

Rollie's chest tweaked, and both hands snapped into tight fists. "No. It's a lie."

"So you've never hit a woman?"

"Who said I hit a woman?"

"You're in Hollywood, Rollie Kemp. The whole town tells lies, and this isn't a difficult question."

"No! Just so you know, Mildred, that answer will never change." Sitting back, a grin floated onto his lips. "Besides, if the woman didn't kill me my grandmother would."

"I don't think you'll have to wait too much longer." She hung up on him.

The following week Mildred sent him out on an interview, to test the waters. The casting director remembered his temper. He didn't get the job. The next day Lance left the paper, returned to Houston, and his family owned pawnshop. Rollie had become a semi-good part-time investigative reporter. Robin Mays found ways to develop dirt on everyone. Because Rollie was so good, the editor sent him out to collect secrets on Sam Delacourt. Sam was the hottest newcomer to join Hollywood's fast lane.

Snooping on Delacourt, Rollie took pictures of the naughty boy naked in the swimming pool with Carol Topaz. Carol was also famous but married to another actor. Rollie got caught. The star's bodyguard, Lou Bays grabbed Rollie by the collar, and tried to take his camera. That was a mistake. Rollie popped Lou in the nose. Lou staggered backwards, managed to snatch Rollie's camera free, and crushed it. Rollie lost his temper and beat the crap out of Lou. The tabloid fired, Rollie. Then, to top it off, Rollie found out Lou worked for Drake Fargo.

Some things Rollie dug up off the Internet found Drake Fargo to be, reportedly, one of the best Private Investigators in California. Rollie stormed over to Fargo's office and demanded payment for the broken camera. Drake Fargo said he was genuinely impressed that he could stomp on a large burly bodyguard like Lou Bays, and live to see another day.

"You got me fired!" Rollie clamored.

"That's two." Fargo smiled.

"Two what?" Rollie stood over Fargo's desk.

"Let me buy you a drink, kid." Fargo got up and came around the desk.

"Why? You got a story for me?"

"No, but I have a job for you," Towering over Rollie, the six feet seven inch monster carried his three hundred pound body well.

Rollie guessed he had less than five- percent body fat, and obviously a lot of solid muscle. Then he caught a glimpse of Fargo's feet. They must've been at least a size fifteen.   Obviously, Rollie thought, the guy made a considerable effect on everyone.

"What kind of job?" Rollie queried.

"Let's talk over a big steak." Fargo wrapped an arm around Rollie. "You hungry?"

Rollie eyed Fargo's meaty hands. "Look, I got a job."

"You had a job. Remember, you just stated they fired you. If they're dumb enough to take you back, you can keep their job and still work for me."

"What about my acting?"

Fargo patted Rollie on the back. "You can keep that too. C'mon."

Fargo headed out the door, and Rollie followed. He was more curious than desperate. The art of game playing was fun, and Hollywood was a perfect place for games.

They sat in a dark corner booth of Anthony's Steak House on Santa Monica Boulevard. Rollie watched Fargo over the candle-lit table. He was curious why this gigantic man was so interested in hiring him. The waitress came by in a big hurry, flipped open her order pad, and pulled a pen from her hair. "What can I get you guys?"

"Porterhouse, medium-rare, and a glass of Merlot,"

Rollie didn't bother to look at the menu even though he had never been to this particular restaurant. "I'll have the same."

The waitress disappeared, and Rollie sat back and waited. Watching Fargo's relaxed demeanor confused him. He wondered what the burly guy actually wanted.

Fargo was thoroughly amused. "What's your back story?"

"Back story?" Rollie didn't talk about his past with anyone.

"Sure. Everyone has a back-story. Basically, Rollie, it's who you really are."

Rollie tightened his jaw and involuntarily closed his fists. He deliberately hesitated for a beat, and decided there was no valid reason he could think of not to tell Fargo about his past. "My old man was sort of related to one of the New York families. He married my mom, and her younger brother was a God Father in-the-making. My dad, his name was Tony, worked the streets, did collections, and stuff. He crossed a line or two, made mistakes, couldn't change what he'd done, and it got him killed. My ma, expecting a block party, packed up and moved us to Charleston. My uncle Charlie took us in. He was retired family. When my mother got cancer, Uncle Charlie said I should go back to New York outta respect for my father. You know, and pick up where he left off. He had markers all over the city. It was suggested I go back to pay off his markers, and make things right."

The waitress brought the wine and quickly evaporated into the dark room.

"Did you go?"

Rollie shook his head, closed his eyes and hoped it would turn off the memories that flashed through his head. He reopened his eyes and watched Fargo. "I wasn't interested. I wanted to do something else. Something legit."

Fargo's eyebrows knotted in disbelief. "So you came to Hollywood to become legit?"

Rollie saw the reaction. "Not at first, no, I came to California to go to college. Stupidly I got married while taking law classes at UCLA. The marriage got ugly and soon ended with a divorced. That's when I dropped out of school and tried the Police Academy."

Fargo was genuinely surprised. "So you became a cop?"

"Sort of a wannabe, almost cop. I got through the academy, second in my class, was a few days away from graduation, from getting my badge, when bam!" It still sounded bittersweet.

"Bam?" Fargo sipped his wine.

"A drunk driver hit my car. The car was totaled, and with help from the jaws-of-life, they extricated me from the wreckage. I was laid up for months. Took over a year to get my legs working. With bad wheels, you can't pass the physical. The guy who hit me drove one of those BMW's. He was heavily insured, and after all the medical expenses, the insurance settlement left me with a few extra bucks."

"How long ago did this all happen?"

"Couple of years."

"So how are the legs now?"

"If I can't out run some argumentative bastard, I take 'em down. Then I hurt 'em for running." Rollie smiled.

The waitress brought the steaks. "Can I get you anything else?"

"No, we're fine." Without hesitation, she dashed off. "So, let me understand this. You're the son of a dead wise guy, almost became an attorney, almost a cop, write bad stories full of misconceptions, had a golden opportunity to become a crook, and now you're a bad actor? Does that about sum it up?"

Rollie's lip twitched. "Yeah, you have a real gift with words."

"This is good stuff. What happened after that?"

"I went back to school." Rollie said. "Studied some journalism, met a thespian, and started a new career chasing' film and TV roles. I'm working my way up from bit parts to starring roles. They say I'm pretty good."

"Whose they?" Fargo asked with hesitation.

Rollie beamed. "My fellow actors."

"Actors lie." Fargo said, positioning the steak on his plate with a fork.

Mischievous sparkle poured into Rollie's eyes. "It took a while to find that out."

Fargo cut into the steak and enjoyed every bite. The candlelight flickered around his face, giving him a strange, powerful exterior. He was a man's man, reeking of masculinity and absoluteness. "So what else have you done to round out this great education?"

Rollie thought a moment. "A little of everything. Women find me attractive. Although I haven't found the right one, I still have some fun. I can bartend, drive cabs, and trucks. On short notice, there are shelves to be stocked, messages to be delivered, and punches to be thrown. I drink a little, attend parties, write some awfully bad stories packed with lies, and I can eat a mean steak." He cut into his steak and chewed on the bite. He gestured with his empty fork, "I suck at telling jokes. Can't remember the punch lines."

"You really are a character, Rollie."

"So what's your story?"

"Me?" Fargo laughed "I carry a gun, legally, follow bad guys, protect stupid people, dig into dirty laundry, force some to take a second look at themselves, and enjoy the hell out of it."

Rollie frowned, "That carrying a gun part makes me nervous. Have you ever had to use it?"

"Once in a while, but mostly not."

"You any good at this?" Rollie kept his eyes on Fargo for a reaction.

Fargo ate the last bite of his steak, gulped the wine glass empty, and watched Rollie. "Rumor has it, I'm very good."

"Is the rumor reliable?"

"Some think so. Truth told. I'm the best. No one's better than Drake Fargo."

"So, who is the real Drake Fargo?"

"Whaddya mean by that?"

"Simple question. You just told me about the detective guy, and now I'd like to know about the other guy, the one you take walks with, sleep with, and look in the mirror at?"

Fargo leaned back, munching on the inside of his jaw. He wiped at his mouth with an open hand and thought about the question. "Drake Fargo's complicated. He's not easy to understand, or get along with. I suppose he's selfish, sort of one-dimensional, opinionated, and sometimes angry as hell about everything." His eyes drifted into a patch of memory. He bit down on his molars to steady the flashes forming in his head. "He's widowed, has an on-going relationship full of frustration, lives alone, needs a dog, and likes to walk in the fog on the beach. What else do you want to know?"

Rollie shook his head and finished the steak in silence. And this guy said he was a character. He flushed the last bite of steak down with the last of his wine. When he set the wine glass down, Fargo reached out and held his arm.

"What?" Rollie's eyes shot up to Fargo's face.

"Trust, Rollie. Can I trust you?"

"Sure."

Fargo tightened his grip on Rollie's arm, and Rollie didn't like it. "Can I?"

Rollie looked deep into his serious, smoky, gray eyes. They focused on each other for a heart-stopping moment. He nodded. "Yeah, you can trust me with your life. Can I trust you with mine?"

Fargo released his arm. "Without a doubt. I've been lookin' for a guy like you for a long time. We'll begin part-time. Start you at a thousand a week, and see how it goes."

"What exactly do you want me to do?" Rollie asked.

"Shadow work. We'll need to get you a permit to carry. Is your record clean?"

"Very clean. What else?"

"I'll have you watching people, maybe do a little recording. Since you write for the tabloids, I'll assume you're good at snooping around, right?"

"Right." Truth be told, Rollie loved to explore. The proposal aroused his curiosity.

Fargo stood up, peeled a few bills from a small wad of cash, and waited for Rollie to stand up. He offered his hand, and Rollie shook it. "Let's get out of here. I'll get you some keys to the office, and show you around. The office is an old house I inherited years ago. It's simple enough, in a great location on Lincoln, and I own it."

"What about my camera?"

"You can afford it, buy another one."

Chapter 8

The Watcher circled through shopping center parking lots in search of a silver Infiniti FX. Identical vehicles were all over the place, and each time she spotted one, she'd wait to see the driver. There were a lot of men in the area, but not the witness she was looking for. Damn! The newspapers covered the wreckage and execution of Louis Baxter for a few days, and then moved on. Breaking news in Los Angeles held press attention for a heartbeat. Relevance faded if a crime couldn't be solved in a few days. The story drifted to the back page, and eventually faded. There was too much violence elsewhere.

Where the hell did he go? She drove around at all hours of the day and night. She followed Infiniti's to no avail, and frustration slammed throughout her. If he lived in Malibu or Santa Monica, she vowed to find him. He obviously didn't come forward when the story hit the papers. Perhaps he hadn't put two and two together? Maybe she was wasting her time?

Missing him in the restaurant parking lot was a whopping fuck-up. It was a good thing she removed the license plate before attempting to run him over. It was by accident she spotted him entering the restaurant earlier. She saw the SUV, circled the building in time to see him enter. Certain it was the same guy, same movie-star looks, and wearing the same sunglasses, she parked in a lot and waited. She should have followed the cute little thing he came out with, but decided to end it right then. Big error. She owed that parking lot attendant. Now wouldn't that undoubtedly be stupid? Yeah. He was lucky. He'd live until he got in some else's way.

Driving north on PCH, she passed the area where the Mustang she used was parked. It was still there, covered with soot that crusted from the ocean mist. The human race continued to amaze her. Everyone had habits. The owner of the Mustang didn't need the car and had moved on like the press covering a story. She had habits. Perhaps the things that fancied her attention would be appalling to others. Her thirst for the next victim wasn't the thrill. The tingling came when a contract had been agreed to. The planning and execution brought satisfaction. To pull off the perfect hit time and time again was where the rush of emotion came from. She had remained impervious to everything. Sonny told her others believed he was heartless, but they had no idea. Sonny was a gentle, loving creature -- her soul mate. Sonny performed a necessary job, and he accomplished it because of his callousness. After every hit, they would celebrate by taking a little vacation. They never talked about victims.

The witness, the guy in the Infiniti could ruin everything, and she had to find him before it was too late – before her clients found out about him. Seeing him twice confirmed he lived locally.

The Watcher circled back, driving through Malibu, climbing up into Santa Monica, and cruised the streets until she felt she might draw attention to herself. She decided to wait. See what he did. If he came forward, she'd have his identity. If not, she'd take her time, find him, and carefully execute him. She would hunt him down and, one way or the other, he would die.

Chapter 9

Rollie wanted to celebrate. Looking back, the day had to rank as one of his best. Traffic on Santa Monica Boulevard was thinning. He passed beneath the 405 Freeway, took a right on San Vicente Boulevard, and headed west. The ride was optional autopilot. He'd surprise her with the excuse of being in the neighborhood. Rollie flipped his cell phone open and pushed number three. He'd placed Tiler's number in speed dial earlier. She picked up on the fourth ring.

"Hello?" Her voice didn't have a lively ring. It was tired and depressed.

"Hey, Tiler, this is Rollie Kemp."

"Hi." She was distracted, yet friendly.

"You up for a late dinner or drink?"

"Sorry, not tonight. Rain check?"

A frown spread yet he tried not to sound disappointed. "Sure." They both hesitated. "Is everything okay?"

"Yeah," she whispered.

"Anything I can do for you?" After the words had slipped out, he wanted them back. If she needed his help, she would've asked.

"Call me next week, okay?"

"Absolutely."

The call ended, but he couldn't stop glaring at the phone. Perhaps she wasn't as crazy about him as he thought. It was a strange conversation, to say the least. He folded the cell phone in his hand. He hoped she'd call him back, but that didn't happen. Calling her back wasn't a good option, so he dropped the cell phone on the passenger seat, and headed for PCH.

Rollie turned left on Ocean, right on Pico and parked in the oceanfront parking lot adjacent to the Santa Monica Pier. Rejection always came hard. A despairing feeling he loathed. The lot was empty. Rollie got out and walked into a fragrant mist blowing in with the fog. The air hung heavy, feeling soupy. The ocean loomed ominous, black emptiness. White-capping waves curled toward shore, creating a base of rolling cotton against the darkness. A glimpse at the fading lights from the pier cast off a rainbow on sparkles, giving birth to the perfect place to pout.

Rollie sat on the sand and watched the surf. Voices from the pier drifted within the atmosphere, bouncing airwaves of laughter and panic from the exhilaration the rides brought in the fog. Loneliness engulfed him. Years earlier he tried everything to move away from a miserable childhood. It continued, however, to follow him into adulthood. The ghosts of yesterday lurked in the shadows, waiting for him to slip, to fall into the abyss. He knew he'd spent the better part of his life ducking responsibility. Afraid to grow up and terrified of staying behind. He tried commitment and got crushed.

Living simple eliminated the creation of chancy relationships, and so far all it brought was negative results of isolation. What was with Drake Fargo? Maybe the tall guy wanted to make him something he wasn't? Rollie shook his head, knowing it would never last. Probably end like all the other jobs and occupations he tried. Nothing stuck. Maybe he'd be better off to tell Drake he couldn't do the job, and move on?

Two men walked out of the fog, one much taller than the other. A beam of light hit Rollie in the face.

The tall guy held a flashlight. "You waiting for someone."

The sudden interruption jarred Rollie. "No."

"Wanna stand up?" the shorter of the two said.

Rollie stood. He'd take both men on if that's what it came to. Involuntarily his knuckles tightened, hands snapping into protective weapons.

"You been drinking?" the tall guy asked.

"Not enough," Rollie mumbled.

The tall guy walked around Rollie. He was shining the flashlight right into Rollie's face. "Rollie Kemp?"

"Who wants to know?" Rollie was surprised. A familiar voice he couldn't place. The shorter guy circled around and stared at Rollie. "Well, I'll be damned."

The tall guy turned the flashlight off. "Long time no see buddy."

Rollie eyed both men, and then it dawned on him. "John Rader. Frankie Mustio." It had been a long time. He hadn't seen either since his days in the police academy. "How the hell are you guys?"

"We're good," Rader said. "Man, it's good to see you."

WILLIAM BYRON HILLMAN

Rollie glanced around. They were alone. "What are you two doing down here? Slumming or looking to get lucky?"

Rader gave Rollie a hug, and then shook his hand. "I'm glad walking isn't a problem."

"We haven't seen you since the accident," Mustio said.

"I know." Rollie didn't mean it as it sounded. They fell into a deafening, guilt-ridden silence. "You guys still with LAPD?" He had gone through the academy with both men. They were set to graduate at or near the top of the class when the accident happened. They came to the hospital to visit a couple of times, called on a few occasions, dropped him a card at Christmas one year, and then went their separate ways. His temper became skittish. Company was awkward and comradely phony. Everyone felt sorry for him. Hell, he felt sorry for Rollie too. Eventually, everyone stopped coming to visit. Phone calls faded, as did letters and cards. No one wanted to hang out with a cripple, and Rollie was a dangerous bird without wings. He was burning charcoal, and took it out on anyone who would listen.

"SMPD. We're both detectives. Work robbery homicide." Rader couldn't stop smiling. "What about you?"

Rollie saw they were genuinely pleased to see him. "I'm working with Drake Fargo. You guys know him?"

The two men looked at each other and laughed.

"Everybody knows Fargo," Rader said. "This is great. You have no idea how good it is seeing you up and around. I'm glad for you. If you ever need anything, and I mean anything, call us. Better yet, stop by SMPD. If they deny knowing us, you're in the right place. Damn, Rollie, this is very cool."

"So what are you guys doin' at the beach in the middle of the night?"

"Union negotiator, a guy buried in organized crime got taken out in Malibu Canyon the other day. No wits, but lots of dots we're trying to connect. He lived in the Palisades, but he also owned one of the condos over there," Mustio pointed into the ominousness area beyond the pier. "We found his Mercedes a couple of days after they shot and ran him off the road."

"Professional hit?" Rollie asked. It was exciting just talking about a real case. He felt a tinge of jealousy. A split second difference and he might be standing there as part of the investigation.

"Yeah, looks as though he pissed some people off." Rader's cell phone rang. He opened it. "Rader. Yeah. We'll be right over." He snapped the phone shut. "We gotta go, Rollie. I can't tell you how good it is to see you. Let's have dinner some night, and do some catching up?"

"Sounds good. I'll give you a call." Rollie said the words, but knew he was all but a stranger to both men. A lot of water passed beneath their bridges. You could never catch up to something so far down stream.

"Whenever you're in town, stop by. Some of the other guys would love to say hello, cause we talk about you all the time." Mustio shook Rollie's hand again and walked into the fog. He was immediately swallowed.

"He's a serious man, and so am I. Don't be a stranger."

"I'll call before dropping in on you." Rollie could see the sincerity in Rader's eyes.

Rader hesitated, "Say hi to Drake for us." He turned and hustled after his partner.

"Yeah, I'll do that," Rollie said more to himself.

Once again he was alone with all kinds of mixed feelings. If that drunk hadn't hit him, he would have been a cop. Maybe even a good one. He'd never know. The wind picked up. Rollie stared over the dark waters, thinking about possibilities. Maybe this PD stuff had some merit?

Rollie watched the giant Ferris wheel spin, the lights casting off eerie specks as they mixed with the thickening fog. The echo of teenage girls screaming soared passed him lifting up into the wind. He walked back to his car and drove home. Rollie's Malibu beach cottage was on the south side of the colony, nestled off PCH and down a rolling hillside -- a one-story, three bedrooms, and two-bath house built in 1954 with a one-car garage. One of the owners along the way added a carport. The front yard was small but sand, and ocean filled the backyard. He parked beneath the carport while a thick mist swirled around him. Visibility had dropped to zero. Inside, he fixed a Johnny Walker Red. Rollie bought the house in an "as is" condition. He tore walls out, opened the house up, and then bored with remodeling. It took on a personality of its own. Rustic modern. Manly details of worn leathers and well-traveled antiques were arranged so visitors could enjoy them.

Outside on the oceanfront patio, he sat on a lounge chair in the fog. He loved listening to the unseen waves crashing on the shore. They sounded close, but in reality the beach was a hundred yards from the house. The surf created a song, echoing from the supernatural pitch-blackness that hung before him. This was part of California he loved. The phone rang. He attempted to block it out, but it kept ringing. On the eighth or tenth ring he snatched it up. His watch displayed 2 A.M.

"Who is this?" Rollie demanded angrily.

"Rollie?"

The moment he heard her voice his lungs became void of air. Hopelessness slammed against him. How long had it been since the last call? Months? He sucked air and held it. Damn her! Why did he continue to let her to eat at him? He wanted to hang up, but was paralyzed.

"Rollie? I know you're there, I can hear you breathing." Her voice was floating sensuality. She purred more than she talked.

He could feel her breath in his ear. Rollie remained silent, trying to focus on spinning memories. What the hell did she want this time? She tore his guts out and stomped all over them. Before that, she killed him as surely as a dagger in the heart would have done.

"Please talk to me?" Her voice brought back the storytellers treasures. The heat from her body surfaced the softness of her skin, and the desirability of her mere existence. She wasn't whispering, but she might as well have been. The assonance of her voice tore him apart. "When you said I do, you made a commitment." She sobbed. "You promised to take care of me."

Oh yeah. Take care of her til death do you part. Rollie could still see his wedding as if it were yesterday. He said the vows and meant every word. She must've been wearing earplugs. He closed his eyes, and saw them running on the beach, making love, and laughing over dinner. All this joy turned into shadows moving in slow motion. They were fighting, saying despicable things to each other, and the darkness cleared with her naked on the bed with another man. Both were shooting drugs into their arms with the same needle. She pointed at Rollie, laughed, and then it got nauseating. She shouted at him, and screeched for him to get out. Her beautiful face contorted into pure hatred. The images lasted but a few seconds, long enough for Rollie to recall the what, and the why, of his failed marriage.

"Rollie?" Her voice popped and closed the door to back memories. She was begging. "You still there?"

"Yeah," he finally managed to get out. "What do you want, Kali?"

"I need to see you."

"That's not an option. Look, I gotta go." He hesitated a beat too long. Heat mixed with disgust sent chills through his guts. He wanted to hang up, and he wanted to listen to her velvet voice at the same time. His heart started pounding. Hang up, stupid!

"Rollie, wait!"

"Why? Why do you want to see me?"

"I'm clean now. It's been seven months." Her voice had a familiar perk.

"I'm glad for you, Kali." He'd heard that so many times he could puke. Every time she wanted something she'd pull that chain. In the past, he fell for it. Not anymore. No way!

"Don't patronize me, Rollie."

He remained silent.

"I love you, Rollie."

"Don't!" His body stiffened.

"I made a mistake. It wasn't me that did all those awful things to you."

"Really? If it wasn't you, Kali, who do you think it was?" He still carried the anger, and the flame. Why else did she get under his skin? Why did he let her? Why couldn't he just walk away? What the hell was a matter with him?

Her breathing became erratic, her sobs soft and pathetic. "Drugs. They took it all away from me. They took me over. Little by little, they destroyed all that I was. All that we were."

Rollie poured his drink into the sink and rinsed the glass. It was time to turn her off, put the feelings in a suitcase, slam the lid, lock the damned thing, and toss the key. If only, but he knew he couldn't get rid of her that easy.

"I can't, Kali. I'm sorry." He put a chill in his voice.

"You still love me." The softness returned. Controlled. "I know you do."

"That may be true, Kali. Most likely I'll always love you, but I'm not in love anymore."

"Let me come see you? I want to see, in person, how much you hate me. You need to prove it to yourself that it's over. You'll never get rid of me until you face it."

"It's over, Kali." He grasped his chest. The pain from his words cut deeply. Even if, it were sick to do so, for some unfathomable reason he still loved her. What he couldn't do was allow her back in so she could finish the destruction. They weren't good together, and never would be.

Her sobs came in heavy gulps. "I'll never stop loving you."

"I know."

He heard her take a deep breath. "Can we at least be friends?"

He got quiet.

"Rollie?"

He waited.

"If I call, will you at least call me back, and talk to me?"

"I gotta go." Rollie finally spoke.

"I'll call again."

"Goodbye, Kali." He hung up fast. Rollie fell in love with her voice when they first met, and he couldn't stand to hear it anymore. They were both nineteen, in college, and fell in love at first sight. They did everything together, and rushed into a marriage they both swore would last forever. He was going to be a lawyer and her, a writer. They would meet in passing, arrange for a romantic rendezvous or two in bizarre places, and laugh until they'd burst. They had the perfect relationship until she started experimenting with drugs. It started innocently, but the need accelerated, and the desire changed from having fun to necessity. She needed drugs for everything, to be awake, study, make love or live life on the edge. Then she started bringing men home. Rollie didn't know about any of that until he caught her. Afterwards, he discovered she'd been doing it for months. How stupid and vulnerable he felt. The solitude about killed him after they divorced. He missed her so intensely. He missed her voice, her whispers, and the way she made love. He missed everything. Life sucked.

Rollie went back to the sink, retrieved his glass, and poured a stiffer drink. He gulped half of it down, and then threw the glass at the wall. The glass shattered, and the liquor splashed. Sleep depraved, Rollie had a hard time putting Kali out of his mind. Visions of happier times reminded him of how fragile life's timing was. One wrong move, one moment of regret changed everything.

Rollie's law enforcement training at LAPD's academy helped accelerate the application to carry a concealed weapon. It was quickly approved. Likewise with his private investigator license and insurance and bonding requirements needed. He excelled at target practice and mastered handling a gun. At the gym, Rollie allowed his frustrations to escape at the punching bag. He almost tore the damn thing off the hook, but always felt better when he finished. Fargo said the job wasn't dangerous, but as with a lot of other myths, that was a lie. He also found Drake Fargo was actually legendary, and had snooped all over Hollywood for one client or another. Studios hired Drake Fargo to protect their investments. Stars feared the famous iron man while gangsters either hated or adored the way business was done. Jocks avoided the ground he walked on. On the other hand, Executives and lawyers, on the other hand, loved the honesty and ethics of the agency and kept it busy year round.

Things changed quickly. The tabloid missed Rollie's cutting edge articles, so they called and said he could write freelance stories whenever he had time. He followed Drake around like a puppy dog and liked how the older man did things. He called Tiler several times, and each call ended as the predecessor – call her back the following week. He put her number in his gym bag, erased the cell phone speed dial, and moved on. He knew she had college, a sick grandmother, and a loving family in the Midwest to keep her occupied. Perhaps Tiler was too busy for her own good. In a paranoid sense, maybe Rollie deliberately pushed her away.

During the week, Rollie had six messages from his accountant, Shelly Bufko. He had put her off too long. He could tell from her messages, she was pissed. He needed to call her back, but dreaded doing so. Shelly was an actress who, like a lot of other entertainers, actually worked at a job. She had a degree in accounting. She did a lot of artist's taxes, saved them money, and was good enough at the profession to earn a living. She also dated lots of fellow actors, often got her heart broken, and shared this info with anyone foolish enough to listen. Usually it was to clients like Rollie. Men she wasn't interested in. Rollie knew he was one of few clients she had that made substantial profits from investments. He stayed with her because she was good. The few times they saw each other in person was at tax time, or to go on interviews together. They never so much as exchanged a romantic thought even though they engaged in lots of extraneous conversations about relationships. Although not Jewish, she presented herself as a typical Jewish Princess. She learned to reveal a fit of petulant sulkiness with the best of any actress around. Shelly could be sultry, even sexy, when she used her hourglass figure to further a goal. Men who didn't know her would walk off a cliff to peek down her ample cleavage. Even Rollie had random thoughts about her chest. On more than one occasion, he daydreamed about getting Shelly in bed. He blamed the wondering thoughts on her chest.

Sadly, Shelly believed she was a brilliant actress. No one could convince her otherwise. Her body had been her primary asset since age twelve, and producers who called her back wanted to see her naked. Callbacks faded because Shelly refused to work without her clothes, and her activities on screen were almost nonexistent. Rollie couldn't help notice she was all business with him. She did his taxes and all but ignored his indiscrete glances at her bursting bust line.

The phone rang. The machine picked up, and it was Shelly, again. Rollie couldn't shun her forever. He picked it up. "Hey."

"Rollie?" Her voice rang with excitement.

"Hi, Shelly. What's up?"

"You owe me dinner."

"Why don't we just file an extension?"

"Meet me at On the Sand at 7:30." Shelly blurted out. "It's on PCH just north of Sunset Boulevard. You know the one?"

"I do." Rollie always used a post office box with everyone. He even filed his taxes with that address, so Shelly didn't know he lived up the road from the restaurant.

On The Sand was a fantastic spot. Ocean view, excellent service and character. It was also frightfully expensive. Rollie arrived early, ordered drinks, and took a window table overlooking the ocean. Shelly arrived a few minutes later, looking fabulous in a tight-fitting, low-cut black evening dress. She bent over to kiss his cheek, and between the cleavage and her captivating cologne, he lost his train of thought. Damn she looked good. And he was sober!

"Seventy eight hundred and twelve dollars is all you owe!"

"What?" The sum got his attention.

Shelly slid in next to him, almost too close for comfort and patted his leg. Rollie looked at her, and she smiled. He wanted to look down at her hand on his leg, but changed his mind. It felt good. Her hand was warm.

"I reworked your returns. Now all you have to do is attached your W2's and ten-ninety-nines." She beamed. "Said I was good."

She kissed Rollie. It was the first time she expressed herself with such exuberance, and Rollie misread her intent. He kissed her back. She enjoyed it for a brief second, and then quickly slid to the other side of the booth. They looked at each other as if they had never paid attention before. He had ruffled her. Her eyes, full of expression, danced with delight. Shelly nibbled on her lower lip, brushed at invisible lint on her chest and snatched up the wine list nervously. Avoiding his eyes.

"How 'bout a good bottle of Merlot?"

"We can do that," Rollie answered as he waved over the waitress.

Not much was said over dinner. Idle chi-chat. They ordered a third bottle of wine, and as the dinner plates were removed Shelly dug into her purse.

"I have a surprise for you, Rollie."

"You never cease to amaze me."

She handed him an envelope. He opened it and read over the enclosed invitation.

He was genuinely surprised. "What's this?"

Shelly gushed. "I got you an invite to the Santino party this weekend."

"How did you...?"

"I do taxes for a little production company that has a deal with him. I said you could use some exposure."

"This is great, Shelly. How can I thank you?"

She reached out and took his hand. The smile lingered. Something in her eyes told him to be quiet. Continuing to hold his hand, Shelly sipped her wine, turned toward the ocean as a blush filled her cheeks. "Can we just sit a while and look at the ocean?"

"Why not?" Heat from her hand felt like a warm fire.

Two hours later, they ordered another snack and were working on their fourth or fifth bottle of wine. Rollie lost count. He didn't want to get drunk, nor did he want Shelly drunk, but they were heading in that direction.

"You know what?" she asked.

"What?"

"Do you know you spent more than you made on your acting career last year?"

"What are you talking about?" He didn't want to hear about taxes.

"Well," Shelly started, bravely sucking down part of another glass of Merlot, "last year you made thirty-two hundred dollars as an actor, and spent sixty-eight hundred for pictures, wardrobe, and union dues."

"Isn't that considered a standard industry thing?

She ignored the comment "So, Rollie, over the last five years, you probably spent more than twice as much as you earned in your chosen field. I think if this keeps up, the IRS will be auditing your classy butt." She slurred her words. "It's a good thing you got that settlement from the accident and made all those profitable investments. You'd be living on the street the way you spend money on your career."

"What are you trying to say?" He slurred back at her. The wine was creating warmth he hadn't expected.

Tax lessons seemed to turn her on. Her breasts filled with a remarkable fullness when she talked deductions. When she noticed he was watching her breasts rise and fall with each breath, rather than look into her eyes, the smile evaporated, eyelids narrowed, nose flared, and the sweet carnality voice erupted like burning snake oil. "You're sick, Rollie."

"Only in my thoughts, and only when I'm tired." He smiled at his joke. "It gets lonely in my bed. I always seem to be alone."

"You belong in bed alone, and, by the way," she slurred over her numb tongue, "you'd think after as many years as you've been trying to get your big break in Hollywood, you'd quit. But I guess you're like most guys, you don't know when to quit, do you?"

"When we read together at the studio, weren't you the one who told me how good I was?"

"Sure, I had to tell you that or you wouldn't have gone to the studio and read that scene with me." She raised a penciled eyebrow in a perfect arch to make her point.

"Are you now saying I wasn't good?" No actor wanted to hear the answer to a vulnerable question blurted from a wine-influenced mouth. He wanted to close his ears.

"Yes, that's what I'm saying. You weren't good, Rollie. In fact, you were terrible. You were exactly what I needed to look good, and it worked. Remember, I'm the one who got the job? You were so bad you made me look wonderful. I forgot to say thanks." She took a deep breath, her breast rising to the occasion.

"Does this mean you don't love me?" He asked with innocent eyes.

Wanting to laugh, the comment turned serious. Frowning in a sexy, liquor-induced expression, "I don't know. I must stink too, cause I haven't worked since then."

"Well, since we both stink, what should we do now?"

She grabbed onto his hand again and looked straight into his eyes. "I think you should take me to your place so we can make mad passionate love. I don't know why it's taken this long, but I've waited long enough for you to make a move."

Without saying another word, Rollie helped her from the booth. He paid the tab, left a generous tip, and they lumbered out to the parking lot arm in arm. They were both too drunk to drive, so he tipped the attendant, told him to put both cars somewhere safe until morning, and to get them a cab.

At Rollie's house, he carried Shelly inside. She started removing her clothes as she staggered toward the bedroom. "Give me a minute to freshen up."

"Take your time."

Rollie waited for her on the couch. Eyeing the shabby furnishings, the desire for a more comfortable environment washed over him. Spending so little time at home, he bought cold leather, glass chairs, area rugs and decorator touches for looks, not comfort. Modern furniture wasn't created for lovemaking. He thought about bedding Shelly for years, and now he had her. She was actually undressing in his bedroom. The idea of making love to Shelly, to hold that magnificent body against his was delirious. Over the years he had undressed her a hundred times, each getting better than the last. He leaned his head on the couch, full of anticipation and fell asleep.

In the morning, Shelly made a dash for his robe. Before she could climb into it, Rollie was standing in the doorway. Eyeing her scattered clothing spread over the floor, and then her phenomenal body. "You were great."

Shelly screamed, covered herself with the robe, and waved him off.

"It's too late for that, Shelly."

"Did we?"

"Yep." And he lied with a straight face.

"Did you use…?"

He shook his head. "No time."

"Oh my God." Her eyes danced everywhere, but at Rollie, as her face twisted in disgust.

"You even said you loved me." Again said with a straight face.

"No!" Shelly all but yelled.

"Yep."

"Rollie, don't you think it was a mistake?"

"Not after everything you said to me."

"Stop!" She darted her large brown eyes in his direction. "What did I say?"

"You said I was the best, most gentle lover you ever had." He felt this might be the best performance he'd ever given. He decided to go for it. "You said you have loved me for a very long time."

"No!" She was stammering.

Rollie pulled her into his arms. Inches from her face he gave her one of his famous Rollie Kemp smiles, and she smiled back. "We don't have to rush into anything, Shelly. We can take our time."

Her nod was a nervous reaction. "Yes, that's a good idea."

He kissed her, and to his surprise, she kissed him back. "Let's do it again." He whispered, brushing the hair from her cheek.

"Okay," she whispered. "I'd like to remember it this time."

When Rollie woke up the second time, it was afternoon, and the bed next to him was empty. All her clothes were gone. He walked through the house, hoping to find a note. There wasn't one.

Chapter 10

Rollie called Shelly and got her answering machine. He hoped she'd go to the party with him, but when he couldn't catch up to her he went solo.

Hollywood parties held in Brentwood mansions were always by invitation. Rollie had never been to one. Superstars roamed the grounds, security over-whelming, and Rollie felt like a turtle a mile from the lake. No one even looked at him. Few knew about the event except those on the A-party list, and the secondary crowd invited to fill empty spaces. The party girls were on a separate list, picked up, and always alone. Drugs flowed like tap water. The inner circle of power players was always on the final list. It was a family. Everyone knew everybody, except new visitors like Rollie. No reason needed to throw a party, they just happened.

Rollie walked through the Bellaire mansion in awe. The place was jammed with bodies, and the over-flow hastily filed out to the pool house. Rollie looked around, and rationalized how a lone coyote must've felt walking down a crowed street. Music throbbed over the twenty- acre estate and the closest of neighbor's wouldn't be cognizant a party was happening.

Rollie passed Shelly in a hallway, and was grateful to see a familiar face. "Hi, Shelly. Great party." He couldn't help notice the sexy dress. "You look very sexy."

She ignored the compliment. "Mingle, Rollie. We can talk later." She gave him a tiny smile while her eyes reached into his soul, and then whispered, "You look good too. Wow." And then she was gone.

Rollie said hello to several producers, directors, and casting agents he had met over the years. All seemed surprised to see him. Phony smiles were everywhere.

Drake Fargo appeared from the shadows in the large game room and maneuvered to Rollie. "I don't remember asking you to join me on this job."

Rollie grinned. "I actually got invited, Drake. Can you believe that?"

"No, but since you're here you can keep an eye on young Ben Parker over there."

"He's a jerk. Why are we watching him?"

"Because we got hired to keep him out of trouble." Drake answered dryly.

"So all that crap I read about him is true?"

"Go rub elbows and pretend you like him. Aren't you always saying you're an actor? Go an act!"

"And what will you be doing, Drake, while I'm acting?"

"Watching' the other jerk. What's his name?"

Rollie looked around the room. "You talking about Andre Garrison?"

"Yeah. These guys are a handful. Don't take your eyes off Ben."

"You know it's my day off, right?" Rollie said.

"So I'll pay you extra! Just keep an eye on him."

Fargo disappeared into the crowd and followed Andre Garrison.

Rollie took a cursory pass in the direction he last saw Ben Parker, but Parker was missing. Rollie remembered meeting Ben, and his inseparable buddy Andre Garrison, at a Christmas party. While most producers in town wanted Ben in their next film, he was almost untouchable. They all had a blind spot regarding the golden boy and overlooked his wretched social habits. His last three films grossed hundreds of millions and his price tag soared. Gifted with blond hair, piercing blue eyes, a throaty voice, and a body every woman wanted, Ben migrated out of Philadelphia and became an instant star. He rode that sudden surge of stardom, using every moment to his advantage. He was offered roles every significant name in town wanted, and he knew about the offer before they did. Every starlet on the "A" list came to party, just to rub shoulders or be seen with Ben Parker. Parker's childhood buddy, Andre Garrison was just downright lucky. He didn't have Parker's talent or charisma, and yet he also worked all the time.

Rollie thought he saw Ben going up the stairs, and followed. At the end of the hallway, Rollie entered a darkened bedroom, and there was Ben chasing after a very pretty, half naked blond. Both were giggling as they ran past Rollie, down the hall, down the stairs, and out into the vast yard. Rollie started to go after them, and bumped into Shelly. She was with a skinny older man who wore his white hair combed forward to cover a protruding, balding scalp. Why she was hanging out with an eighty year old, Rollie wondered?

"Rollie!" Shelly was all giggly. "I'd like you to meet Arnold Aronjelovich, the director. Arnold, this is Rollie Kemp, the actor I was telling you about."

Rollie shook hands with the little man while his eyes searched for Ben. "I'm glad to meet you, Arnold."

"Likewise, Rollie. Shelly here, she's a big fan of yours. Give me a call next week and we'll do lunch." He handed Rollie a business card. "I might have something for you in my next film."

"I'll do that." Rollie said as he took the card. He tried to keep his eyes with the conversation and still look for Ben Parker. Everyone knew Arnold Aronjelovich. He'd won two Academy Awards, and been nominated numerous other times. The old man still had his pick of the crop from the studios, even though he hadn't had a hit in years. "Nice meeting you."

Arnold wrapped his arm around Shelly, and they took off down the hallway. Rollie watched them for a moment, knowing the only thing down the hall were bedrooms. Shelly being with that old man... He took off down the stairs in pursuit of Ben. He spotted Fargo tagging along with Andre, and then he saw Ben outside. As he rushed through the doors, he watched Fargo get stopped by an exquisite young actress in an exceptionally low-cut dress. Andre disappeared into the crowd, and before Fargo could blink the kid was gone. Rollie caught a glance from Fargo, talking to the cutie cost him -- a child getting caught with his hand in the cookie jar. Fargo returned Rollie's smirk with cutting daggers before migrating in the direction Andre vanished. Rollie couldn't help smile as he moved back to the staircase. The house was a mansion-sized castle with over twenty-five thousand square feet, so it was easy to lose someone.

The mansion belonged to Drego Santino, and Rollie knew all about the capo from New York. Santino worked his way through the ranks of the Castellano crime family, and then the organized crime syndicate boss became an executive producer. Magically he was known to arrange financing for many hard-to-fund motion pictures, and was thereby given the ability to specify whatever lead he wanted for the films he financed. Ben Parker seemed to be one of his favorites. Santino originally built the chateau for his young starlet wife, but that marriage ended in divorce, so he turned the place into party-boulevard. He added caves, in-door-out-door swimming pools, slides, fun rooms, sex rooms, and other extensions you needed a pass to get in. Santino, in his late sixties, continued to behave as though he was twenty. Rollie ran into him on the stairway. Santino was going up with another blond on his arm while Rollie was coming down. The girl looked familiar to Rollie, but she turned away to avoid recognition. From what he could see of her she was utterly beautiful or imposing makeup created an illusion in the hallway lighting. She was statuesque and extremely hot. Rollie couldn't remember whom she was or where they met, but was sure they knew each other.

Santino stopped and pointed at Rollie. "Aren't you Bobby Moore?"

"No, I'm Rollie Kemp." He answered, still looking for Ben.

"Too bad," Santino added, "I have financing for Bobby's next film."

"Yeah, that is too bad. If I see him, I'll tell him."

"Thank you. You have a good look, kid." Then Santino lowered his voice. "Could you help me up the stairs? That last drink has slowed me down."

"No problem." Rollie took his arm and helped him climb the stairs. The girl avoided his stare. "Stairs can be a bitch, can't they?"

Santino made idle conversation climbing the stairs. "Are you enjoying the party?"

"Absolutely." Rollie had seen the girl on his arm before. As they climbed the stairs, his mind raced trying to remember where they had met. He tried to get another peek at her face, but she buried it into Santino's shoulder.

At the top of the stairs, Ben Parker charged out of nowhere and took hold of Santino's arm. "Hey Drego, great party." He looked at Rollie and frowned. "I've got him from here."

Rollie let go, and Ben led Santino and the girl down the hallway. He was about to follow when Diz O'Lare came up from behind Rollie, and grabbed him.

"Hey slugger, how's it goin'?"

"Hey, Diz." Rollie thought control. "How's it hangin'?"

"Whoa dude, you're not still angry at me are you?"

Rollie wanted to punch his lights out. "No, of course not." He tried to look around Diz, to see where Ben was taking Santino and the girl, but Diz was in his face.

"That's good 'cause we might work together again, and I wouldn't want ya mad at me, right?" He faked throwing a punch.

"Right." Rollie nodded, tossing a punch into the air.

Diz flinched. "So, come with me."

Diz grabbed Rollie's arm and pulled him down the stairs. When he finally got a look down the long hallway, Ben, Santino and the beautiful blond were gone. Diz led Rollie over to a cluster of couches where Luke Waters sat with a group of fellow actors and agents.

"Luke, look what I just found?"

Waters frowned. "Still tryin' to make it, huh kid?"

"I'd love to chat with you guys, maybe later okay?" Rollie gave Diz a nod and dashed back up the stairs.

Over the next few hours, Rollie and Fargo bounced around, like riding inside a pinball machine. Ben and Andre changed partners every few minutes. Party guests continually bashed against one another to the music, drugs popped up everywhere, and escorts did what escorts do best. Memories blurred, bodies blended together without explanation, and the night became morning. Throughout the entire evening, Rollie got dizzy trying to keep up, and Fargo ran from one room to another, chasing after the two loose cannons. The two actors, who took being mega stars to a new level, were certifiable. They drank, used drugs and bounced from one room to another without thought. They were both jerks, and somehow Fargo, without Rollie's knowledge, got talked into watching them. Rollie laughed at the idea of attempting to keep these two from making a mistake. The last part was a joke. Nobody could keep these two from doing what they wanted. Sometime, in the wee hours of the morning, both Rollie and Drake lost sight of the boys again. Rollie searched everywhere and couldn't find a hint of their ever being there.

Empty bottles of the most expensive liquors were scattered throughout the mansion and tossed over the grounds like discarded paper-plates. Bodies slept where they fell or passed out. When the morning sun peeked over surrounding hills, partygoers woke up. Bodies moved, most were half-dressed, and all seemed to rush to their cars. In a synchronized moment, the cars then vanished into the morning haze.

Rollie found Ben Parker sleeping outside on the lawn. He had crawled under a clump of bushes, unnoticed and passed out. He wore a skimpy thong and nothing else. He clothes were scattered over the bushes. Rollie rolled Parker over and in a half-assed attempt, dressed him. Then, he picked Parker up and tossed him over his shoulder. Parker reeked of stale booze and urine. When he entered the house, carrying Ben like a sack of potatoes, he found Fargo with Andre Garrison. Andre was so slammed from a drug-alcohol-cocktail mix he didn't know where he was. He whimpered about going home, so they took the two renowned stars out to Fargo's SUV.

"How'd you get here, Rollie?"

"Cab. I thought I might have a good time."

Fargo nodded. "Get in the car."

His sleek black BMW SUV sped off into the morning dew. They drove in silence out of the hills. When they hit Sunset Boulevard Fargo sped out the entrance of Bellaire Estates, turned right, and headed west towards Santa Monica. Rollie reached into the back seat and prevented both actors from tumbling to the floor. When he sat up, he saw them. Coming from the opposite direction, passing without seeing them, John Rader and his partner Frank Mustio were following a black and white police-car. Rollie watched it turn left, into Bellaire Estates. Right where they had just come from. The two cops didn't see Rollie.

"Think someone called the cops?" Rollie asked.

Fargo looked in his rearview mirror. "You call the cops, Ben Parker?"

Rollie spun around and watched Ben Parker start to giggle. He started mumbling some gibberish, and then he whispered, "Maybe your friends came to kill Drego?" He laughed, coughed, "Play some cops and robbers." He closed his eyes, started to laugh again, and then he ejected a missile of multicolored vomit all over Fargo's backseat.

"Shit!" Fargo blurted out.

"No," Rollie said, "it came out the other end."

Chapter 11

Rader drove through the Bel Air gate as a parade of exotic cars and limos passed them. "The wedding must be over."

Mustio craned his head around, watching the departing vehicles. "So where the hell's everybody going?"

"This is L.A. Frank, where does anybody go?"

"This is gonna be a waste of time, isn't it?"

Rader nodded and followed the squad car onto the grounds of a magnificent two-story mansion. When they drove through the open gates, Rader noticed the name on the mailbox read, Santino. He knew the name, and suddenly the visit took on a whole new meaning. Both locals and the feds watched, and waited for, Drego Santino, to make one mistake. They'd been watching him for years without so much as finding a hair out of place. The mysterious film executive, in spite of his organized crime connections, was squeaky clean. His financial connections came from offshore banks and couldn't be traced back to crime families.

More cars passed them in the opposite direction. Rader glanced over at Mustio, "Looks like a mass exodus. Santino must throw one hell of a party, and then toss everybody out."

Mustio watched the passing cars with intense curiosity. "Maybe it wasn't a prank call?"

"Desk Sergeant said the caller was drunk, giggling throughout the whole conversation." Rader drove up the long driveway. What he genuinely needed was a few more cups of coffee. This wasn't the way to start a new day. One more cup and he might wake up -- or at least feel alive. "She told the nine-one-one operator never mind. We wouldn't be here if it wasn't for the Captain insisting we check the place out."

"Maybe he recognized the address?" Mustio surmised.

Rader doubted it. "I think his mean-spirited attitude was working overtime. This is an early reminder he's still in control."

Rader parked behind the black-and-white in a circular driveway. Two uniformed cops where already waiting for them.

Rader flashed his badge, "You been inside?"

The oldest of the four cops shook his head. "We just got here." He looked around, "Doesn't look like much of a crime scene does it?"

Rader surveyed the grounds. The lush lawn was covered with debris as if a parade had passed through. Grounds keepers were busy collecting the mess into large black plastic bags.

"Let's check it out anyway," Rader mumbled, moving to the front door. Over his shoulder, he said to the older cop, "Why don't you have one of your guys stop the yard cleanup until we see what's up?"

The older cop nodded and quickly gestured for another officer to take care of it. The young cop walked outside and moved toward the gardeners. Mustio and the uniformed cops followed after Rader.

On the second ring, a maid opened the door. In broken English, "Can I help you?"

Rader flashed his badge. "Someone called about a dead body?"

The maid nodded, her expression calm, puppy-eyed wide. "Si."

"Could you show us the body?" Rader asked.

"Yes," the maid said opening the door wide, "please come it. My name is Maria."

Rader guessed she was in her early twenties, a pretty little thing. He made a mental note to check her background. She seemed too calm, disconnected, almost uninterested.

Inside the foyer, a group of maids were cleaning the house, dusting the furniture, vacuuming the floors, washing the banisters and windows, preparing for another party or wedding. Fresh-cut flowers were in several colorful vases, casting out sweet, aromas, and exotic scents. The house smelled like a hospital room, or mortuary. Maria gestured, and the detectives followed up the stairs.

Rader couldn't take his eyes off the cleaning staff, "Maria, can you ask them to stop cleaning until we have a look around?"

"Si, ah, yes, of course." Maria scampered into the largest of rooms and spoke softly, in Spanish, to the group of maids. They stopped cleaning and gathered around her like school children do with teachers. They listened, all nodded, and then turned to stare at Rader. Maria ran back to the detectives and led them up the wide staircase.

Rader noticed all eyes were on them, watching their every move. The maids chattered nervously in hushed whispers.

The entire second floor had already been sanitized, dusted, swept and manicured. Both Rader and Mustio stared in disbelief. Down a long hallway, decorated with antiques, priceless art, paintings, and movie posters, Maria, hurried to a closed door. She paused, and then opened the door in one jerky movement. The room was one of many bedrooms on the floor. They stepped through the door and froze. The bedroom, furnished like a Presidential Suite, had been purified to perfection. In the middle of a king-sized poster-bed, the body was positioned ever so eloquently -- waiting for a photo shoot. A lush, earth-colored, down-filled comforter surrounded the once beautiful young woman. She had long blond hair, which was picturesquely spread over a fluffy pillow. Her face, however, was colorless, skin placid, hazel eyes turning into a chalky gloss. The eyes stared into emptiness, exposing neither surprise, or fear. She had obviously been dead for several hours, but both Rader and Mustio ran to the bed to check her vitals. Advanced rigor mortis had set in, and both detectives backed from the stiff corpse.

"Dammit to hell!" Rader jerked open his cell, and punched the buttons. "This is Rader. I need a bus, the ME, the crime scene boys, and lots of hands. We have a crime scene that's been so fuckin' compromised it will make us all sick!" He spit out the address and slammed the tiny phone shut. His eyes danced over the entire room in an angry sweep, and then he turned to one of several cops standing behind him and lashed out, "Get everyone out of here! Take 'em all into the big room downstairs, and tell the gardeners to stop what they're doin' and to get their ass in to join the others. I want the entire house taped off, and tell everyone to watch where they're walking!" He took a deep breath to calm his blood pressure. He thought he had seen everything.

The older cop nodded and carefully backed out of the room. As he went he mumbled. "Yes sir." He then turned to the other cops, "You heard the man, let's secure this place."

Rader, with Mustio tagging along behind him, took Maria into the kitchen. This was beyond stupid.

Mustio flipped his notebook open, "Where you from, Maria?"

"Monterrey Mexico."

"Illegal?" Rader watched her reaction. She didn't answer the question. He could tell she'd been around a while. Her English was too transparent. He knew she would understand significantly more of what was said than she'd admit, and probably got the job because of her ability to speak broken English well enough to be understood. It also assisted owners to have someone who could communicate with other help. He'd seen the look before, the look behind the eyes, the art of playing fox. Maria was an instant challenge. Obviously she didn't like or trust cops.

"Who cleaned the room?" Rader asked in a raspy voice he thought sounded pleasant.

"I don't know." Maria answered with a shrug.

Rader knew her explanation might actually be the truth, working with a team of ten, mowing through the house like a herd of buffalo. Perhaps she didn't know exactly who cleaned the room, but he wouldn't bet on it. "Who found the body?" He watched her body language. She had rehearsed. He'd get nothing from her unless he played her game his way.

Maria cleared her throat. "She was like that when I came to work." Her dark brown eyes teared up when she looked from one detective to the other.

"The owner, Santino is he home?" Mustio asked.

The terror in Maria's eyes grew, and Mustio turned away. Rader could see her issues coming. He quickly stepped in front of his partner. If Maria freaked on them, whatever information she had, would be sealed in a world of silence. Rader smiled and closed his little black book.

"No," Maria finally answered, "Mr. Santino is in New York, I think."

"So, who was at the party?" Rader asked.

"Party?" Maria seemed surprised.

"What was your name again?" Rader asked, his voice changing, adding a no nonsense edge. Angrily he flipped his little black book open again.

"Maria," she said quickly, "Maria Gomez."

Rader wrote her name down. "So, are you illegal, Maria?" He glanced up from the book. He knew, and he knew she knew he knew. He loved silent answers. People always gave themselves away. "Let's say we over-look reporting you," Rader smiled again. "Let's also say you will help us build a list of people who might've stopped by. You understand what I'm saying?"

She shook her head, agreeing too quickly. "Si, ah, yes."

"Good." Rader gave a nod, knowing she would never tell on Santino's guests. Loyalty to the master created a false security, not to mention a relationship between the lead maid and her staff. Rader assumed there was a implicit threat on her life if she opened her mouth. His observation of Maria was a replica of others he'd questioned in the past. She didn't know what truth

111

meant, and was most likely taught to lie about everything since she learned to talk.

"Do you know who the dead girl was, Maria?" Mustio pressed on.

Rader caught Maria's eyes, the nervous tick. She knew the girl. He tried to get passed the code of silence. "You didn't know her by name, but she was a regular, right?"

Maria hesitated answering. After a beat, she mumbled. "Yes."

Mustio smiled with his best fatherly tenderness. "Was she, you know, -- ah, paid?"

"Maybe the girl tried too hard to become an actress?" Maria whispered.

Rader glanced over Mustio's shoulder, and saw the ME enter with the Crime Scene boys and the Scientific Investigation Division team. "Why don't you take the ME and his team upstairs? We're gonna need a warrant to search the house."

Mustio nodded, "I'll get things in motion." He walked off.

Rader turned back to Maria. "Where does Mr. Santino work?"

"I don't know," Maria answered distantly "I just work for him here at his home."

"Well," Rader said real slowly, "might you know where he went?"

"I'm sorry," Maria whispered.

It took Rader a few minutes to clear his head. He took Maria by the arm and led her out by the pool. They stood alone. She started fidgeting while Rader toyed with his notebook. He was deliberately being clumsy and slow. He finally opened the book and thumbed through the pages. From the corner of his eyes, he watched her, trying to get a read on her body movements. She couldn't take it any longer, and turned to face him.

"What do you want?" Her English suddenly became prolific, and full of anxiety.

"I was thinking, guessing how many in your crew would be deported."

She stammered. "We work very hard." He was quiet. "What can we do to avoid deportation?"

"Start by telling me what you know?"

"The girls name was Tawny. I never heard her last name."

"What about Santino?"

Maria faced the pool, glancing down at her reflection. "I've been in this country for ten years. I like my job."

"Yeah, I like mine too." He held the book open, and waited her out.

Tear well up in her eyes. She glanced into his eyes. "What do you know about mister Santino?"

"Not enough."

She gave him a sardonic smile. "I do not know what the meeting was about. He met with two men I've never seen, and then they got together with some of the actors. Later, I saw them with some of the younger women, girls really. I don't know anything else."

"Yes you do."

"You play poker, detective?"

"I do."

"Will you keep me, and my crew out of this?"

He waited before answering. Her eyes bore holes into his soul. "What did you hear?"

"Promise me first?"

"I don't know if I can make that promise."

"Then I heard nothing." She turned, and started back into the house.

"Maria?" Rader hated himself for giving in.

She turned around, her face drawn tight with fear. Her head spun violently from side to side. "My life must be worth something, no?"

"You have my word. I'll keep you out of it."

Maria walked back to him. She glanced around nervously, to make sure no one heard her, and then looked up, studying Rader's face. "I heard the two men talking after mister Santino left. I only heard some words they spoke. They talked about pension funds and laughed. Then twice, angrily, they said something that sounded like, explosion, and without warning. I couldn't hear any more. If I moved closer they would have caught me."

"That's all you heard?" Rader pushed her.

"No." She looked deep into the pool. "I heard one of them tell someone I couldn't see that the price had doubled. They walked off laughing."

Rader watched her movements. "What do you think they were talking about, Maria?"

"I don't know." Tears dribbled down Maria's cheeks. "If I run, I know they will find me."

"So don't run." Rader said. "Just do your job, and tell the others to do the same thing."

"When I am dead and gone, detective, will you watch out for my children?"

Chapter 12

Fargo drove north on PCH, and a bunch of cop cars caught Rollie's attention. They passed the area where the Mustang that almost hit Rollie a few days earlier was still parked. Rollie spun around in his seat, glanced out, and stiffened when he saw the Mustang being lifted onto a flatbed tow truck. The car was covered with dust, and the side he hadn't seen before was badly dented. A For Sale sign was still visible in the Mustang window. Rollie craned his neck until they were out of sight.

Fargo tossed him a look. "She must've been a looker?"

Rollie turned away, frowning at the memory. "No big deal."

Eddie Rosewell's beach office, a small house off PCH was no longer used as a workplace. Instead, it served as a crash pad, or used in emergencies. When Fargo parked in the rear, Rollie waited for an explanation.

"This is Eddy Rosewell's old office."

Rollie frowned. "What's that supposed to mean?"

"We were hired to keep them out of trouble, right?"

"Isn't this sort of like, you know, kidnapping?"

"No." Fargo thought about it for a second. "Get out of the car and drag his ass inside. Hurry it up before snooping eyes see us."

Rollie got out and tossed Ben Parker over his shoulder. Fargo picked Andre Garrison up like a rag-doll, and they carried the two actors inside. Rollie put Ben Parker to bed, pulling off his shoes before he covered the fully dressed celebrity. Mini-malls and fast food restaurants surrounded the old house. It was one of the last single-family homes in the immediate area. The front functioned as an office with a reception area, and two private rooms. The back of the house had never been changed, and still had two bedrooms separated by a bathroom.

Andre Garrison was mumbling incoherently while Fargo tied him into a waiting-room recliner. He bound his hands and feet, and then wrapped his body so the kid couldn't possibly move. Rollie and Andre watched him with considerable interest. When Fargo finished, he stepped back to admire his work.

Andre looked at Fargo. "What if I have to take a leak?"

"Go where you are." Fargo snapped. "You can clean it up later."

"Maybe we should do the same thing to Ben?" Rollie said

Fargo tossed Rollie the rope. "Tie under the mattress."

"Why?"

Fargo shook his head, like any dummy should understand him. "'Cause if he decides to go anywhere, he'll have to take it with him."

"Clever." Rollie added sarcastically.

Rollie went to check on Ben. In the bedroom, he found the actor slowly getting to his feet. Rollie pushed him down, but Ben popped up, a bit off balance, and took a swing at Rollie.

"I'm gonna sue you," Ben slurred, taking another wild swing.

Rollie blocked the wayward punch, just as Ben threw another. Tagged in the chest, Rollie angrily popped Ben Parker in the nose. It wasn't a roundhouse blow, just a short vicious jab, but enough to knock Ben out. Rollie stood over him for a moment, clenching his fists. He caught himself and put both hands in pockets. Then, embarrassed, he looked around to make sure Fargo didn't see him. He tied Ben to a chair and then to the closet door. To hell with a mattress, he'd have to take the door with him. Rollie waited to see if the actor would protest. He didn't.

Rollie returned to the front room just in time to watch Fargo sit on a small loveseat, trying to reduce his gargantuan body into a comfortable position. Rollie opened the fridge and took out a jar of peanut butter. While he looked for utensils, Fargo's cell phone rang. Rollie found a spoon and scooped out a glob from the jar. He sucked on the tasty, brown thickness and listened to Fargo with idle curiosity.

"What are you yellin' at?" He shot a look at Rollie. "We got both of 'em here at your old office on PCH." He shook his head. "They ain't goin' anywhere."

Rollie sat across from Fargo. The burly man nodded, and then his smile vanished. "You're kidding?"

His face tightened, his eyes darted from Rollie to the bound Andre, who was out. "I'll see ya when you get here."

He closed the phone and looked at Rollie.

"I don't like that look." Rollie said taking another spoonful of peanut butter. "What happened?"

"An actress was murdered at the party. The cops are all over the mansion." He gestured toward Andre with his head. "Their attorney is on his way over here. He wants us to stay with them, and move 'em out of town as quick as it can be arranged. How much stuff did you touch at the house, Rollie?"

"I don't know, probably everything. I touched the banisters, doorknobs to various rooms, glasses when I had a drink, tables I leaned on, and stuff. Why?"

"Cops will be getting prints off everything in sight."

"Wow, so they'll know we were at the party."

"They'll ask lots of questions we don't want to answer 'cause of client privilege, and all the other nonsense." Fargo shook his head. "We gotta be on the same page, understand?"

"Absolutely, but I have one question?" Rollie said thoughtfully.

"What?" Fargo was getting testy.

"Who's writing the page?"

Fargo glared at him. "You can be a real ass, you know that?"

"I've heard that before. So who was the dead girl?"

Fargo shrugged. "Don't know yet."

Eddie Rosewell arrived, covered in sweat. Rosewell stood a couple of inches taller than most midgets, and carried that height complex wherever he went. His voice was raspy, nervous squinting pig-eyes, considerably overweight, and he only represented major stars and studio execs. Some of his more elite clients remained nameless, even to Fargo. The upper echelon of Hollywood power players kept him running day and night. While most people hated Rosewell's guts or were jealous of his victories, Fargo told Rollie he liked the guy, and worked lots of gigs for him. Rosewell was amusing at times and otherwise was a significant pain in the ass to everyone. To add to his repertoire, he had an excitable, humorous movement. He extended limbs into frozen positions, and held them still as he spoke or made his point. All of this was overlooked because the little guy was a significant source of income for the agency – he paid well, and his checks were always good.

"Come on in, Eddie."

"Not now, Drake. This is serious business."

"Meet Rollie Kemp, my new associate." Fargo gestured to Rollie.

Rosewell stared at Rollie. "Don't I know you?" He snapped his fingers, remembering. "Your that actor! The one in the bunny movie, that Hip Hop one."

"That's me," Rollie answered dryly. "One of my bigger roles."

Eddie turned back to Drake. "He's an actor, Drake, can we trust him?"

"We can."

Eddie pulled out a chair and sat across from them. "These two bums are under contract at the studio, and they are my best-paying clients. These guys could be in a shit load of trouble."

Rollie tossed half an eye at Drake. "What am I missing here?" He deflected his scrutiny back at

Rosewell. "You're thinking one of them killed the girl, aren't you?"

Rosewell shrugged, his protruding belly bouncing with the rapid hand movements, "Nothing surprises me, kid. Drake knows. Drugs and enough booze make this type think they're invincible." He glowered over Andre Garrison, took a peek in the back room at Ben Parker, and dropped his shoulders. "Sometimes I wonder if there isn't a better way to pay the bills. Did they ever get out of your sight?"

"Every ten minutes," Fargo answered. "We're good, Eddie, but we're not magicians."

"You guys need to help me out of a very deep hole." Eddie was a nervous wreck.

"How deep is the hole?" Rollie asked. "This is getting' good."

"No one needs to know how long they were at the party, ah – we," he laughed at his own joke, "You should get them out of town until this blows over." He took out a small black notebook, and flipped it open. He thumbed through page after page of notes. "You ever heard of the Rainbow House?"

Rollie knew the place well, but Fargo had to think for a moment before nodding. A quick glance towards Rollie brought knowing eye contact between them. They were both thinking the same thing -- a bigger payday.

Fargo gestured with his hands, doubt. "Babysitting gets expensive, Eddie."

Rosewell gave a sympathetic pout, "A thousand a day plus expenses."

Rollie looked at Fargo and shook his head.

Fargo turned to Rosewell, "There are two, Eddie. Two real pain in the ass pricks."

Rosewell turned a distinctive shade of red, bordering on purple. He loosened his tie as veins grew from the tight collar around his neck. "Don't break my balls here, Drake. I throw you a lot of business."

"And I take care of things for you, but this is different. If one of them killed the girl, I'll be hidin' a murderer. The cops will be askin' a lot of questions, and we'll have to give 'em answers. I don't know, Eddie. This is dirty stuff."

"Don't back out on me now, Drake."

Rollie frowned. "You're asking us to take some serious risks."

"Okay." Eddie sounded as if he had just been stabbed in the heart. "Twenty-five hundred a day plus expenses."

"What's the Rainbow House?" Rollie acted like he'd never heard of the place.

"It's a first-class rehabilitation center, on a secluded ranch up the coast. It was designed to protect the privacy of the rich and famous. Everyone's heard of Rainbow. What'd you do, fall off a turnip truck?"

"I don't use drugs," Rollie tossed back.

Fargo became all business. The usual affable manner changed. His facial expression tightened, and the eyes sharpened into focus. "Let's get back to what you want us to do?"

"You take both boys to Rainbow, and stay with them through detox. They have cabins at Rainbow. When the boys complete their detox, you'll move them to one of the private cabins, and stay with them until this blows over."

"What if they take off?" Rollie asked.

"Then I'll fire you! Fact is if you lose either one during the treatment I'll never use your agency again. That sound fair, Drake?"

Fargo instantly had a look of doubt. Rollie saw him watching Rosewell's nervous behavior. "Why do I feel there's more to this than you're telling us?"

"Okay!" An actor Rosewell wasn't. "It could get messy." Again he got a sympathetic look, freezing an arm in the air. "Take your guns."

Eddie said this almost too quietly. Rollie expressed his feelings with a simple nod, but Fargo's face changed from being a buddy to distrust.

Rosewell put up his hands in defeat, and then did a gyration with both arms, freezing in mid-movement. "I hear the girl had a past." He opened his palm, disclosing information he didn't want to share. " Santino is angry, and God knows you don't want a guy like him mad at you. The fact a murder happened in house, well, ah, now the studio is furious, the cops want a suspect, and need to close the case before the Mayor craps purple balloons, and everyone, Drake, everyone has an opinion." He dropped his chin and stared at the floor. "Okay, I'm sorry. It could be dirty. Santino's people don't play nice, but I doubt he'll create a problem with all the attention this thing is getting. The biggest problem is these two idiots. For whatever reason, Santino and his bankroll make these two, I don't know, ah, different." He looked directly into Fargo's eyes, and then turned to face Rollie. "Are we okay here?"

"No." Rollie stood up and walked to the window. He glanced at Andre and got a lunatic smile in return. Out the window, without looking at Rosewell, "What haven't you told us?" Rollie knew he hadn't heard everything. He knew Santino. Knew all about him, all about his connections, and his obligations.

Rosewell pleaded with his hands, like a moronic mannequin, "That's it. I swear. If there's more, and there probably is, I don't know what it might be." He took a peek at Rollie, then abruptly begged Fargo, "Please, Drake. Help me out here. If I lose these two, I lose the studio as well."

"Okay," Fargo answered quietly. "I'll help you out, and take your word there's not more to this than you've told us."

"You know what I know. If I smell a rat, Drake, I swear I'll call. Okay?"

Fargo nodded. Rollie just stood there, feeling as though he just got sucked into a vacuum cleaner. The situation reeked of vulnerability.

"I'll have a cashier's check for twenty grand by the time the limo comes to pick you up." Rosewell nervously warmed up and even forced a smile. He gathered his notebook, his twenty-four-carat gold pen and stood. He tucked the notebook into his breast pocket and turned the pen to retract the point. "You said your name was Rollie, right?"

"Right."

"You remember when the cops raided Nicole Thrasher's party a couple of weeks back?"

"Sure."

"Then you heard about the cop who was pushed out the window?"

Al thought that was just a story." Rollie added.

"Nah, Andre Garrison pushed the cop, then grabbed his arm, and held him."

Rollie's eyebrows rose. "Twenty-two stories above Wilshire Boulevard?"

Eddie nodded, looking at Fargo. "Yeah, he's lucky the other cops pulled their buddy to safety. The others didn't see what happened, and thought Andre was a hero for saving their comrade. The cop was so grateful to be alive he never said a word. Had he fallen, they would have called it murder -- even here in Hollywood? I only mention this because I want you to know what you're dealing with. These two came from the sewer."

* * * *

When Eddie was gone, Rollie turned to Drake. "So one of these guys could've killed the girl, right?"

"Right."

"Well, gee, this outta be fun. You gonna give me permission to whack them if they get out of line?"

"Whack away."

Chapter 13

In the two hundred block of Park Avenue, on the forty-third floor overlooking the heart of Manhattan, Fabrio Tallagi stepped out of the walnut-paneled elevator and into the marble lobby of Pataglia Brothers Properties. The receptionist immediately notified JoAnn Carter, and she appeared as if by magic, through the ten-foot tall double-door entry. The greeting was silent, the smiles absent. JoAnn Carter, a tall statuesque beauty in her early thirties had executive secretary written all over her. A perfectly tailored Gianni Versace suit moved majestically with her every step.

Fabrio Tallagi followed JoAnn into the executive suite. Standing just inside the door, Gi Carlo, the ever-present bodyguard watched Fabrio enter. The two men nodded at one another, and then Fabrio turned to Anthony Pataglia, who was standing at the window peering over the city of New York below. Miles of endless rooftops reached for the clouds, but only a few had the stature and presence of standing alone above the others. Off in the distance, Central Park sat in the middle of cement and bricks. A strange island of green was a welcome site in the midst of mindless construction expertise. Fabrio, however, wasn't here to look at the scenery. He could see Anthony Pataglia's reflection in the window. A distraught emptiness coated Pataglia's eyes. Tears stained the God Father's flushed cheeks. This was family business. Without turning around, Anthony Pataglia spoke in a near whisper.

"Thank you JoAnn."

"May I get you anything else, Mr. Pataglia?" Her voice carried a slight sensuality.

"No, thank you." Pataglia answered, staring out at nothing.

"I'll be at my desk if you need me." JoAnn backed to the door and left. The door closed without a sound.

Fabrio waited. He was a patient man. He'd worked for the Pataglia's long enough to know when to be quiet. This had to be the most painful meeting he ever had with Anthony Pataglia. Earlier in the day, William Drone had called with the news that Pataglia's only daughter had been raped, and murdered. Fabrio waited for the call, knowing he would be summoned to the office for this meeting. There was no one else Pataglia would call. Fabrio stood alone. Trusted and loyal, he would take care of business quickly, and efficiently.

Finally, Anthony Pataglia wiped the tears away with the back of his hand, and turned to face Fabrio. His one-of-a-kind eyes, dark, and vacant, were surrounded in bloodshot, all cried out. The agony was gradually replaced with intuitive animalism. "Sit down, please." Anthony Pataglia gestured to a large burgundy leather chair. "Someone killed my daughter, Fabrio, and I want the bastard who did it." His eyes warmed, flushing again.

"I understand." Fabrio lowered his powerful physique into the soft luxurious cushions and waited.

Pataglia sank in the chair behind the desk, "You spoke with William Drone?"

"Whatever we need."

Pataglia felt the pain from his broken heart. He closed his eyes, breathing slowly to regain composure. "Has Santino been located?"

"He thinks he'll be next, so he's ah, indisposed."

"He's a good man. Santino didn't kill my daughter." His eyes drifted. "He may be careless, but this wasn't his fault."

Fabrio watched, and patiently listened.

"They want me to retaliate don't they?" Pataglia's eyes penetrated Fabrio's. "This has Moe Brayden's fingerprints all over it."

Fabrio felt uncomfortable, "Should I confirm that with Mr. Drone before...?"

Pataglia cut him off, "Yes, please. I want revenge for my little girl, but if we retaliate wrongly, the cost of living will increase." His eyes focused, narrowing to a squint. "What else did Drone tell you?"

"Louis Baxter was deliberately run off the road after they shot him, and Ronnie Mauten is on the run. Drone said he left everything but essentials."

"Stupid coward." Pataglia glanced at Gi Carlo, watching the thickset man move his weight from one leg to the other.

Fabrio cleared his throat. "Lipesky was at Santino's party."

Pataglia's eyes drifted up to receive Fabrio's gaze. "What was he doing there?"

"Claims pension funds are missing." Fabrio said.

"That sonofabitch! Nothing's missing. They're starting, and we need to end it."

"I agree."

Gi Carlo shifted his body again.

Pataglia rose from his chair, gesturing to all his expensive possessions. "All of this means nothing, Fabrio."

Fabrio didn't have to look around the room. He knew the art was priceless. Right now the only thing that mattered was taking care of Anthony Pataglia, and hoping a conflict between the families could be avoided. "What would you like me to do, Mr. Pataglia?"

Pataglia shrugged his massive shoulders, "Someone has taken my Tawny -- my most treasured gift in the entire world. When our heavenly father was gracious enough to bless me with her, I promised myself, and God, I would take care of her…, and I failed." He sank into his chair, and covered his face with massive hands that, a long time ago, were filled with calluses from working the docks in New York harbor. Anthony Pataglia was fifty-nine, in excellent health, a body rigid with muscle, head full of black hair, and lonely. Then, as if a light went off in his head, he pounded the desk with a closed fist, "All of this over a proposed low-budget contract? No! They want change. Want me out in the open, to react, and give them a chance to take the reins. "

Fabrio was confused. "Why would they…"

"Control. Moe Brayden and his little shit sidekick Mark Lipesky want to control the unions, the pension funds, and the waterfront. They know they can't do it if I'm in the way."

Fabrio shook his head, "With all the potential terrorism, Homeland Security will take a serious look at us if we go to war." The muscles in his jaw tightened. He saw Gi Carlo open his stance, spreading his legs. He gave Fabrio a nod as his eyes watched everything.

"First, you will take an out-of-the-way trip to Philly. We'll start with Mark Lipesky, and then you'll head to the west coast to find the man who actually killed my daughter. I want whoever did this to know the real meaning of pain, and suffering." He looked deeply into Fabrio's eyes. "You comprehend?"

"Yes." Fabrio nodded. "Anything you want to know from this person?"

"Yes!" Anthony screamed as he pounded the desk again. His face twisted with hate, the anger gushing from within. "I wanna know why the piece of shit killed my innocent little angel. I want to know why he snuck off in the middle of the night, and left her to die." His voice grew angrier as each word got louder. "I want to know who took my little Tawny to the party, and I want to know what he's sayin' before he closes his eyes for the last time!" Anthony leaned back in his chair, and turned to look out the window. "I want you and only you to make sure my only daughter's body is shipped home in the best coffin you can buy. Find Santino, and talk to him. It's important he knows we'll protect him, and the others. Talk to everybody. We need to stop this before it escalates. If it's war they want, then we'll be the sneaky little bastards who will win it." Pataglia suddenly knew the reason for the whole mess. "This is all about greed. Hollywood's a sick town, Fabrio, and somebody out there is gonna pay. JoAnn has your ticket, and some expense money. I'll have Billy, and his crew, meet up with you in Philly. Gi Carlo here will take you to the airport." He got up and circled the enormous desk. The two men hugged, then Anthony Pataglia held Fabrio out at arm's length, "Call me?"

"As soon as I have my first conversation."

Fabrio turned, and walked to the door that Gi Carlo held open for him.

"Fabrio?"

Fabrio turned back. "Sir?"

"I'll want to know the last thing Lipesky says."

"Of course."

Fabrio didn't look back, and neither did Gi Carlo, who followed him out.

Chapter 14

Rollie needed a break from babysitting, and told Drake he was going to his house for a change of clothes. Fargo was attempting to take a nap, and waved Rollie off. He drove Fargo's SUV to PCH, and turned south instead of north. He drove past the lot where the Mustang was, and found it had been removed. On his way into Santa Monica, Rollie kept replaying the near accident with the Mustang. The driver was a kid wearing a baseball cap on backwards. He wasn't going to be much of a witness. What the hell was that? It was all he could remember, other than the guy drove like a lunatic. He crossed over to Fourth Street and found a parking space behind the police station. Maybe it wasn't important, but Rollie felt compelled to tell Rader about it.

Inside the station house, Rollie showed his I.D. to the desk sergeant, and ask to see Detective Rader. The cop told him to have a seat, picked up the phone, and quietly said something unheard by Rollie. Within minutes, Rader came out.

"I didn't expect to see you this soon." Rader shook his hand enthusiastically.

"You got a minute?" Rollie asked.

"Sure, absolutely. Let's go back to my desk."

Rollie followed him through a locked door, down a hallway, and into a vast area full of desks. The desks formed little cubicles, each one backing up to the next. It was lunchtime, and they were alone. Rader took him to his desk, pulled out a chair, and they sat down.

"I don't want to take up a lot of your time, John."

Rader glanced at his watch and shook his head. "We're okay for a few. What's up?"

"The other day, when we ran into each other on the beach, you mentioned a guy was run off the road. I think I saw him."

Rader sat up. "Whaddya mean?"

"I was on my way to the studio, and in a hurry to get there."

"Okay," Rader said, trying to get to the point.

Rollie shrugged. "I finally got a speaking part, and was really nervous, ya know?" Rader nodded, but Rollie could see he didn't have a clue where the conversation was going. "It was foggy as hell that morning. There was an accident on the ten, so I took the long way to Universal Studios, and cut over Malibu Canyon to the one-o-one." Rollie knew he was taking too long to get to the point when Rader glanced at his watch. "I got cut off. Hell, a whole bunch of us got cut off when this crazy kid sliced through the lanes, driving on the wrong side of the road. He just missed hitting my car."

"What was he driving?"

"A maroon Mustang." Rollie answered

Rader tried to be polite. "And what does all this mean, Rollie?"

"About an hour ago, me and Drake were driving on PCH, and I saw cops lifting the maroon Mustang up on a flatbed. It was still on the lot where he parked it."

Rader's interest renewed. "You saw the driver?"

"Yeah, that's what I'm trying to tell you. It was a kid. He wore all black, a baseball cap on backwards, and had a pair of those reflective sunglasses on."

"Did you follow him?" Rader asked as he made notes a small notebook.

"No, I was slammed in that traffic jam, and all I could think about was being late for my role in the TV show. My first speaking part." Rollie wore a bittersweet smile.

"Yeah, yeah, you said that already." Rader sounded in a hurry.

"You know my temper, John. I knew if I lost it, and went after the kid – I wouldn't stop until I caught him. By the time I thrashed his ass, the job would be gone, and I might not ever get the chance again, ya know?"

"So, you just drove off and left him there?"

"Hell of a witness, huh?"

"Wait a minute," Rader turned away from his notes. "How do you know what the guy looked like? Did he get out of the Mustang?"

Rollie remembered. Dah, how stupid could he be? "Yeah, he got out and threw me a look. You know as if he had time he'd kill me too." Rollie closed his eyes. The guy was crystal clear. So was the look. "He left the Mustang and got into a dark blue Audi."

Rader interrupted Rollie. "You see the model Audi?"

"Yeah, it was an A8. Nice car. I wouldn't mind owning one."

"Right," Rader said. "Then what did the guy do?"

"He drove off."

"Just like that?"

"Yep."

Rader looked at him through narrowed slits, "Rollie?"

"What?" Rollie frowned, knotting his brows. "He drove off and left the Mustang in the lot. That's it."

"And you didn't think that was weird?" Rader asked.

"Not really. The Mustang had a For Sale sign in the window, so I figured the guy was giving it a test drive. A real good test."

"You didn't see the damage?"

"Nope."

Rader was exasperated. "Can I ask why not?"

"Sure."

Rader set his notebook down, raising his hands with an open palm gesture. "Okay smartass, why couldn't you see the damage?"

"Cause he cut me off, and the only thing I saw was the passenger side. Hell, I forgot all about the Audi. That's something, isn't it?" Rollie knew he should have come in sooner. He could see it in Rader's eyes. His buddy was thoroughly frustrated.

"Thanks for coming in. It's a start, and it's more than we had before."

"That's the car that ran the guy off the road, isn't it?"

Rader nodded. "Yeah, it is."

"Damn, I'm sorry. I didn't connect this until I saw your guys picking the car up."

"The guy was a pro, Rollie. It was an organized crime hit." Rader thought for a moment. "Were you driving your personal car that morning?"

"Of course." Rollie saw the worried look cross Rader's face. "Why did you ask that?"

"Cause if he got a look at you, and your car, he might get the urge to come after you."

"But I couldn't make him." Rollie felt his blood pressure surge.

"Does he know that?"

"No," Rollie shook his head, "I guess not."

"They don't like witnesses, Rollie. You can count on it. He'll be coming for you."

Chapter 15

Rollie drove home, stuffed a change of clothes in a small duffle bag, and returned to Eddie Rosewell's house on PCH. Inside, Rollie found Drake in the same place he left him. The tall man was sound asleep. He looked like a giant, curled into a child's crib.

Rollie went into the bedroom, untied Ben Parker, and moved him into the front room across from Andre so he could keep an eye on both. Andre was still wrapped like a mummy, so Rollie pushed Ben into an office chair and moved it against a wall. He wrapped Ben Parker around a large, empty fish tank. Watching Ben Parker in constant, restless sleep, made Rollie sick with ghostly visions. Damned images he thought he had successfully pushed to the bottom of memory lane. Not so. Fargo woke up, strained to stand up, and groaned from tweaking his back. He grabbed his cell phone and went outside.

"You're too damn big." Rollie called after him.

"Zip it, kid." Fargo was in a sleep-persuaded, bad mood.

136

Rollie turned to the drugged out actors. "Well, that leaves us to chat alone."

Neither responded to him. Out on the small patio, Drake talked incessantly on his cell phone. Rollie watched the large man pace. He slammed the phone shut, and stormed into the room through the open slider.

"The limo won't be here for hours."

"Swell," Rollie said.

"A short drive from here is a great deli. I'm going to order us a couple of sandwiches. What's your pleasure?"

"Turkey." Rollie answered.

"Care what's on it?"

"Lots of turkey."

Fargo smirked and stormed toward the door. He turned back. "You okay here?"

"Sure. When they wake up, we can try to talk nice to them again."

"You can whack 'em if they give ya trouble."

"I know."

"You're a jerk, Rollie."

"I know that too."

All the way out the door, Fargo shook his head.

Rollie sat on the couch and stared at the actors. They made him sick. Drool was dripping from the corner of Ben Parker's mouth. Andre Garrison wore a silly grin, had urine stains around his crotch. Superstars reduced to drug-infested punks. Rollie remembered his only drug use. He was fourteen. He'd buried his mother, and found living with Uncle Charlie intolerable. He snuck into the alley with Billy Zafra, to smoke a joint. Rollie became nauseated and puked all over his clothes. Millie Jefferson found him, took him home, and poured chicken soup into his delirious, earthly container. He never touched drugs again, even though Uncle Charlie used perennially. Rollie closed his eyes and instantly fell asleep.

Uncle Charlie was standing before him, staggering in a stupor, urine discoloration on the front of his tattered beige slacks. He was grinning, congratulating Rollie on graduating high school at seventeen, without the use of drugs to help him. Uncle Charlie convinced himself, with the help of a little heroin that Charleston wasn't for him. He thought it was safe to go back to New York. It wasn't.

"If a man's gotta die, he should be able to die where he grew up." Uncle Charlie said.

"I thought you said they'd kill you if you came back?" Rollie asked.

"So all they'll do is take me outta my misery. Ticker's gone, Rollie, and the kidneys are starting to go south. They want me on dialysis, but once ya start that crap, you go from once a week, to three times a week, and then ya die. If I'm goin' down, I wanna do it in New York. You comin' back with me?"

"No, I'm going to California."

"Ain't any family out there, Rollie. Fact is nothing's out there 'cept crowds. You can't run away from whom you are."

"Who am I, Uncle Charlie?"

"The nephew of Uncle Anthony, that's who."

"He doesn't know me, and I'd like to keep it like that. I'll get a new start in California."

Uncle Charlie angrily waved him off. "Suit yourself."

Rollie watched Uncle Charlie pack his drugs up. He went back to New York, and a week later was killed. They caught up with him as they promised. Rollie drove west. Months earlier he had applied to UCLA and was accepted. His four-point average all through high school was good enough to get in, and he had Millie Jefferson to thank for that. She made him study, dished out plenty of discipline, and warned him about drugs. For once he listened to someone.

Then Kali appeared -- crying.

A car backfired. Rollie woke, shook off Kali's vision and walked out on the patio. It was a strange house. Built right across the street from the ocean, and yet you couldn't see water from anywhere. The view from the back patio was surrounding hillsides, houses on stilts, dried chaparral, and a few dead-end streets. Rollie watched a young woman, wearing a low-cut white blouse with spaghetti straps, and a full, powder-blue-skirt, sneak up on a man working on a motorcycle. She embraced the guy from behind, bent over for a kiss, and teased his masculinity with her cleavage. He was distracted enough to try and grab her, missed, and ended up chasing after her. Rollie smiled, remembering when he first met Kali. She used to sneak up on him, jarring his intense concentration in law books. He never heard her coming until she was either sitting beside him, or bending over him like the girl in the blue skirt had just done. When he studied law, all he could concentrate on was the book, and its contents. He learned early to block things out, but Kali's cleavage and sultry voice carried the type of heat, and sexuality that could stop a bullfight.

"Hi," she whispered, the first time they spoke. "I've been watching you."

"Really?" Rollie stopped reading. He studied her beautiful face, intense green eyes.

"Every day you sit out here alone. You read your books, make startling observations in that notebook, and go back to class."

"You're good." He pointed out.

"No, I'm vigilant." She held her hand out, "My name is Kali."

Some women spray cologne, and never gage how much is too much. Kali had a scent that was both captivating and alluring. Rollie shook her hand, and her breasts jiggled with a wonderful, sexy freedom. He felt an peculiar shudder. She smiled, and behind the smile her eyes spoke of a woman's secret that love-at-first-sight emits. A moment of pure carnal lust passed through him. He had a hard time releasing her hand.

"Rollie Kemp."

She teased with her hair, fluttering her eyes, daring him to be adventurous, "And how old is Rollie Kemp?"

"Nineteen."

"Married?"

"No."

"A man of few words. I like that. What are you studying to become?"

"A lawyer."

"Mmmm." She looked him over, her gaze slowly taking every inch of him in.

She had his attention. "Mmmm? Translate Mmmm for me?"

She purred. "An expression of preference." With one, finger, she played with the edge of her hair. Everything about her was erotic.

"Okay." He said.

"Do you want to know what I'm studying?" Kali batted her eyes at him.

"Men?"

She laughed. It was pure innocence, like hearing a small child giggle. "You are very cute, Rollie Kemp. Should we have dinner?"

"Tonight?"

"And you work fast. My, my."

He turned to face her. Her satin-smooth skin was flawless which made her remarkably beautiful. She had the biggest, widest green eyes he'd ever seen. The eyes danced, inquisitive, and full of sensuality and pleasure. Her hair was golden, not yellow or brash. She wore a full skirt, a silk blouse with spaghetti-straps, and sandals.

Rollie couldn't take his eyes off her. "I should pick you up around seven."

"You didn't ask if I was married."

"You're not." He answered in a cavalier way.

"You didn't ask my age, or what I was studying?"

"You're eighteen, taking double classes in Journalism, your full name is Kali Rocha, you're single, live alone in a small apartment on Veteran Avenue, and you want to be a famous writer."

She loved it, chewing gently on her finger, "You're a stalker!"

Rollie nodded. "Yeah."

She leaned over and kissed him. It started out as a fun kiss, but when they looked into each other's eyes, it was instant meltdown. The second kiss was the one that made a statement.

Ben Parker coughed. Rollie snapped out of his trance and looked inside. Ben Parker turned his head to the clean part of his shirt, and tossed what was left in his stomach all over the area that wasn't already covered. He briefly opened his eyes. "What's that weird smell? His words were slurred.

"Nothing." Rollie answered

"Good, that's good." He closed his eyes and drifted off again.

Rollie turned back to the limited view. The young woman in the full skirt continued to move around the yard. This time, however, the man tackled her. They kissed, rolled over each other, and as he carried her into a house -- they were undressing each other.

Rollie closed his eyes. Kali was so light in his arms. He carried her into her apartment. The apartment was fresh and clean. The furniture came with the place, so nothing was distinct. What stood out were the little feminine touches, flowers, tiny knickknacks, a collection of miniature kittens, and decorative beads hanging where the void of a kitchen door might've been. Even on an apparent limited budget, everything matched with decorator taste. He set her down, and realized she wore high-heeled shoes with tiny spikes and thin straps. With the help of her high heels, she could look Rollie right in the eye. They stood close together. He could taste her.

She whispered, "I bought us some steaks."

"Saving me money already."

"Yeah." She giggled.

"So?" He asked the dumb question.

"Not once in my life have I shown my bedroom to a man. For some odd reason, I have this compelling urge to invite you in before dinner."

"Okay." It was an invitation he'd never turn down.

She took his hand and led him into the bedroom. He sat to remove his shoes, and before he could get them off she was standing naked before him. He touched her breasts, and she gasped. For the life of him, he couldn't remember what happened next. They made love, cooked dinner, and made love again. They became constant companions over the next six months, and flew to Las Vegas where they got married. She was everything that was missing in his life. Their joy ran over the brim. He continued his studies, worked nights, loved every minute of life to the fullest, and for the first time was truly complete. She experimented with marijuana, and a little coke. She convinced it was only once in a while. He soon realized she was dependent on them. He wanted her to get help, but she refused and laughed it off. Then he found her in bed with Professor Thomas Layne. They were both juiced, naked, and in the middle of a wild and intense moment. She was covered in sweat when she yelled at Rollie, demanding he get out. She accused him of ruining everything. He bolted and never went back. He abandoned his things and moved on. During the divorce, he discovered she had a tryst going. Many professors and fellow students had been to his apartment. She'd kept a journal of her activities. Rollie dropped out of school, needing a change. He applied and was quickly accepted into the LAPD. He trained hard and breezed through the academy at the top of his class. Three days before graduation, three days before getting his badge – it happened.

Rollie saw the car for an instant, just before it hit him, a brand new Mercedes, black, sleek, and fast. They were on the Hollywood Freeway. The Mercedes changed lanes, from the fast to the slow lane, all in one swift motion – tried to reach the exit before running out of space. Only problem was Rollie's car. The Mercedes slammed into his driver-door, sending Rollie's car head-on into a light pole – nearly tearing it in half. His legs were crushed beneath the metal, and it took the jaws-of-life to get him out.

Ben Parker started coughing incessantly. Rollie ran back into the house and found more of the same. Ben Parker contorted his handsome face into a loathsome panic as chunks of regurgitated food spurted out the

143

corner of his mouth. Rollie didn't see Ben Parker though, he saw Kali. She looked just like Ben Parker, when food wouldn't stay in her stomach. In his mind, he could envision Kali as clearly as though she were in the room with him. Her pretty face contorted. Sick dribbling from her beautiful lips. Rollie flinched -- seeing the memory so clearly. Drugs could take anyone down to ground zero. Ben Parker continued to cough, and then in one violent eruption, he spewed the contents in his stomach all over himself. He laughed, turned his head the other way, and drifted off again. Rollie waited, but Ben disappeared into a drug-infested sleep. Rollie's first instinct was to clean him up, and then he thought better of it. It's what Ben deserved, to wake up covered in his own puke. A lasting memory Ben needed to enjoy first hand.

The door opened, and Drake came in with sandwiches, drinks, and chips. He took one step in, and his nose wrinkled from the stench. "What happened?"

"He barfed all over himself." Rollie was breathing hard, clenched fists at his side.

Drake studied him. "You okay?"

Rollie shook the memories. "Yeah, the smell gets to you is all."

"Why didn't you clean him up?"

"Why would I do that?"

"Good answer. Let's go out on the patio, and get away from this mess. The sandwiches look too good to be interfered with."

Rollie relaxed his hands and trailed after Drake. He glanced down Ben Parker with contempt. "Thanks for the memories, asshole."

When Parker opened his eyes, squinting up at Rollie. "They didn't pay me enough."

"What?" Rollie glared at him.

"It was supposed to be easy." Ben Parker raised one eyebrow, and then passed out.

Chapter 16

The Watcher spotted the man in a black BMW SUV and followed him to a little shack in Malibu. It was Infiniti man, a positive I.D, sunglasses and all. She waited. Hated to wait. A short time later he came out and drove off. From a distance, The Watcher followed him to his beach house. While he was inside, she checked the mailbox. Everything inside was addressed to Rollie Kemp. She was angry it took so long to recognize him when he was right under her nose. Oh my God, she was unequivocally losing it. She just made it back to her car when Rollie came out and drove off. He was in a hurry, and she lost him. It didn't matter. She knew where he was going. She couldn't do him on PCH. She'd already tried that. Now that, she had a positive I.D., knew where he lived, and that he lived alone, she'd be more careful next time. Her cell phone vibrated. She had a text message. It was short and to the point. What's wrong with your computer? Respond ASAP.

She used a computer café in Santa Monica to connect her laptop to the Internet. She logged in to Yahoo and opened her account. Her clients were pleased with how the Louis Baxter event concluded, and made an offer she couldn't turn down. Five hundred grand had already been transferred into her account. Rollie Kemp would have to wait. Too many interruptions meant getting rid of him could prove dangerous. The Watcher didn't do danger, she just did. The thrill of playing with Rollie Kemp was overwhelming. She planned to tease him a little, watch and wait for the right time. Part of the thrill was to fly out in surprise, savor the brief moment, and then kill him. When the email came in, her first instinct was to turn the job down. She hated New York, but this time the contract was a two-for. The payday was too humongous to ignore. They were paying her five hundred large to take out two scumbags. A glance at her watch said it was time to go. Rollie Kemp would be revisited upon her return. There was new business to attend to, and a plane to catch. The Watcher drove back home, packed an overnight bag, and headed for the airport.

The Watcher took the 10 Freeway and cut over the 405 to the airport. She took her time. Her purse was packed, and the silenced Glock she carried would be left behind. The gun had all ID numbers burned off. It was untraceable. She pulled into the long-term parking lot and drove to the floor directly beneath roof parking. Her first victim was a creature of habit. He drove an old Silver Cloud Rolls Royce, and always parked a zillion miles from other cars to avoid door-dings. The roof was a fantastic place to avoid other vehicles. The info they sent her was always correct. She didn't have to give it a second thought. She studied his picture -- handsome guy.

The Watcher retrieved a suitcase on wheels from the trunk. Inside the case were pension fund receipts, and two hundred thousand dollars in cash. She heard the engine. No mistaking a Rolls engine. She ducked behind the cement pillars and waited. The long, white sedan purred into the garage. Slowly the Rolls Royce rolled quietly up the ramp to rooftop parking. Making sure not to be seen, she made sure the parking lot was virtually void of traffic. Then with a casual movement pulled on black gloves and strolled up the ramp to the roof. Like a typical traveler, she tugged the wheeled case in one hand and carried the Glock down at her side.

At the end of a row, near the elevator entrance, the Rolls stopped. A man got out and opened the trunk. He removed a suitcase and then checked pockets for ticket and boarding pass.

"Ronnie?" She walked briskly, closing the distance between them.

The man turned to face her. "I beg your pardon?"

"Ronnie Mauten?"

"Do I know you?" Ronnie Mauten was over and out striking. His silver hair cast off a distinctive look, and his well-tailored suit fit perfectly. Too bad.

"It's been a long time." She said with a smile. His appearance was exactly like the photos sent. No doubt about it. This was her man. Narrowing the gap. Fifteen feet. Close enough.

"I don't believe we've ever met." His voice trailed.

It dawned on him. She saw it in his eyes, but it was too late. She raised the gun and fired two soundless shots -- one into the heart, and the other between the eyes. Ronnie Mauten died with a startled look on his face. A quick scan of the area returned no surprises. They were still alone. It took only seconds to stuff both the body, and the suitcase into the trunk. She opened his case and carefully inserted the pension files along with two hundred thousand bucks inside. She zipped and locked his suitcase. The silencer came off easily. She wiped the gun from barrel to handle and dropped it inside the trunk next to the body. She wiped up what little blood there was with a rag from the trunk. With loose ends tossed inside, the trunk lid closed quietly, and she made sure it was shut. Moving quickly the Watcher locked the Rolls and walked away with her suitcase on wheels. She would dump the keys before she boarded the flight to New York. The silencer she'd keep.

The first hit went smoothly, but the second would be far more antagonistic. She needed to prepare, scout things, and see the inside of getting the head of an organized crime family alone.

Chapter 17

Rollie was annoyed at Drake. The tall guy refused to help move the two actors into the limo Eddie Rosewell had sent. Drake used the excuse he had a bum back, but in reality, Rollie knew he didn't want to touch either actor. They both reeked of nausea and urine, and Rollie had no desire to pick them up either — but someone had to carry them out. The limo arrived with two drivers. The second guy was to take Drake's SUV to Rainbow House. It didn't take Rollie long to figure out a way to keep his hands clean. Both drivers were hesitant when Rollie asked for help, but given a generous tip — both promptly lifted and carried.

The drive up the coast was quiet. The limo driver had the glass behind him raised for privacy, and to avoid the stench from Ben's regurgitation. It took him ten minutes to wash his hands, and was still pissed Rollie hurried him. The second driver tagged along behind them, handling Drake's SUV judiciously. Rollie and Drake played poker. The actors remained out of it. The highway clicked beneath them from grooves cut into the pavement by Cal-Trans. They said it was for tire traction, but Rollie figured they did it to annoy everyone who had enough money to live in the Santa Barbara area.

"This Vicks stuff works great under the nose," Rollie said as he dealt the cards. He witnessed Drake palming a card.

"A friend who works at the morgue told me about it." Drake looked at his hand with all the deviousness he could muster. "Full house."

Rollie glared at him. "You cheated."

"I'm good."

"I saw the card up your sleeve."

"Which one?" Drake held both sleeves up.

Rollie grabbed Drake's left hand. "This one."

"What about the other one?"

"Nothin' there." Rollie was sure it was the left hand.

Drake removed a card from his right sleeve. "See how much better I am than you?"

"If we were playing' for money, I would've caught you." Rollie sulked, a look black as thunder. He hated to lose, even in jest.

Rollie stared out the window, looking at what little scenery there was. To the west was the ocean, but on the right were dried out weeds and brown grass – as far as the eye could see. Up on a hillside, Rollie watched a herd of cattle. They were all following one giant fat bull. Then Rollie did a double take. In the middle of the herd, two deer strolled along with the cattle. Rollie appreciated their braggadocio. Free meals, lots of water, and forbidden to be shot at. The deer were winners and took Rollie on a journey. He remembered taking Kali out for a picnic. They drove over Highway 154 and found a fantastic canyon near Lake Cachuma. They sat beneath remarkably beautiful oak trees, and mile after mile of lush greenery. They ate lunch, played cards, and were surrounded by a herd of deer. The deer roamed nearby for a look-see but never came too close. Kali was another one who loved to cheat at cards every time they'd played. Rollie decided both should be naked but Kali still found ways to cheat. When caught, she'd giggle, and tease him. It wasn't so much the cards, but her presence he loved. The cards, however, relentlessly led to foreplay, and intense, passionate lovemaking. The longer the pursuit, the fiercer the near-violent bundling became. She suggested he should slap her, but he couldn't. She always seemed disappointed with his reluctance. Part of that void turned her to using, and the thrill drugs gave her. She later said she kept a list of things he couldn't do. He knew not hitting or doing drugs were at the top of the list.

Drake poked Rollie on the arm, pointing out the window. "Here we go."

Rollie rolled his eyes toward the Rainbow House, and when he turned back both Ben and Andre were waking up. Being in the presence of these two was dragging dirty laundry back into his head. He resented the actors all the more, and hoped to get this part of the job over quickly.

The Rainbow House was on a secluded piece of property that overlooked the ocean. The estate was behind ten-foot walls, and massive steel gates. Rollie could see rooftops from a cluster of buildings behind the gate. The guard who stood watch at the barrier was armed. He smiled as he glanced over the paperwork handed to him by the driver of the limo, then he took a peek inside.

Ben Parker was starting to come off the stuff, and his eyes filled with dread when he looked out the window. He smelled himself, "I can't go there like this."

"Sure you can," Rollie said.

Ben shook his head. "They'll think I'm some kind of addict or something."

"Probably." Rollie agreed.

"Damn you!" Ben looked at Andre. "We're not going into lock-down either."

Rollie calmly turned to Ben and grabbed hold of his arm. Drake just watched. "We're going inside, Ben." Rollie said it quietly, "So I suggest you behave and lower your voice."

"Fuck you." Andre Garrison seethed.

"Fuck you." Kali shouted. "I'm not going in."

Rollie had done this before. He held Kali's arm, the same way he held Ben. She was pulling away with all her strength, shaking her head so violently it made her dizzy. Kali pouted, and grudgingly entered the rehab center. It was the best he could afford at the time, and nothing like Rainbow.

Kali shouted when they took her away, "I hate you, Rollie! You've turned into a total piece of shit!"

"I love you," was all he could say to her.

"You don't know what the word means! Fuck you!"

He was embarrassed. "I'll see you in a few days."

"Go to hell, Rollie. Do you hear me? Go away and don't come back!"

Rollie and Drake calmed the two actors, and gestured to the guard that things were good.

"Droppin' 'em off?" the guard asked.

"We're checking' in," Rollie called out to him. "The car behind is also with us. Can you show him where to park our car?"

"Sure." The guard waved both vehicles through the gate.

153

The limo pulled around a circular driveway and stopped in front of stairs leading into an English Tudor Mansion. Drake's SUV continued down a steep driveway and disappeared. The Rainbow House was right out of Gone With The Wind. The spiral staircase was ten feet wide with a generous incline. Rollie looked down into a deep ravine where two-stories below he saw the wire fence with razor caps. The stiles were solid marble, and the railing was polished brass. A large front porch hung precariously beneath massive white columns leading into a gateway. The expensive windows were covered with a white-mesh. No one could escape through a window. A large metal plate covered the front door. Once inside, you needed permission to come out. Rollie was glad he wasn't paying for it.

The driver got out and opened the back door.

"I have a film starting next week," Andre mumbled.

"They're going to delay the start of production," Drake said.

"I can't do this," Ben said as the steel door slammed behind them. He looked at the windows and jerked free. He took a wild swing at Rollie, who ducked. Ben reared up, took several more wild swings, and finally Rollie had enough. He tossed a crisp jab and popped Ben in the nose again. The punch brought immediate damage. Blood trickled down over his lips.

"Don't do that again." Rollie shook his hand from the sting of the punch.

Drake smiled. "So that's what punch first and ask questions later means?"

Ben held his nose and pouted. He turned to Rollie, apologetically. "I won't use anymore, I promise."

"Sure you will," Rollie said.

"No, you don't understand." Ben was stammering, moving in small circles.

"I understand perfectly." Rollie remained calm. "Too late."

Andre was waking up. "Who are you guys? Do you know who we are?"

Drake shrugged. "Pretend we're your big brothers."

"I don't have a brother." Andre sulked.

They moved into the foyer, and two burly attendants joined them. The large black man wore a nametag that announced his name was White. He gestured for them to follow the second attendant. White held out his hand, but both Ben and Andre ignored it.

Rollie shook it instead. "Rollie Kemp."

"I'm White," the attendant answered.

"Very funny," Ben added sarcastically.

"Cleavon White," the attendant went on. "If you gentlemen follow, Raymond will take you down to admitting."

"I don't think so!" Andre shouted.

Both actors bolted back toward the entrance. The two attendants stood back and watched. Drake caught Andre and slammed him into the wall. Rollie easily tripped Ben before he ran two feet, and then helped him get up off the floor.

Ben shouted in Rollie's face, "Whaddya think you're doing? This is kidnapping! It's against the law." He spun to the attendants. "Call the police."

Rollie remained calm. "Last night, while you two were partying, someone murdered an actress who happened to be with both of you clowns at one time or another during the night."

Andre shouted, "And you think one of us killed her?"

"Did you?" Rollie asked.

The actors glared at Rollie.

"Doesn't matter what we think," Drake replied. "It's what the cops will think, and how the press will deal with it."

Rollie asked, "Do you really want the press looking into your backgrounds."

"Okay!" Ben shouted almost too quickly. "Did Eddie hire you two?"

"No, your agent did," Drake, answered. "He asked us to tell you guys your contract with the agency will be canceled if you don't complete this visit."

Andre snapped, "We can get another agent."

"When the Wilfred Mondell Agency dumps you, nobody in town would touch you," Rollie stated quietly. "Now why don't we put this episode behind us?"

Andre finally asked, "Who was the girl?"

"You remember the blond?" Rollie was guessing 'cause half the girls at the party were blonds. Maybe these two did kill her? Not a good thought.

"No," Andre mumbled.

"Which one?" Ben asked.

"The tall one," Rollie answered. "She was taller than you, I think."

Ben shook his head, trying to remember. "I don't remember a tall blond."

"It's called short-term memory loss," Drake rubbed it in. "Drugs cause it."

After a moment, the two actors caved in and stared at the floor. Rollie watched them, and believed both would go back where they started if they couldn't get their acts together. Hollywood had a habit of spitting inadequate blood out, and had little trouble moving on. Everyone was replaceable because of the crowd waiting to be discovered. Raymond led the way, and Cleavon White trailed behind.

Raymond sat behind a small desk and handed various paperwork, attached to a clipboard, to Drake. While Drake filled out the admission worksheet, Ben sat next to Andre. Andre was sweating like a pig, and Ben started shaking. Withdrawals. Raymond was impassive. He was as thick as he was tall, and carried a manner you didn't mess with.

Andre pulled away, knocking everything on Raymond's desk to the floor. He jerked toward Rollie, eyes full of hate, "What did you do with my stuff?" He tried to run, but Rollie held him. Andre slapped Rollie's face.

Kali slapped Rollie with both hands, and it stung like hell.

Rollie held Kali's arm down after she brushed dinner plates off the table. He cooked a fabulous dinner only to see it splattered on walls. Kali looked at Rollie, eyes narrowing.

"Why don't you believe me?" She always yelled when he caught her.

"I know it's yours." He said looking at the stash he found in her purse.

"I'm just holding it for a friend." Kali justified.

"Kali, I saw you use it."

"So I'll stop."

"Good. Then flushing this crap should help you."

"Fuck you, Rollie! What happened to the guy I married?"

"He's right here."

"No. You're the other guy, the guy who won't try anything. Mister straight lace, do good that's nothing but a bore, that's what you are. I'm not going back to rehab."

"Then maybe the cops will know what to do with you?"

"So do it asshole, flush the stuff down the toilet."

"Okay."

Rollie dumped her stash in the toilet and flushed it. Kali screamed and exploded into a ballistic fury, beating and punching Rollie. She fell to her knees and reached into the toilet in an attempt to stop the water in the toilet bowl from swallowing the drugs. Kali stood up, her back against the wall, and begged with trembling hands. Then her face twisted into a hateful glare.

Andre had the same look on his face as he backed against the wall. Nurse Clements, along with an even larger man whose nametag identified him as Cactus, came from a door behind the admissions desk. She was enormous and filled the doorway. Not an ounce of fat appeared on her athletic body. She didn't smile, and her voice sang each word in a monotone straight line. She looked to be in her early thirties with black hair cut so short it made her head appear super-sized. Her dark eyes were colorless and empty. Her breasts looked like rocks ready to burst through the uniform, and her arms carried various tattoos of snakes, and other slithering creatures. Her face wasn't pretty or attractive, and yet Rollie couldn't help but study her look. No doubt she was one-of-a-kind.

"Welcome to Rainbow House, gentleman. Will you please follow me?" Nurse Clements gestured with her hand, and reluctantly the two disgruntled stars got up to followed. The two attendants tagged along behind them.

Cleavon White took control of Andre's arm and led him off in the opposite direction – away from Ben.

The other attendant, Cactus had a Native American Indian appearance. Obviously he didn't have a sense of humor either. When he took Ben Parker's arm, Ben jerked it away from him, only to have Cactus clamp down much harder than necessary.

"I can't do this!" Ben blurted. "You're hurting me."

"I understand," Cactus answered, and took a firmer grip on Ben's arm.

"Don't touch me!" He contorted his face, spitting in Cactus face, his eyes growing wide in an attempt to intimidate Cactus, but it didn't work.

"I understand," Cactus repeated, wiping his face as he led Ben down another hallway. When Ben tried to yank his arm free, Cactus walked faster, and half-carried Ben like a tow truck hauling a reluctant wreck away.

Rollie watched the admissions lady come from a private office. She relieved Raymond, who silently bowed, and disappeared down the hallway. Attractive in a business sort of way, her suit was meticulous as was her makeup. Her smile was genuine and sincere. Probably in her forties she was unmarried. Her appearance reeked of sheer pre-occupation. She was serious. No time for a man.

She pointed down the hallway. "The cafeteria is at the end of the hall, and your rooms are just beyond the eating area. I had your things brought in. We had your car parked in the garage downstairs." She smiled. "We hope your stay with us is pleasant. My name is Price Felton. If you need anything whatsoever, please ask for me."

Drake shook her hand. "Has everything been taken care of?"

"Oh, yes. The studio called before your arrival. They delivered fresh clothes and personal items for the young men earlier. I have their histories, everything is in order." She glanced at her watch. "I believe they are still serving, so if you gentlemen are hungry, just tell the cook what you'd like, and it will be prepared for you. Have a lovely evening."

As Drake and Rollie walked down the hall, they both watched Price Felton disappear into her office, and shut the door.

"Wonder how long ago her last date was?" Drake said.

"What makes you think she ever had a date?" Rollie asked.

"Good point. You hungry?"

"Yeah, I think my appetite is coming back. Let's see what they have."

"How's your hand, Mighty Joe?"

Rollie rubbed over his knuckles. "It's hurts."

"Yeah," Drake mumbled, "punchin' people does that."

Chapter 18

The old rusted van, its white paint faded years ago was parked at the curb adjacent to the parking lot of Sparks Steak House. Fabrio Tallagi, wearing a unique disguise that remarkably changed his appearance, sat inside the van. He wore a gray wig that made him look much older. He added a neatly trimmed gray beard, wide-rimmed glasses with clear lenses, and clothes befitting a retired schoolteacher. He looked older, and nothing like himself. He sat with Frank Masseria, an electronic surveillance genius, and Billy Davis. They were watching and listening to the images on a bank of TV monitors embedded in the van's wall. Behind them, Sal Lucchese, a soldier for the Pataglia family cleaned two handguns. Before the meeting between Fabrio and Mark Lipesky had been set, Masseria wired cameras and mikes inside the restaurant, and the parking lot. His cousin, Joey was the night bartender at Sparks, so access to the site was easy.

They watched Mark Lipesky arrive with his son, Drew, his driver, and family captain, Albert Spatola, and three soldiers. There were six cameras covering everything. The sound was excellent. Lipesky waited for over an hour, with men from Moe Brayden's crew hiding everywhere. They were ready to take Fabrio out, but when he didn't show they smelled a rat. The group gathered around Mark Lipesky.

Drew Lipesky was a baby-faced kid with lots of black, unruly hair. He looked to be in his early twenties, and carried angry narrow eyes over a pouting, withdrawn face. "I'm outta here, pop. I said they were teasing' with ya. Scared shitless of us, is what they are. Maybe I should just go over to New York and kill the fuck for ya. Get it over with."

"No, we'll draw him out."

"I'll leave Al here to keep an eye on things." He tossed a salute at his father. "See ya."

Drew Lipesky, hugged Mark Lipesky, and left, taking his soldiers with him. Outside, the cameras stayed on them. Drew loaded his men up in two cars and drove off. Spatola sat in the shadows, by himself. He kept his eyes on the door, and a hand buried in a jacket pocket. Fabrio smiled. The guy actually thought he had things under control.

On other monitors, Fabrio watched Mark Lipesky go to a pay phone on the wall, dial a number, and wait. Lipesky appeared to be a little pudgy man with thinning hair.

"Here we go," Fabrio, said, "Can you turn up the sound?"

Frank Masseria nodded, "Sure." He made a few adjustments and sat back. The picture on the screen was crystal clear. The sound was crisp, as though they were in the restaurant.

Mark Lipesky waited, and then spoke into the phone, "He didn't show up." Irritated, he strummed his fingers over the top of the phone as he listened. "Yeah, I'll wait for ya." He hung up, returned to the table, and gestured for the waiter. Pataglia watched him order a streak, rare, with french-fries, and a beer. He ate half of it before a well-dressed man in his late forties showed up. Fabrio figured he was waiting a few blocks away. The suit the man wore cost more than Fabrio's entire wardrobe.

"Is that Moe Brayden?" Fabrio asked.

Billy nodded, "Yeah."

Brayden was known as Dapper Brayden in the press. One of several east coast bosses, Brayden always wore two thousand dollar suits. He carried himself like a corporate executive. Underboss Johnny Wade, his constant companion was at his side. Even from the small monitor, Johnny Wade looked deadly. Fabrio knew all about Johnny Wade. Wade was a twenty-eight year old contract killer. He was a brutal, coldhearted eliminator, and he looked the part.

Lipesky stopped eating when Brayden and Wade sat down.

Brayden looked around the restaurant, his jaw muscles working overtime, and then he leaned in close to Lipesky, and whispered, "Are you outta your fucking mind?"

Frank Masseria enjoyed his handiwork. "You want me to zoom in, Fabrio?"

Fabrio was impressed. His thick, black eyebrows involuntarily rose in surprise, "Yes."

As if by magic, the images on the monitor grew tighter, clearly defining Moe Brayden, and Lipesky. Brayden was dressed to perfection. He combed his short cut solid black hair straight back. A handsome man who knew he looked good. Brayden wore a light beige suit made of exquisite silk, with a matching vanilla shirt and pale yellow tie.

Lipesky threw out his hands, "What?" He chewed. "Pataglia's on the way out, and you know it. He's forgotten how he made all his dough."

Brayden looked around the room, took several french-fries off Lipesky's plate and munched them slowly. For a brief moment, he looked right at the camera, but Fabrio could tell he didn't see it. "First you do Baxter, and then," his livid lips pursed tightly while his eyes scanned the room, "and then you have the balls to do this daughter thing -- all without telling us." He turned away for a moment. His face suddenly revealed controlled anger as his voice dropped to a whisper, "This is not how we do things."

Fabrio could see the look in Lipesky's eyes as he watched Moe Brayden eat fries off his plate. Lipesky couldn't handle it and looked away. "We never see Pataglia any more Moe. He won't give up on the union change, and he's made so much money for the pension fund – those union suckers love him. If we didn't have new ways to make dough, he'd suck us dry." He glanced around the restaurant, nervously expecting someone to hear him, "It's time to draw him out, and get rid of the bastard once and for all."

"And how do you proposed to do that?" Brayden asked.

Lipesky smiled, a confident man. "Either way, New York or California. If he's still alive, he'll go to California. People will start turning on him when things don't add up. By the time, he figures it out it will be too late. He'll have this need, you know, to take care of his daughter? While he's thinkin' about who did her, it'll be over. We have lots of friends in New York who will welcome the change."

"You already send someone to New York?" Moe Brayden asked.

"Anthony Pataglia loves surprises, so I arranged one." Lipesky answered.

Fabrio squirmed in his seat as he watched two men develop Pataglia's demise. Frank Masseria glanced at him.

"You all right, Fabrio?"

"Yeah, Frank. It's hard to believe it's come to this."

They watched Moe Brayden looked into Lipesky's eyes. "If this New York thing doesn't work out, you have someone in California?"

Lipesky nodded, "The best."

Brayden's voice remained indifferent. "Don't make me come lookin' for you and your kid, Mark. You seem to be on a roll, makin' one mistake after another. I have a great idea. From this moment, until the dust storm you've created settles, you're on your own. I'll deny knowing anything about this." Brayden wiped his fingers clean with Lipesky's napkin.

Lipesky shook his head, "How come you are so upset, I don't understand? We've talked about this."

Brayden got right on Lipesky's ear, "You acted alone. We didn't talk first. Perhaps things could've been handled differently, and the girl would still be alive. I'm not happy, and now you're gonna have to make me happy."

Lipesky's lips curled at the corners of his mouth, "It'll be taken care of."

Brayden abruptly grabbed Lipesky's face, and turned it with his hand, grinding into his cheeks with sharp, well-manicured fingernails, "Buy a ticket, and take a trip." Brayden said it slowly to make sure he was heard.

"Where am I going?"

"California, where I hear the weather is fabulous year round. The people suck, full of liars and cheats, but then again, you're not going out there to stay, are you?"

"I have good people ..."

"You have nothing but a potential headache. Make sure, first hand, that it goes down smoothly. If Anthony comes to me for help, I'll provide whatever his needs are."

"When I get back...."

"Won't be back if things don't work out." Brayden gestured, and Johnny Wade got up.

Frank Masseria adjusted the controls and zoomed out. Brayden slid out of the booth and brushed his two thousand dollar suit off. Fabrio watched a man he called a friend with downcast eyes. It was unbelievable.

Lipesky glared up at Brayden, "I won't let you down."

"You already have." Brayden whispered as he walked off.

Lipesky turned to his driver, "Get the car."

Fabrio Tallagi sat back. Disappointment rose into his face, the darkness resurfaced as he watched the screen. A dull rage was building inside. It was time to go back to street law.

In the parking lot, waiting in the shadows, Fabrio put on a pair of gloves. When Lipesky came from the restaurant, his driver, Albert Spatola, open the back door of the large Cadillac sedan. Lipesky slid into the back seat. Fabrio came up behind Spatola and pumped two, quiet, bullets into his heart. His body slumped over the back seat. Lipesky, with the shadow of death covering his face, looked up. He knew what was coming.

Lipesky recognized Fabrio. "I didn't kill her."

Fabrio understood. "You just gave the order."

Lipesky shrugged, "Nothin' personal, Fabrio. She was becoming a liability."

Fabrio felt the pain in his chest. He winced, and closed his eyes, "It was business."

Lipesky agreed. "Business. Things are changing, Fabrio. You're a good man. You should come work for me."

"Yeah," Fabrio whispered, "only that won't work out." He felt his body shutting down, going cold and numb. "Who'd you send to New York?"

"It will be quick and painless, I promise."

"You're right about that." Fabrio shot Mark Lipesky in the forehead.

Quickly he placed Spatola's body next to Lipesky and slammed the door. He drove to the Vander Towers construction site in silence. Billy Davis met him, dressed like a construction worker. He hugged Fabrio and ushered him to a waiting car.

"Ray will drive you to Baltimore." Billy said.

Fabrio looked the site over, "How soon is the cement getting poured?"

Billy smiled, "In just a few minutes." He gestured with a nod of his head toward Lipesky's car. "We'll take Lipesky's car to the wrecking yard, and turn it into a ball of metal. Give me the piece you used, Fabby. I'll spread it around Philly for you."

Fabrio retrieved the gun he used, and handed it to Billy. Billy handed it off to another one of his men who swiftly took the gun apart.

Billy turned back to Fabrio. "I'll need your coat, gloves, shoes and pants for furnace fuel." He offered a reassuring nod. "You have fresh clothes waiting in Ray's car."

Fabrio undressed down to his boxers and T-shirt, handing everything to Billy. "I appreciate the help, Billy. Tell others the same."

Billy nodded and looked at his watch. "You should have plenty of time to catch your connecting flight west. Have a safe flight to L.A. I wish your visit was under different circumstances."

"Me too." Fabrio said.

Fabrio took out his cell phone and called Anthony Pataglia. He filled him in on the events, told him about the contract Lipesky put out on him, and suggested he get out of town for a few days. Pataglia told him not to worry. To go to California, get things in order and come back home.

Billy Davis hugged Fabrio again as his cousin Ray opened the back door of his new ride.

Fabrio hesitated. He knew this might be the last time he would see Billy. It left a strange emptiness inside. Billy was family, Part of the only family Fabrio had ever known.

"You worried that Moe Brayden will start something?" Billy asked.

Fabrio shook his head, "No, I was wondering how many of us are gonna die."

Chapter 19

Rollie walked down the hallway to the soda machine. As he was putting coins in the slot, several attendants ran down the hall. First came a scream, not of anger but frustration, followed by lots of commotion, distant yelling, someone blaming others. Rollie couldn't understand, and then more attendants followed after the first group. People darted every which way. Rollie's cell phone rang. The action disappeared behind closed doors. He opened his phone. "This is Rollie."

"Aren't you supposed to check in with me?" Mildred Wanamaker's raspy voice asked.

"Sorry, I got busy and forgot." Instantly Rollie regretted saying it.

"Busy?" Mildred bellowed angrily.

Rollie's cheeks burned. "I was helping a friend out."

"So, you're too busy to call me?"

"No." He frowned, slapping the wall with his palm. "Believe it or not, I was going to call." He never was good at telling a lie. The blush continued to sting.

"Right! You're not even a good liar. Let's leave it at you forgot."

"If you insist." He cleared his throat. "So, what's up?"

"I had a job for you."

"Had?" Rollie could feel his chest tighten. "As in the past tense?"

"Yes, and yes. Your past is still catching up with you. The lead actor's name was Luke Waters. You know him?" Mildred was good at hitting her target.

"Yeah, we've met." Bittersweet feelings raced through Rollie. He wished he could hit Luke Waters all over his pudgy body.

"So you punched him out too, huh?" Mildred egged him on.

"What did he say about me?"

"Said he wouldn't work with you, even if you were dead." She coughed, a deep sounding cigarette rumble, cleared her throat, "He said it was either him or you."

"I guess they went with him, right?"

"Right. I have other things in the fire, so stay in touch, hot shot."

The sudden hang up brought silence. Rollie folded the cell up and put it back in his pocket. Chairs squeaked over linoleum down the hall.

The noise brought Drake from his room. "What's goin' on?"

Rollie gestured down the hall with his head as he added the last coin in the machine. His soda arrived with a loud thump. "Got me. Rainbow House is full of crazies. Must be action like this all the time in here. The place would drive me nuts."

"Really?" Drake wrinkled his face.

170

"I don't have to live here to be crazy. I have you."

"You can say that again." He planted his hands in his pockets, "I'm not a good babysitter. Maybe we should go out for a drink?"

"Great idea, Drake, and if I listen to you, you 'll become a bad influence on me." Rollie didn't finish. He caught Price Felton running toward them in his peripheral vision. Her clothes looked rumpled from distress.

Drake saw what Rollie was looking at. "Why does this look like bad news coming?"

The color had drained from Price Felton's face. Her once radiant demeanor had turned ghastly. She had a possessed look about her, gullible and disheveled.

Rollie's smile disappeared. "Looks a bit crazed, doesn't she?"

Price Felton was out of breath. She shook her head in disbelief. "They're gone!"

Drake spoke with an incredible calmness, "Both of 'em?"

"Yes!" She was half-screaming, nodding, pointing down a darkened hall, utterly astonished such a thing could happen on her watch. She looked from Rollie to Drake, finally stammering, "This never happens at The Rainbow House, never!"

Rollie smirked, "There's a first time for everything."

"Not here!" Spittle ran down her chin.

"How'd they get out?" Drake asked as his eyes tried to follow her pointing fingers down the darkened hall. He frowned at her confusion.

"It was therapy time. Her arms fluttered wildly. The attendants went to their rooms, and discovered they had simply vanished without a trace."

"Vanished?" Rollie repeated to Drake.

"Without a trace," Drake added. He turned to Rollie. "Whaddya think?"

"I guess we'll have to go and find them?" Rollie gave Price Felton a cursory inspection. "Any idea where they went, or how they got out with all this security you have?"

Felton Price raised a hand to her lips, "Good Lord, our insurance, our reputation."

"In the dumpster," Rollie said.

"You think?" Price Felton turned on him with fire in her eyes.

"The studio sent them," Drake said. "They'll want to know things. Is anything missing, Miss Felton?"

Price Felton hesitated, avoiding Rollie's stare.

Rollie assuredly didn't want to ask. "What's missing?"

"Lexus. They took the company Lexus. Oh my God. This is awful."

"I'll get the car," Drake said to Rollie. "Why don't you take a look in their rooms? When was the last time they were seen?"

Price Felton hesitated again. "Ah...bed check last evening."

"Bed check?" Rollie glanced at his watch. "It's 2:30 in the afternoon!"

Price Felton mumbled, "We were behind on a few things,"

Rollie tried to decipher. He stared Price Felton down until her embarrassed eyes oscillated and dropped to the floor. "You get the car, I'll check the rooms." He caught Drake's eyes. A payday was slipping away. Drake reluctantly followed after the nearly hysterical woman.

Price mumbled as she hurried away, "I thought you'd be more upset than you are?"

"I have high blood pressure," Drake answered.

Rollie watched them go down the hallway and disappear. He turned and walked right into Cleavon White. They walked down the hallway together.

"Shit happens," White said.

"On your watch?" Rollie quizzed.

"I was home with my lady. They were in locked rooms on the third floor."

Rollie glanced up the stairwell. "And nobody saw 'em leave?"

White shrugged his shoulders, "Nobody was watchin', I guess."

"Can you take me to their rooms?"

"Sure." White ambled up the stairs.

"How'd they get out the front door?" Rollie asked as he hurried after White.

"I know for a fact they didn't go out the front door." White said.

Rollie stopped walking. "Then how'd they get out?"

White grew a smirk, his hand gesturing openly, "Don't know how they got out of their rooms, but they took the dumbwaiter down to the laundry room in the basement. They walked through a maze of hallways to the emergency door." He raised his shoulders in a silent question, "Someone gave 'em directions or they'd never know about that exit, or our underground garage. The keys to the company cars are hung on hooks in the broom closet. I guess they found 'em."

Rollie thought it over. "Any staff missing?"

"Raymond."

"When was the last time you saw Raymond?"

White thought about this for a minute, rubbing his cheek as if that would help his memory." Last night. Yeah, as I was leaving, ah, he was coming up the stairs."

"Stairs?" Rollie looked up at the maze of stairs.

"Yeah, the back ones that go up to the third floor."

Rollie followed White's eyes up. "The third floor where their rooms are?"

"Yeah, the same floor. Raymond had keys, and now he has money."

"What money?"

"The money they offered me and I turned down." White gave Rollie a sarcastic smile, "Raymond's not too smart."

"Why didn't you say something?"

White theorized for a moment, formulating his thoughts. "I'm not getting paid to say stuff." He vindicated himself, "They tell me to look the other way all the time, and that's what I did."

Chapter 20

Rader was summoned to the Captain's office. Captain Ed McBride was one of the last hard-liners in the department. He fully expected closure on all cases, and when they dragged on, shit hit the fan. McBride was late fifties, one beer-belly over weight, a few strands of snow-white hair, and enough mileage on his face to re-write the maps of the California freeway system. He didn't give a rat's ass about procedures. He demanded results.

Rader and his homicide squad stood in the conference room. McBride looked over the file, notes, the murder book, and pictures of the crime scenes. When he finished, his eyes found only Rader. It was like the rest of the squad didn't exist.

"Okay," McBride started. "Tell me how these cases connect."

Rader cleared his throat. "Louis Baxter was known for his organized crime connections, and the girl was the daughter of a crime boss."

"How does that connect them?" McBride asked. The edge in his voice was deliberate.

175

Rader ignored the sarcasm. "We believe Baxter was skimming funds from pension money, and the girl…"

McBride cut him off. "You believe? Is that what you said, detective?"

"Yes sir," Rader answered.

"So if I take this to the DA, there's no question he'll file?"

"I didn't say that, sir."

"Excuse me, detective Rader, but did I just hear you used believe and the word skimming in the same sentence?"

"Louis Baxter had two hundred forty thousand dollars in a briefcase." Rader sounded defensive even to himself.

"Ah," McBride said with a indication of his head. "Now I understand. Good work, team." His eyes bore right through Rader. He looked at the other detectives. "Frank Mustio. What do you have on either case?"

"We found the car that ran Baxter off the cliff, sir." Mustio answered proudly.

"Where there prints, detective John Miller?"

Rader watched Miller squirm. He couldn't help his fellow detective.

"No prints, Captain." Miller said.

"But you're sure it's the right car, ah, detective Tanya Wilson?"

Detective Wilson stood rigid and conferred with notes written in the folder. "The damaged car parts match as does the paint from both cars. Without a doubt, sir, the car we found is the right car."

McBride turned his attention back to Rader. "What do you have on the girl?"

"Her stage name was Tawny Brock, legal name Tawnia Pataglia, daughter of New York crime boss

Anthony Pataglia. Autopsy report shows she died from forced trauma, a broken neck. The body was then posed at the crime scene. We have over five hundred sets of prints from that location, all being worked on. There was blood in the bathroom, but the DNA didn't match the girl, nor did it match skin taken from beneath her nails. So far we have no matches for the DNA. Apparently the maids at the location thoroughly dusted and wiped the house down before our team got there."

McBride's eyes narrowed. "What did you get from the Baxter house?"

Rader answered quickly. "We found pension fund files, bank accounts, cancelled checks, more cash, several weapons and a binder containing dates, deposits, withdrawals, and wire instructions. The bank is not cooperating with us yet. In his condo at the beach, we found a picture portfolio of the female Vic, Tawny Brock. It was a nude photo layout."

"So," McBride prodded, "you figured he knew the girl, and somehow their deaths are connected?"

"Yes," Rader said.

"Prove it to me, detective?" McBride demanded.

"I intend to, Captain." Rader said.

McBride turned but stopped short of the door. He looked back. "This Pataglia fella, what's his name again?"

"Anthony Pataglia," Rader answered.

"We expecting him to visit our fair city?' McBride's eyes darted around the room, waiting for a response.

Rader shrugged. "He'll send a soldier first. This girl was his only daughter. Whoever he sends will be on a deadly mission. They'll move quickly, so we'll have to ramp up, to stay in front of him."

"Have you called LAPD organized crime or the Feds yet?" McBride asked.

"No sir. They'll take the case, and I'd prefer we kept it in house. It's our case." Rader sounded in charge but waited for the Captain's approval.

"Okay for now, detective Rader. But if these mobsters come out here and start killing people we might have to make that call. You think that soldier is here yet?"

Rader knew. "Yes sir, he's here in town as we speak."

"Then let's find him and take his ass down." McBride walked out of the room.

Chapter 21

When Rollie got to Ben Parker's room, he quickly searched through everything. The room had been cleaned out. About to leave, Rollie spotted a document under the bed. He picked it up, glanced at White, who gave Rollie a shrug. White didn't seem to care what Rollie did, so he opened the file and thumbed through the pages. He turned a page, and used a finger to sweep over the lines. Why wasn't he surprised?

Ben Parker's real name was Vince Castiglia, born in New York City. His family, before the untimely deaths of his mother and father, had moved to Philadelphia in the early 1990's. His contact in Philly was Elizabeth Brayden. Elizabeth Brayden was Moe Brayden's wife, and that meant the kid was connected to the Brayden crime family. The bottom line, Parker was related to the Castiglia family. Rollie knew from his own people that Francisco Castiglia was part of the extended family of Frank Costello, the notorious fixer. Frank Costello was the payoff king, nicknamed the Prime Minister of the

Underworld. Until The Chin, a Genovese crime family soldier better known as Vincent Gigante, shot Costello in the head, Costello was considered an elder statesman of the Cosa Nostra. If what he just read was true, Ben Parker was distantly tied to more than one of the crime families. Regardless of the distance, Ben Parker was either a target or a valuable prize to one of the waring families. Either way, he and Drake had to get Ben Parker to protect their payday.

"Your face is red." White broke the silence.

"Red?" Rollie pulled his eyes from the file, and found White standing at the doorway. "Whaddya mean?"

"Dude, if you can't feel that, you better have yourself checked. A bright red face like the one you're wearing means your blood pressure is soaring."

Rollie suddenly felt the heat and took several long, very slow, breaths. "What did Ben Parker offer you?"

"Ten grand."

"How could you turn that down?"

White smiled. "First, I'm an honest man. Second, my fiancée is pregnant. Third, I'm gonna marry her, and fourth, I like my job. The pay is great, and for the first time in my life I'm doing something good. No jail time for Cleavon."

"So Raymond got ten grand to help them get outta here?" Rollie asked. The heat returned. This time his cheeks tingled.

"No." White answered in a slow drawl, "He asked me what I turned down, and I told him. He went back to the actor and said he wanted twenty-five."

"Ben Parker agreed to pay Raymond twenty-five?"

"Not exactly." White shook his head.

"What does that mean?"

"Raymond don't trust anybody. He expected the actor to rip him off, so when Parker agreed, too quickly mind you, Raymond said forget it."

Rollie was confused. "So, Raymond didn't help them escape?"

"I didn't say that. The other actor said he would double the fee if Raymond drove them back to L.A. Said he had cash at his house."

Rollie was stunned. "Raymond got fifty grand to drive them to L.A.?"

White shook his head. "Not exactly."

"Oh, for God's sake, just tell me what happened." Rollie was about to lose his temper. He realized both fists had closed into tight little knots.

"Raymond said he'd drive 'em, but that he'd stop to pick up his two brothers on the way. If the actors planned to rip him off, he and his brothers wouldn't hesitate to kill 'em, and dump their bodies in the ocean."

"And they agreed to that?" Rollie couldn't believe it. Were the actors that stupid?

"Sort of." White looked perplexed. "The Parker kid said he had to make a phone call to have a friend move money over to Garrison's house, cause it was closer to the airport. This phone call made Raymond nervous, and the actors could see that, so they upped the offer to seventy-five. Said it would be all cash, so Raymond let them use his cell phone."

"You think Raymond picked up his brothers?"

"Raymond doesn't have a brother."

"That's not good." Rollie closed the file and tucked it beneath his shirt, in the small of his back. To Rollie's surprise, White didn't object to the new location of the file.

"I told Raymond they'd probably kill him before they'd pay him that much money."

Now that, Rollie knew whom Ben Parker was, nothing would surprise him. He walked past White and headed down the stairs. Over his shoulder, he asked, "Did Raymond say anything else?"

White followed after Rollie. "Yeah. Said once he got the money, the actors would be the only ones hard to find."

"That's great. You think it meant it?" Rollie asked.

"Sure. Like I told you, Raymond's not too bright. He'll pick up two boys from the hood, and they won't care much about anything. Seventy-five big ones can buy lots of stuff."

Chapter 22

The Watcher hated New York airports, so she landed at Newark International. She drove to Jersey City in a rented car. In a seedy warehouse district, she found where her weapons source lived. She knew him by the name of Wally, and she was Brenda. Wally was expecting her. He was a short, fat slob. His face was scared over, hair thinning, and eyes that squinted at everything though thick-lenses glasses. She picked out three untraceable handguns, an Uzi, a Glock and a little thirty-eight. She also grabbed enough ammo to start a war, and asked Wally about listening devices. He showed her the newest gadgets on the market, explaining he only carried high-end things with the latest technology. She believed him, paid his exorbitant prices, and drove to Anthony Pataglia's waterfront mansion in Long Island. The Watcher was surprised not to see a small army of bodyguards. She parked, waited, and watched a parade of vehicles emerged from the mansion gates. The first car had four men inside and was followed by a black limo. Behind the limo, another car trailed with four more men. Unless she got lucky, The Watcher would have to take out more than

WILLIAM BYRON HILLMAN

her lone target. She was sent to eliminate Anthony
Pataglia, not a bunch of thugs. Risky. She hated the
thought of risky. She didn't mind going out of her depth
once in a while. After all, she was a wildcat – wasn't she?
The involuntary smile grew -- a significant challenge. The
thrill of trembling in the balance before lying oneself open
to an untimely demise was exhilarating.

The procession drove into South Brooklyn and
stopped at Paully's Steak House on Diggs Avenue. The
Watcher stayed far enough away not to be seen. She
parked, and watched the front and rear cars unload.
Everyone converged on the limo as three men
materialized. The Watcher peered through small,
powerful binoculars. Two were dressed in dark-blue suits,
the third guy built like a door. The Watcher lowered the
eyeglasses, and stared down at the picture she had of
Anthony Pataglia. She raised the binoculars just in time to
get one last glimpse before they all entered the
restaurant. The two men in suits looked like Anthony
Pataglia. They looked like twins. Damn! Did he have a
twin? Was this a set up? What the hell was going on? The
contract was contaminated.

Two men stayed at the front door of the
restaurant. The only way The Watcher could get in was
through the back. Not a good choice, unless she could
park by the back door. Even that wasn't good because
there was still only one way out. She shrugged her
shoulders. If its the only way, she would make it work or
die trying. She put the Explorer into gear and turned the
corner. Around the block, she found a dingy alley. It was
primarily used for deliveries. Parking in the back meant
she would have to block the alley. If another car entered
from the wrong way she was screwed, and probably be

shot at or killed. She'd have to back out of the alley. She took her only option -- plug the damn alley.

She parked the Explorer in the middle of the alley. The back door had been left open, and there were no signs of his guards.. Either they needed ventilation or were expecting a delivery. She'd surprise them with a new wrinkle on delivery.

She inserted the tiny earpiece into her left ear. The mike was supposed to pick up sounds from two hundred feet. She turned the receiver on and promptly got whacked with mumbled dialog, glasses tinkling, water sloshing, traffic down the block, and men laughing. She screwed a silencer on the barrel and tucked the Glock into her purse. She'd carry the Uzi at her side. She slipped through the backdoor, and found she was in a storage room. The stench was a combination of booze and spoiled food. Trashcans were cluttered together next to the door. The sounds in her ear narrowed to those of the restaurant. Food sizzling on the grill, a room full of undistinguished garble utensils banging against plates, laughter, and a little Spanish from workers in the kitchen. She inched closer.

Anthony Pataglia and his look-alike were sitting in a corner booth. The man built like a door, stood guard at their side. Four other men sat at the table, all with their backs to her. The Watcher waited in the shadows. The restaurant was crowded, and this pleased The Watcher. Once she opened fire, pandemonium would reign. In the middle of mayhem, they wouldn't know where the shots came from. People instinctively would run or duck. Bodies would be everywhere. The unfortunate would be dead. She watched waiters scramble from one table to another, refreshing drinks, serving food, and taking orders. The wall behind Anthony Pataglia was brick, and to his left was a large, open fireplace. Between the fireplace and the bar was a series of TV monitors, a big-screen TV, stereo components, a small dance floor, an enormous fabric sofa, and matching chairs. There were no windows on the side where they sat. She turned her head, and heard some of what was said.

"Ronnie Mauten...yet." One person said.

Another added, "No...disappeared...word."

A third said, "...thony...we gotta...quick."

She couldn't determine which of the two men Anthony Pataglia was, but now she knew he was there. She didn't have time to distinguish which one was Anthony. Not a problem. She'd take them both out. She needed to get the guy built like a door too. The men with their backs to her were of no concern. If they survived, she'd be gone before they got up.

Years ago, her teacher did work for the Pataglia brothers. Since then, Anthony Pataglia had created enemies with various families. He had grown too powerful, too strong and successful, and had embarrassed some others by living an principled life, running legitimate businesses. The dark side was accomplished so covertly, not even close business associates suspected any wrong doings. He had turned the once illegal activities into legitimate holdings and comprehensive investments. The limited criminal activities he continued to deal in bore no resemblance to the old days. Yet, wounds everyone hoped had healed long ago, continued to permeate. Relatives of those who had been eliminated years ago remained wronged in their eyes, and still harbored hatred that demanded retribution. She knew all about Anthony Pataglia, and his mistakes. She had never worked for him, and he was about to regret that. His death probably would create a war, which would be good for her business, or, quickly end discrepancies and a long peace would follow. That wouldn't be good for her business.

The Watcher stepped into the room, Uzi in one hand and Glock 17 with its Brugger & Thomet silencer in the other. The attached magazine carried nineteen hollow-point bullets. She raised the Glock, in rapid fire and a near silent splat-shushing sound, The Watcher put rounds into the two men who looked like Anthony Pataglia, and two quick pops into the guy built like a door. Within seconds, all three dropped to the floor. The Watcher then raised the Uzi and sprayed bullets everywhere. People screamed, pandemonium broke loose, tables overturned, everyone was shouting, men and women dove for cover, and the four men sitting with their backs to her dropped to the floor. It didn't matter if she hit them or not. She got the target, and that's what counted. The Watcher wiggled back into the shadows of the storage space and emerged unscathed out the back door. Without incident, she drove to the airport and caught a flight to Los Angeles.

Chapter 23

The moment Rollie saw Drake coming, he knew the tall guy was dragging more distressing news. He had a look Rollie identified immediately. He was pouting.

"Tell me from where you are?" Rollie called out.

Drake stopped walking, shrugged his hulking shoulders, resembling a Gorilla doing symmetric exercises. "Wires cut. All of 'em."

Rollie didn't understand. "What wires?"

"All the wires that start and keep a car engine running."

"Including your SUV?" Rollie knew the answer, but had to ask.

"Yeah, smartass, mine along with everything else that has an engine.

Rollie glanced at White but got nothing from him. He sized up Price Felton and found her near tears. All she could do was gyrate.

"You can use the phone in my office to call the rental agency," Price spilled out before loud sobs took over.

Rollie and Drake waited on the front steps of The Rainbow House. It took over two hours for the car rental company to send a car to pick them up. Than the kid had to drive back to Santa Ynez to get their rental. The agency girl went to retrieve their car, and returned in a tiny compact. Rollie stared at the minuscule vehicle while Drake towered over the coupe. Getting in would be a challenge.

"What is this?" Drake inquired.

She offered a whopping, cheerleader smile. "All our full-sized cars have been rented. This is the only one left. It's a Ford Focus 3-door hatchback. Isn't it cute?"

Rollie took the keys. "Thanks." He watched the girl skip back to the office, and turned to admire the car. "It is, sort of, ah, cute, isn't it?"

"No!" Drake opened the door, and had to bend his body in half to get in.

Drake moved the seat all the way back, and adjusted the height, but it didn't help. "Didn't you call the Santa Barbara agency?"

"Yep."

"Then why'd we have to drive to Santa Ynez to get a car?"

"Convention in Santa Barbara." Rollie answered humorously.

Drake tried to adjust in the seat, bashing elbows and his head against the headliner. "Before you signed the papers, did you inquire if any cars would be returned soon? Did you ask?"

"Yep." Rollie tucked nicely behind the wheel. "And nope, no cars were coming back. Hey, would you rather drive?"

"Are you kidding? Just get us back to the office!"

"My, are we testy or what?"

"Did you remember to have my car towed?" Drake was talking to avoid thinking about riding all the way back to the office bent in half.

Rollie watched him twist and turn, trying to get comfortable. Nothing worked. Drake Fargo was too bulky for his own good. "Yeah, they'll pick it up later today. They asked why you cut all the wires. I said you had a bad day."

"If I could move, Rollie, I'd punch your lights out."

"Sure, always the tough guy." He eyed the enormous Bally slip-on loafers Drake wore, "You should take those size fifteen's off so your feet will have more room."

"You're not funny, Rollie."

Rollie started the car, and because he hadn't driven a stick shift in a long time, lurched forward. Drake rumbled in his seat, whacking his head on the interior. Rollie wasn't easily amused, but damn if he didn't find Drake touching his funny bone. He tossed the car's gears from one to the next and enjoyed the sound coming from Drake with each one.

Drake groaned, "You're an actor. Where would you go to hide out?

"You can't ask me that. I don't count."

"Why not?" Drake tried to move his knee so he could see Rollie.

"I don't consider myself a dope and those two guys are certifiable." Rollie wasn't sure if he should tell Drake about the information he found. Ben Parker's background was way beyond what Rollie had left behind. This kids relatives were killers. He thought about that for a moment and realized his uncles weren't that much better. Rollie hated to admit he had more in common with Ben Parker than he wanted to admit. Maybe Parker was running too? No, that didn't' add up. Now he knew how Ben Parker just came out of nowhere. They were funding his movies with laundered money.

"Rollie, talk to me?"

Rollie put the metal to the floor. Nothing happened. The two-cylinder engine was already peaked out. Where would they seriously go to hide? "I'd go up to San Francisco, and get lost."

With his knees cutting off circulation, Drake couldn't breathe. "That where you think they went?"

"No." Rollie wouldn't run if he had the kind of friends these two had. Wouldn't they go back to town and ask for protection?

"Rollie?"

Rollie gave Drake a cursory look. "They went back to L.A. Probably think hiding out in Marina Del Rey or maybe Long Beach is cool. While they wait for help, I'm sure they know the nightlife is pretty active down there. It's a perfect place to hide in plain sight, and maybe get laid while they hang in a state of suspense."

"Why not just check into the Bel Air hotel?"

"Too obvious, even for their mentality." Rollie kept rolling what he found around in his head. "You know they have at least eighteen hours on us, right?"

Drake ignored him, and started analyzing. "If they call friends …"

"They already have. By now they might have an army available to them, and none would be nice guys."

Drake looked over at him. "That's not a good thing."

"Not if their friends are bad guys."

"What aren't you telling me?"

Rollie didn't take his eyes off the road. The ocean to his right rolled turbulently with the wind. The sky took on an ominous darkness, and that's what raced through Rollie. He didn't know whom Ben Parker's old man was, and it didn't matter. Rollie's old man was stupid worthless, and a wife-beating coward. Rollie's uncle started out defiant, and only God knows what he did over the years. Rollie knew all about Ben Parker's relatives. They were notorious, infamously evil that flesh is heir to. They were the beginning legs of the Mafia.

"Rollie?" Drake was persistent. "You know something, don't you? Something you haven't shared with me and you're starting to scare me, kid."

Chapter 24

The jumbo jet taxied to the terminal building, and Fabrio Tallagi, along with several hundred other passengers, wandered down the tarmac into the expansive tentacles of Los Angeles International Airport. Fabrio was on a mission. When young Drew Lipesky realized his old man wasn't coming home, he'd go ballistic. Fabrio knew he didn't have much time, and would have to move quickly. Drew Lipesky would go after everyone he thought was an enemy. The terminal was crawling with cops. The guys in suits were easy to spot, but organized crime units from the locals were different. Fabrio could smell them. Even dressed down, they had a look, anxious eyes taking in everyone, and heads bowing into their chest so they could communicate with their fellow officers. Fabrio wasn't flustered. He wasn't on their radar -- hell they didn't even know about him. Fabrio carried only one overnight bag to the area where limousines waited for their passengers. He spotted Barko Fontaine, waiting for him at the end of the ramp. Barko had worked for the Pataglia's, on and off, for years. He was a good man who could be trusted.

Barko Fontaine tipped his hat and took the overnight bag. "Welcome back to L.A., Mr. Tallagi. You have a good flight?"

"As good as a flight can be when you hate flying, Barko. Thanks for asking."

Barko opened the back door of the limo and closed it behind Fabrio. He placed the overnight bag in the trunk and zipped out of the airport. They drove in silence until they reached the 405 Freeway heading north towards Westwood. Every once in a while Fabrio would casually look around to see if they were being followed. They weren't.

Fabrio felt his knuckles relax for the first time since he left New York. Flying was the only thing in life that scared the living blush-of-life right out of him. He was known as the family enforcer, and if word got out he was a cupcake on an airplane, he'd never live it down. On every flight, his fingers buried into armrests, and he'd cling to them during the entire flight. He couldn't eat, sleep, read, or watch a movie. He was a virtual prisoner in his own mind, paralyzed as others moved about the cabin having the time of their lives. Every time the plane took a dip, or God forbid it shook a little too violently, sweat ran like a river down his back. Damn airplanes! Kids giggled and laughed, thrilled that the bumpy ride was a roller coaster in the sky. The departure sent shivers throughout his body, and when they came down to land, he closed his eyes and held on for dear life. The one and only fear Fabrio had was flying. He couldn't breathe normally until the plane landed and stopped rolling. Fabrio could face a shootout more comfortably than to get on an airplane. He only flew when dire necessity required it.

"Where am I staying?"

"The Beverly Wilshire." Barko smiled. "That is your favorite hotel, isn't it?"

"Yes, thank you. Let's stop at the hotel first. Do you have the list?"

Barko produced an envelope from his breast pocket and handed it back to Fabrio. He read it over carefully. It contained guests, agents, lawyers, managers, producers, directors, and actors who had attended the Santino party. Also on the list were doctors, girlfriends, and other closely related friends of friends. Fabrio studied it while Barko drove in silence. Good drivers knew when to shut up, and when to speak. Fabrio watched Barko, and wondered how much this man knew about their business. The act of silence was a dedicated driver's credo. They were blind, deaf and dumb to their surroundings. The road was their only ally.

Fabrio studied the list. "Were you there?"

"Yes," Barko answered. Al stayed with other drivers in the garage quarters. That's how I got the list."

"See anything I should know about?"

"Nobody dares to come near the garage, unless they want a ride. Me and the other guys watched baseball on TV. Both the Dodgers, and Angels played that night. Music was loud. We heard laughter, clinking glasses, and conversations we couldn't understand."

Fabrio asked as if he didn't care, "Who did you take home in the morning?"

Barko cleared his throat, a nervous habit. "Alex Foster, that comedian kid. He is so funny, and that gets him on everyone's guest list. A real life of the party."

"Alex Foster?" Fabrio knew who he was.

"You know him?"

"I know who he is, yeah, I've seen him on TV."

Barko nodded. "He was really out of it."

"Drunk?"

"No, he was floating in another world. Feeling no pain."

Fabrio leaned forward. "Did he say anything to you?"

"He kept mumbling he was sorry about something. I asked what he was sorry about, and he said he couldn't remember. He finally fell asleep, and said nothing when I helped him into his house."

"Thanks..." Fabrio wondered what the kid was upset about. Did he kill Tawny Brock-Pataglia? If he didn't, did he know who did? Could it be this easy? Maybe. He looked at the list and found Alex's name, address, and phone number.

"You okay?" Barko asked.

"Lets run by ol' Alex Foster's place, and surprise him." He looked at the list. "Where's Mulholland Drive?"

"Up in the hills."

"Secluded area?"

"Yeah, he lives out in the middle of nowhere."

"Perfect." He glanced at the list again. "Who's Drake Fargo?"

"P I, usually does bodyguard work at parties. He's a good guy."

"What about Rollie Kemp?"

"Actor with a temper." Barko laughed, "He's known as, punch first and last." He glanced in the mirror at Fabrio, "I heard he's working part time for Drake Fargo. You know him?"

Fabrio nodded. "Yeah, I know him." He made a mental note to call Rollie Kempanelli. "What about Santino, Barko. Who drove him out?"

"Drove himself. He was in one helluva big hurry."

Fabrio peered out the window, watching the freeway traffic. It amazed him how Los Angeles hadn't changed over the years. Cars smashed together, barely moving, going nowhere and switching lanes to speed it up. Smog lingered over the entire city. Most who lived here hadn't seen a perfect blue sky in God knows how many years. He glanced through the perpetual clouds and caught a glimpse of the sun, orange, brown, ugly, like a lamp burning out. Hollywood, a place where dreams were created to the desire of writers, then corrupted by directors as they used their creative juices to manipulate the words into totally obscure meanings. Actors and actresses came to town with hopes of stardom, and if they were lucky enough to get out, left with tails snug to their underbellies, their heads down, hearts defeated, and morals forever shattered.

Little Tawny. Fabrio remembered the gifted girl with golden hair, and crisp blue eyes that spoke oceans in her silence. The delicate girl he bounced on his knee. As she grew into a young woman, she called him Uncle Fab, always hugging and kissing him. She was like a daughter to him, a girl he could never have. He flinched with that sudden memory. No one actually knew what happened to him so many years ago. He kept it to himself. It was nobody's business. He could still see the blood between his legs. Still felt the numbness and the end of his manhood. "Yeah" he mumbled, "that was a long time ago."

"I'm sorry," Barko looked at him in the mirror, "did you say something?"

Fabrio spoke up. "It's been a long time since I've been to L.A."

"Lots of changes, all the time. Town doesn't know how to stop growing."

197

The limo exited the 405 Freeway at Mulholland and turned right into the hills. They passed estates, mansions and hillside dumps. Another colorless road, Fabrio thought. Brown dried hillsides, palm trees in need of a manicure, and a thickness in the air that made it difficult to breathe. This was Brentwood, and extension of Hollywood. Crime families were the forbidden lot, unless, of course, they financed or manufactured celluloid dreams. Up here, the rich mixed with the poor, the con man with the clever liars, thieves and back-stabbers, and amazingly many sunk beneath the principals of honesty and good. On the top of the hills, lived a multitude of idealists. Some fabricated dreams. Others had materialistic demands and suffered through multiple marriages with friends and neighbors. Most lived beyond their idiotic assets and socialized with the depraved. It was an intriguing mix. Fabrio watched the fancy cars and gated homes with views of the ever-present smog. Most paid millions for the view. There was no manual to assist these people through lunacy. A parade of numerous vehicles passed them on the other side of the road. He watched, Mercedes, Porches, Roll Royce's and a Lexus or two go by. "Busy place."

"Yeah, even up here it's overcrowded." Barko agreed.

"Then they won't miss one or two of 'em, will they?" Fabrio said as he flipped open his cell phone and punched in a number. He felt Barko's eyes on him, and then he saw the gesture. Whatever he did, would stay within. Barko was one funky dude.

Chapter 25

Rollie's cell phone rang. He struggled, from lack of space, to get it out. On the third ring, he managed to extract the tiny phone, and flip it open. "This is Rollie."

"Rollie the actor?" The voice was strange, raspy, and unfamiliar.

"That's me. Who's this?"

"Rollie Kempanelli, right?" The voice had an bite of sarcasm.

Rollie swallowed hard. No one knew him by that name, except those who worked for his uncle. He glanced at Drake, and then turned his attention back to the road. They had just cleared the hills between Buellton and Gaviota, heading south on the 101 Freeway. "Who wants to know?" Rollie glanced at Drake.

"I heard you were at the Santino party." The voice was cutting, angry.

"Look, if this is a joke…"

The voice cut him off, "No joke, Rollie. You remember Tawny Pataglia, don't ya?"

Rollie hadn't heard her name in years, not since he was in his early teens. He felt his arms go numb, the

199

hair standing on the edge. Drake was now facing him. "I remember."

"You there when they killed her?" The voice asked.

"What?" Rollie blurted it out. He almost lost control and quickly pulled off the road. "Who the hell is this?"

"I work for your uncle, but I ain't your uncle, understand?"

"No, I don't understand." Anger flared in Rollie, he clenched his fists. "You threatening me?"

The voice dropped to a whisper. "Listen you little shit. You went to that party, and as far as I'm concerned everyone there is a suspect -- savvy?"

"You think I'd kill Tawny?" It was preposterous just to say it.

Drake twisted in an attempt to sit up. Rollie had his attention. He gestured for Rollie's cell phone, but the gesture was waved off.

The voice became controlled, level, monotone. "I don't know what you'd do since you deserted your family. One thing's for sure." He hesitated, breathing slowly but profoundly into the phone, "I'll be comin' to see you."

"Who the hell do you think you are?" Rollie was shouting.

"You get in my way, I won't hesitate to take you down." The call ended.

Rollie closed the phone with a loud snap.

"Who was that?" Drake asked.

Rollie mumbled. "The murdered girl was my cousin, Tawny."

"Tawny?" Drake gestured with open hands, "Am I supposed to know who Tawny is?"

* * * *

200

Childhood flashes zipped into Rollie's head. He saw Tawny at five, eight, ten and twelve. She grew up right there inside his head. She was beautiful, golden hair, ocean blue-green eyes that sparkled, and a smile that did everything but embrace you.

* * * *

"My mother's youngest brother's daughter."

"Okay," Drake glanced out the window.

Rollie's eyes glistened, a waterfall of tears cascading down his cheeks. He looked over at Drake, sucked air, grasping to control of emotions. It dawned on him where he'd seen the blond on the stairs, going up with Santino and Ben Parker. At the time, he couldn't place her, but she sure as hell remembered him – that's why she turned away. "Tawny was my childhood friend. The daughter of Anthony Pataglia."

Drake spun around as best as was possible, "Crime boss Pataglia?"

Rollie nodded, "That was one of his enforcers."

"He thinks you were involved in your cousin's death?"

"Forget what he thinks about me. What if...?"

"Actors?" Drake cut him off. "Did you see either one of them with your cousin?"

"Yeah," Rollie remembered Ben chasing her through the house, and then Andre in the backyard. "Both were with her."

"You didn't recognize her?"

"It's been years, Drake. She was fourteen the last time I saw her." Rollie regretted not remembering her. If he'd of said something, maybe... No, it wouldn't change anything.

Drake pounded his fist on the dashboard, making the whole car vibrate. "Tell me what you found back at the Rainbow House?"

"What are you talking about?"

"Your father."

"He's dead."

Drake wrenched his neck, "The rest of the family."

"Ma and Uncle Charlie are dead."

"I'm not talking about them!" Drake was exasperated, "I'm talking about the rest of the family. The ones you're running from."

Rollie's mind raced with unpleasant thoughts. "They're all bad guys. They went legit years ago, and now what they do is considered good business."

"You know how they think, and I need to know what you know."

Rollie's cheek muscles bungled. "They kill people when they get crossed. Family is family. Why are you busting my chops?"

"Cause you're holding out on me."

Rollie dug the file out from the small of his back and handed it to Drake. Fargo snatched it out of his hands and thumbed through it. "Ben Parker's real name is Vincent Castiglia? I don't get it?"

Rollie almost smiled. Too much time had gone by. Old mobsters were being forgotten. "Have you ever heard of Francisco Castiglia?"

Drake shook his head. "No."

"Better known as Frank Costello?"

"Oh shit!" Drake's blotched face turned red.

"No one knows what alliance the kid actor has, but I'll bet all of his films have been financed with washed bills. If Tawny found this out…"

"What if your uncle is financing them?" Drake asked.

"Then it wouldn't make sense to kill her."

"Was she Anthony Pataglia's only child?"

"Yeah." Rollie could feel his chest tighten. The last thing he wanted was a family reunion. If his uncle thought he was involved, there was little doubt Anthony Pataglia would have him killed.

"Let's get back to town." Drake said. "Put this piece of crap in gear!"

Rollie started the car and sprayed gravel racing onto the freeway. In a blink, he was speeding. The car rocked over every pebble, and each time it felt as though they were going a hundred miles an hour. They were barely going sixty. He gripped the steering wheel with caged anger. Few people knew what extent a crime family would go to, to even a wrong. Rollie knew all about the Pataglia brothers. Anthony's older brother Vincent, started out on the docks, became a union force, and then the boss. He brought his younger brother, Anthony, in to organize the family, build a business atmosphere, and keep them beneath the radar. Anthony was masterful, turning illicit funds into legitimate, entrepreneurial, enterprises. Although both brothers started out on a violent path, they quickly changed course, under Anthony's guidance. The tentacles of the FBI continued to stomp on crime families. They successfully shut down the Gambino family, sent John Gotti, John Gotti Junior, and Salvatore Gravano, to prison. Law enforcement hadn't gathered enough evidence on any of Pataglia's activities, to build a solid case against them. The government couldn't find a sequence of mistakes leading back to them, but Rollie knew more than he wanted to. The Brayden family in Philadelphia would move out to confront the Pataglia's for control. Each had a spider web of units all over the country, controlling waterfront docks, unions, transportation and film crews. The pension funds alone had to be worth billions.

They drove in silence to their office where Drake unfolded his body. Several long minutes passed before he could walk. Even in a hurry, Rollie had to wait – to see if his partner needed help.

"My feet are numb." Drake said. He leaned against the little car for support.

Rollie couldn't resists. "I told you to take your shoes off!"

Rollie hurried inside before Drake's outstretched hands could reach him. Both were surprised to find detectives Rader and Mustio in their reception area.

"How'd you guys get in here?" Rollie checked the door to see if they broke in. There was no damage or signs of a break in.

"Front door was unlocked, so we came in thinking you guys were hard at work." Rader offered a slight smile, acknowledging what he just said was bullshit.

"I locked it when we left." Rollie said.

Rader ignored him and shook Drake's hand. "Drake."

"They picked our lock!" Rollie said to Drake.

Now Drake ignored him. "John." Drake took Rader's hand. It's been a long time." He shook Mustio's hand, "Frank."

Mustio glared at Rollie. "Rollie. You know, I didn't put two and two together."

They shook hands. "I didn't know you could count to two, Frankie?"

"Not funny," Mustio said but couldn't help the inevitable grin.

"We found your prints up at the Santino house." Rader wasn't smiling. "Mind telling' us what you were doin' there, and why you didn't tell us before now?"

"What happened to the long-time-no-see stuff?" Rollie said

"We'll do that later." Rader's face had a strained, tight look. Dark circles beneath his eyes created a bizarre, haunting glare.

"Went by invitation," Rollie answered.

Mustio almost laughed out loud. "You'd never get invited to that kind of party, Rollie."

"Just the same, I did. As a matter of fact, I think I still have the original invitation in my desk drawer. Wanna see it?"

"Yeah," Rader said, following Rollie to the desk.

"What about you, Drake?" Rader tossed out.

"I was there to protect and serve."

Rollie pulled out the invitation and handed it to Rader.

Rader studied the invitation and shared it with Mustio. Mustio turned it over, insinuating it might be a fake. "So what do you know about the girl that got herself killed?" Rader asked.

Rollie couldn't talk about family matters, regardless of how long it had been since he was around them. He knew the FBI or Homeland Security would come breathing down his neck -- so the less he shared about his past, the better. He assumed they already knew some, but why feed a hungry crocodile?

Drake sat down and rubbed his feet. "Just what we read in the papers."

Rader couldn't take his gaze off the huge feet. "You should try getting a foot reduction, Drake."

"Very funny, Rader. What brings you guys all the way over here? What is it, Rollie, two or three miles?"

Rollie nodded. "Yeah, it's quite a drive."

Rader glared at them. "We're trying to put a guest list together."

Rollie asked, "Why don't you ask Santino?"

"He's out of town, and his domestic help doesn't have a clue." Mustio shot back.

"So you're running prints from the house?" Drake asked. "Damn, that sure sounds like a big waste of time."

Mustio said, "We found you, didn't we?"

"And mighty good police work it was." Drake said. "Out of, what, five hundred people, you found us? What are you thinking, Rollie?"

"I think they're good." Rollie was at home with Drake. They thought alike and lied as good as anyone.

"All right!" Rader was clearly not in the mood for jokes. "Who was at the party? If you two were there, you must've been watching someone, right?"

Rollie chirped in, "You're forgetting the invitation."

"Don't bullshit me. Do you guys know who that girl was?"

Rollie looked at Drake, and the muscular guy shrugged. They both turned back to Rader, waiting for him to tell them.

Mustio was genuinely surprised. "You guys don't know do you?"

"Haven't a clue," Rollie said.

"You recognize the name Anthony Pataglia, right, Drake?"

"Yeah, so what's he got to do with this?"

"The Vic was his daughter."

206

"Aw gee," Rollie blurted out. "You gotta be shittin' me?"

Rader turned and gave Rollie the once over with his eyes. "You know Pataglia?"

"Everybody from New York knows about the Pataglia family." Rollie couldn't bring himself to think of telling them that his old man worked for the Pataglia brothers, and worse, that Anthony Pataglia was his uncle. If they weren't related, Tawny, his childhood buddy, would have been his first love. They adored each other.

Rader turned back to Drake. "The brothers have been quiet for years. This girl was Pataglia's only child. The shit hasn't even started to hit the fan."

"We need a list with real names on it." Mustio tried to be serious with Rollie. "The maids gave us a list of people who don't exist. That party was a who's who event so everybody that's anybody, no offense Rollie, got invited."

"Without breaking that client-privilege crap, what can you tell us, Drake?"

Drake hesitated for over a minute. His forehead crinkled, a man in deep concentration, trying real hard to remember names that would help these guys out. Rollie watched the master at work. Finally, Drake shook his head. "You know, I see their faces on the big screen, but the names. You guys know how I am with names. If I don't write 'em down, I forget 'em. Studio hired me to make sure no one got out of hand. I couldn't watch everybody."

Rollie perked up. "I've got an idea. If you put some heat on the agents, you know William Morris, and the kids over at CAA? They'll tell you who went, and who didn't. You're good at this stuff, Rader, go there and bust some balls. I'll bet half their clients were there."

Rader considered.

Mustio agreed. "That's a good idea, John. We could take a team with us?"

"Yeah, that's not a bad idea, Rollie, thanks. You'd've made a good cop, Rollie. Too bad about that damned accident."

Rollie said, "If I had to pass a physical, I wouldn't be here either."

"Okay, we'll visit some flesh peddlers. You guys learn anything, you'll call, right?" Rader waited for their answer.

Rollie shrugged. "Sure."

"You bet," Drake added. "Any idea how she died?"

"Not enough drugs or booze in her, so we're guessing an old boyfriend or something like that. She'd been busy with unprotected sex. They're tryin' to sort out the DNA downtown as we speak. She must've been up for a big role or something?"

"Her neck was broken," Mustio added. "She died quick, like someone yanked her head back too far, and it snapped."

"We'll call if we hear something." Drake stood, and shook their hands.

Mustio gave Rollie a hug, patting him on the back. "You take care, hear?"

Rollie nodded and shook Rader's hand.

When they were gone, Rollie felt guilty lying. Drake angrily snatched the phone and dialed. Rollie could feel his passion from across the room. He'd never known anyone like Drake. One minute he was mister charming, and the next explosive.

"Eddie?" Drake started pacing. "You lied to me. No, you listen. If either one of these punks are guilty of killing that mobster's daughter, both are dead men walking. If I find out you knew what they did, you'll curse the day you met me." Drake changed ears with the phone and continued pacing. "The cops are lookin' for us and don't ask how I know, I just do. I expect you to call my cell and fill in the blanks. If either one of these clowns gets to a phone and calls you, I better be your first call, got it? Good, our fee's going up by the minute!"

He slammed the phone down and glared at Rollie. "Let me get this straight before we go out there, and get ourselves killed. Your uncle has a soldier after you, your cousin is murdered, the actors we're watching are connected, and, and they might have killed the girl. Is that everything so far?"

"No, there's a big piece of the puzzle still missing."

"What are you talking about?"

"The man who was run off Malibu Canyon worked for my uncle, and that means he must've known Tawny."

"There's more isn't there?" Drake was fuming.

" I saw the hit man."

"What!" Drake yelled.

"I was on my way to the studio, my first speaking role. I didn't want to be late, so I cut over the canyon. That's when I nearly got run off the road." Rollie didn't like the look in Drake's eyes, so he looked away and continued. "I didn't put this together until we were on our way to Rainbow. I saw the cops picking up the Mustang, the car that cut me off. It was still parked where the guy dumped it. Remember when you thought I was looking at a broad?"

"Yeah, I remember, so?"

"I was watching the cops lift it up on a flatbed."

"Oh this is good." Drake was smoldering

"Before I got my clothes, I went to see Rader. When he told me who the dead guy was, I knew the man worked for my uncle."

"And you're telling me this now because?"

"I forgot. By the time we got to Rainbow, well things started happening."

"Is that it?"

"No. I took this girl I know out to dinner. We went in separate cars. She drove off, and before I could get in mine, this car, this little sport thing tried to run me down."

"So the hit man knows you?" Drake sounded exhausted.

"We saw each other, Drake."

"You can identify him?"

"No, he was several hundred feet away. Sunglasses covered his face. He wore a baseball cap, so I didn't see his hair. I couldn't ID him if my life depended on it."

"Your life might depend on it, Rollie, because the hit man knows you. You are a loose end, my friend. Hit men come back and kill loose ends!"

Chapter 26

Fabrio waited with disciplined patience. He studied the list of names, and made plans to visit a few. The light of the day was fading after a spectacular sunset had the smog filled sky burning in saturated oranges, yellows and bluish reds. The color presentation drifted into gray and Fabrio could no longer read under the remaining light. Barko had parked beneath low, over-hanging oak trees, half a block from Alex Foster's house. Down the road, he saw headlights coming toward them. The glow started as quivering candles, and exploded in brilliant halos as the approaching vehicle climbed the hill. Recklessly, the car didn't brake until it had turned into the circular driveway of Foster's home. The house, probably built in the late 1930's, looked like an old movie star's pad. It had the appearance of a Mexican Haciendas with patched stucco, and a red-tile roof. Fabrio recognized Alex Foster the moment he climbed out of the Mustang convertible. He stumbled all the way to the front door, fumbled with keys, and staggered inside. He closed the door behind him. Fabrio waited until darkness swallowed the surroundings, and then he got out of the limo.

Fabrio Tallagi didn't believe in doorbells. He just dropped a shoulder and blasted his way in. Alex Foster was on the back patio watering plants. The moment he heard the door split apart he ran inside to see what happened. Fabrio grabbed him. In his late-thirties, Alex Foster, was a small man. He made a living ridiculing mousey men of which he was one. The house was sparsely furnished, like someone just bought items to fill in empty spaces. Nothing matched a leather couch under the window, fabric recliner of a different color in the corner, a coffee table that didn't go with anything, and several lamps that were just flat ugly. Alex Foster had no inside plants, or pictures on the wall -- just lots of dirty plates, and food wrappers lying everywhere. He was a slob.

Alex shook his curly head assuming this was all a colossal mistake. "Whoa, big guy! You must have the wrong house."

Fabrio held Foster at arm's length, took a good look, "No, this is the right house!"

Alex pointed at the door. "I think you better get out of here before I call the cops."

Fabrio punched him in the lower stomach. Alex doubled over, gasping for air. "You think?"

"Wait!" Alex whispered, holding his arm up.

Fabrio grabbed his collar and dragged Alex into the kitchen. He scanned the room for a chair, found one with stacks of papers and magazines on it, and brushed them to the floor. Angrily he pushed Alex down in the chair. He looked around. What kind of pig lived like this when he had all the money this guy had? Fabrio was disgusted and felt dirty touching anything.

"What did I do? Am I late on a bill? I got it. I'm late on the car. Hell, take it."

Fabrio slapped his face. "I'll ask you a few questions, and you'll give me answers. I'll keep 'em simple, okay?"

"Whatever you want." Alex was breathing hard.

Fabrio pulled another chair out, dumped a pile of clothes piled on the seat to the floor, and sat right in front of Alex. "Tell me about the party?"

Alex didn't understand. "Party? I'm not having a party."

Fabrio slapped his face again, drawing blood from inside the mouth. Alex felt his cheek as it turned from red to purple.

"I don't have much time. You went to the Santino party, yes?"

"Yeah, but I didn't take anything." Alex Foster's lip puffed up.

"You know Tawny Brock?"

"Sure, everybody knows her."

"How much time did she spend with you that night?" Fabrio asked.

"We were together for a little while. She likes to share her happiness."

Fabrio slapped Alex again. Each blow was worse than the previous one.

Fabrio looked straight into his eyes. "You take her to bed?"

"Is that what this is? No! We're friends. I bounce jokes off her. She's a great audience. If she doesn't laugh, the joke doesn't work. Did someone say I did something to her? It's a lie, man. I wouldn't."

Fabrio reared back to slap him again, and Alex put up his hands. "Who was she with?"

"Lots of people. I didn't pay attention, you know? It was a party."

Fabrio grabbed his shirt and pulled Alex within inches of his face. "But you did see her at the party?"

"I said I did. What's this all about? Did something happen to her? Is that what this is all about?"

Fabrio's face relaxed. He was genuinely surprised. Her murder had been all over the news. He looked around the house but didn't see a television. "Where's your television?"

"Don't have one." Alex said, wiping blood off his lip with the back of his hand.

"You don't know." Fabrio watched for a reaction. There wasn't one.

"Know what? Did someone hurt her? Oh no, don't tell me this shit. How is she?"

"Dead." Fabrio said in disgust. This was a waste of time.

Alex Foster shook his head violently, his kindly hazel eyes filled with tears. "She's one of my best friends. Oh, God, no. This is awful."

Fabrio calmed. "Who was at the party?"

"Everybody that's lucky enough to be on the "A" list."

Fabrio stared at him. "What does that mean?"

"Hundreds," Alex Foster answered. "Producers, directors, actor and actresses, hell I don't know, hundreds."

"Okay, let's try a different question, the names you saw Tawny with?"

Alex drifted off, withdrawing, closing his eyes to escape the madness. Over and over he shook his head, trying to wake from a bad dream. Fabrio slapped his face again and got immediate attention. Tears gushed down the comedian's cheeks. His nose got drippy.

"Ah, I saw her with Dylan Taylor, on the stairs with Rollie Kemp, and then she was with Ben Parker, and Arnold Aronjelovich."

"Anyone else?"

Alex wiped at the tears. "Ah, yeah. She was dancing with that director guy, Diz O'Lare, and then, the next minute she was with Andre Garrison." His eyes traveled over Fabrio's face, "She's really dead?"

"Yeah, she's really dead." Fabrio stood up, and started pacing. "You know these guys?"

Alex nodded. "Yeah, we all hang out, you know?"

"No, but that doesn't matter. Where do they live?"

Alex shook his head. "Listen, man, I can't give you a star's address."

Fabrio yanked Alex to his feet. His punch sent Alex across the room. He slid down the wall and curled into a fetal position on the floor. He peed his pants. Fabrio moved with the quickness of a cat and jerked him to his feet. He pulled Alex back to the table.

"Write 'em down." Fabrio tried to control his anger, but he'd had enough of this jerk, and his patience vanished.

Alex nodded. Fabrio released him, and he sank into the chair. Alex scrambled for a pen and paper. In total panic, he scribbled addresses. As he wrote, he gulped air and took several deep breaths. "Are you going to kill me?"

Fabrio was surprised. "Do you want to die?"

"No." Alex was almost whimpering.

Fabrio picked up the list and read it over. "Anyone missing from this list?"

"I don't know where Rollie lives. He's not a regular."

"What does that mean?" Fabrio marked time. Was everyone in this town on a list? What the hell did you have to do, to get on the list? What kind of trouble did Tawny get into?

Alex stammered. "Rollie's, ah, you know, a peripheral actor trying to make a living."

Fabrio made up his mind. "I'll tell you what, Alex. Stay off the phone, and forget I stopped by. Can you do that?"

"I can do that."

"If the cops question you…"

Alex shook his head. "I won't know anything."

"Good." Fabrio kept his eyes on the comedian. He might be beneficial later. He made a decision. "If you disappoint me, I'll come back. If you run, I'll find you. Trust me; you don't wanna see me again. Am I right?"

"Yes." Alex had a hard time keeping his eyes dry. The room fell into a deafening silence. Finally, Fabrio pulled a wad of bills from his pocket, peeled a few from the stack, and dropped a bunch of hundreds on the kitchen table. Alex stared at the money, and then his gaze traveled up to Fabrio.

"That's to repair the front door. The rest is for you to get outta town for a week or two without having to stop at your bank."

"Why?" Alex whole body shuddered. He couldn't keep his hands from shaking.

"You're gonna have visitors, and the cops will be lookin' for ya."

Alex Foster curled up. "But I didn't do anything."

"That might be true, but will anyone believe you? Keep your mouth shut, except for when you're on stage. You're a very funny guy. Maybe Vegas would be good for a few days." Fabrio smiled and moved toward the splintered front door.   He stopped and looked back. "Who broke your door?"

"I don't know," Alex mumbled quietly, "it was like that when I got home."

"Good answer.   Have a good life, Alex." Fabrio took one last look. He'd seen lots of guys like Alex -- weak, soft in the brains and scared to death. The guy would die before he said anything. "The only way you'll see me again is if you let me down."

"I won't." Alex whimpered.

Chapter 27

It didn't take long for Rollie to find out where Louis Baxter lived. Drake had gone off to meet with John Rader, and get a feel for how much trouble they were in. Rollie wanted to know what Louis Baxter might've left behind. He heard uncle Charlie discuss Baxter, about how sneaky he was, and how stupid uncle Pataglia was for trusting a punk like Baxter.

The Baxter house was on Mandeville Canyon Road off Sunset Boulevard. Up a long driveway, the house was secluded on ten acres, and buried behind towering trees, shrubs and electronic gates. Rollie had little trouble getting in. The property had been turned inside out. Expensive furniture was cut open, drawers emptied, pictures shredded, and clothes from the closets on the floor. It looked more extensive than what cops would do. Someone was looking for something Louis Baxter had, and wasn't supposed to have. It didn't look as though they found whatever they were looking for. Rollie read about the union problems, and the low budget deal everyone was fighting -- but this went deeper. Rollie was convinced Baxter wasn't killed over a contract. The pension funds were another matter, depending on how much was taken.

Rollie spent several hours in the house, and searched places no one would think about. In the garage, among a pile of old tattered books, Rollie found what he was looking for -- Baxter's ledger. Baxter was brilliant. He'd made a copy of the records that most likely got him killed. He probably thought if they knew he had it, his life would be safe.

Rollie got out of Baxter's house and drove to the office. As he thumbed through the ledger, he discovered how money flowed from dubious activities into offshore banks. When funds were washed, they returned to various businesses as venture capital. They funded a variety of projects -- buildings, leaseholds, films and cash-flow businesses like fast-food restaurants and Laundromats. Most of it looked like the kind of activity you'd expect, but mingled within the notations were sums of money wired to unnamed entities. The amounts were enormous, but the recipient's names were initials. The money didn't recycle either. Whom did they pay off? A worse thought, what was purchased? Millions had been transferred.

When Drake came back, Rollie knew things he wished he didn't. His uncle was a hands-off investor. While his name wasn't spelled out, his initials were there, as were companies he either owned or controlled. Rollie showed Drake how Louis Baxter had crossed the lines, and did business with more than one crime family. He had double-crossed the hand that fed him.

"Whatever this means," Rollie said, "part of it must be connected to Tawny's death. What did you find out from Rader?"

"They know enough about the girl to paint a very unpleasant picture." Drake answered.

"Like what?" Rollie wasn't sure he wanted to hear dirt on Tawny.

"It seems she told everyone about it. Her old man hated the guy she wanted to marry. Your uncle threatened her boyfriend's life, so he went and join the army. Got himself killed in Iraq, and your cousin never forgave her father. Fact is she vowed to make his life miserable."

"Great. That's just dandy. So what now? None of this will help us find two actors."

Drake picked up the phone and walked off. Rollie watched him make a call, talk in whispers, chuckle, and hang up. He came back to Rollie. "Let's go."

Rollie was oblivious to Drake driving like a maniac. To avoid traffic on the 10 Freeway or on PCH, Drake took every shortcut he could think of. Nothing helped, and he ended up behind a procession of vehicles all going in the same direction. Rollie was fighting back emotions long ago buried. He ran from what was left of his family, and never wanted to look back — but now all that had changed. The family was damaged goods, and with Tawny's murder, there was no choice but to fight back. As hard as Rollie tried to stay away, he somehow managed to position himself right in the middle of their mess. Dull of feelings, he watched nightlife in Venice and the outskirts of Santa Monica turn into dark, eerie shadows. Traffic was slammed. The usual hookers and drug dealers worked their corners. Clients felt no shame when they drove up, right out in the open, and bought their pleasures. Not a cop in sight. They headed west, finally ran out of side streets, and were forced to cut down to Pacific Coast Highway.

Rollie, with a heavy heart, closed his eyes and shut out the world. On her twelfth birthday, Rollie gave Tawny flowers he picked from a neighbor's yard. They were the only flowers in the yard, and the woman who grew them would've surely killed Rollie had she caught him. She didn't see him, however, and Tawny was thrilled that Rollie would do such a brave thing. Rollie was thirteen, and thought he was in love with Tawny, even though she was his cousin, whatever that meant. He didn't know about incest or things like that. He was never told it would be inappropriate for cousins to mess around. Tawny took his hand and led him to a secret place beneath the back stairway in their apartment building. While all the Brownstones in New York looked alike, most were vastly different inside. The old stairwell had once been used as an office, then a spare bedroom when tenants had relatives stay over and didn't have room for them upstairs. Packed in the small, murky area were several fold-up beds and lots of fantastic places to mess around. The exact reason Tawny brought Rollie there. Joe Lucky, the older boy down the street told Rollie all about how he taught her a few tricks, and bet Tawny couldn't wait to show Rollie what she had learned. Joe Lucky told Rollie to go for it. Tawny led Rollie to an old couch where she opened her blouse and gave Rollie a glimpse of her breasts. At thirteen, she was fully developed, and proud of it. She teased him exactly the way Joe Lucky said she had done to Joe, touching Rollie where he'd never been touched before. She introduced him to French kissing, and how to be gentle with her. She unbuttoned his pants, and allowed them to fall down around his ankles. Just when she started kissing Rollie on the part of his body that was growing rapidly, Rollie's mother came into the storage room.

The veins in her neck instantly swelled as she screamed, "What are you two doing?"

Rollie scrambled to pull up his pants, and had trouble getting everything in.

Tawny calmly buttoned her blouse and smiled innocently. "I was thanking Rollie for the flowers."

"No!" Rollie's mother waved her arms in a frantic motion. "Not like that!" Her eyes were wild. Hysterics swallowed Rollie's mother. She shook her head and licked her lips to calm down. Furious, she turned her back to the kids, dropped her head in shame, and started crying.

"It's okay," Rollie bravely added.

She spun around to face him, "No, it's not okay, Rollie. My brother is Tawny's father, and that makes you two cousins. Cousins don't touch each other, especially like that! It's sick and wrong." Tears poured into Rollie's mother's eyes. "It's called incest. It's wrong! Relatives don't do that."

"You gonna tell?" Tawny asked.

"Never!" Rollie's mother whispered, and crossed her chest wildly looking up at the ceiling. "He'd kill the both of you." She looked at the two kids, wiping at her eyes with the back of a hand, and shook her head. "You are never to do this again, is that understood?"

"Ma!" Rollie protested.

She smacked him up the side of his head. "Don't ma me. You are never to kiss, hold hands, touch each other, or do that thing you were doing, not ever. I catch you again I'll go straight to Anthony. I will agree with whatever he decides to do to both of you. You will never be forgiven, not ever!"

"You wouldn't," Tawny said through clenched teeth.

"Test me." Rollie's mother spat. She turned to Rollie. "Now get upstairs. You aren't going out for the rest of the week. And you," she pointed a wavering finger at Tawny. "Go home, and leave my boy alone."

Drake spanked the horn, jerked the wheel, and miraculously avoided hitting another car.

Rollie looked over at him. "That was close."

"Where you been?" Drake asked.

"What are you talking about?"

"I was watching you. Your eyes were closed, but you weren't asleep, kid."

Rollie watched people walking faster than they were driving. "A long time ago, I was very close to Tawny Pataglia. It's not right, what happened to her."

Drake drove in silence for a few minutes. "On a need-to-know basis, Rollie, how bad a guy is your uncle Pataglia?"

"One to ten, ten being totally unreasonable, he can be an eleven."

"His only daughter is dead. So you must be thinking eleven?"

"Fifteen would better describe the anger he must be feeling."

"You think he'll come out here?"

"Yep. If he's not already here, he's on his way."

Drake had to stop for the traffic light. Evening traffic on the coast highway was in the usual stranglehold. The moon hovered over the ocean like a dancing ball of cheese. The reflection caught the tip of the waves just long enough to create crashing waterfalls. A well-lit restaurant parking lot exposed a flying team. Floating just above the rising ocean swells, came an assemblage of Pacific Brown Pelicans. The leader, bold, and wearing his white chest proudly, soared over the tip of the waves as

223

he led his followers to their last snack of the day. Like silent jet airplanes, they continued on their journey down the coast, creating a perfect V formation before they vanished into a black hole.

"How well did you know her?" Drake asked.

"Well enough."

"When was the last time you saw her?"

"I was thirteen." Rollie could still see her, standing before him -- giggling, teasing and wanting him.

"What about her father?"

"Not since I was fourteen."

"Did your mother still talk to him after you moved?" Drake persisted.

Rollie remembered the calls. His mother begged for help. "Yeah, she couldn't let go."

"He knows you're out here?" Drake looked over.

Rollie could feel Drake's eyes. "Yeah, he knows."

"He'd know soon enough anyway, after that call you got."

"When I got to California I changed my last name. Had it done legally, and the next day I got a call asking me why."

"Changed your name from what to what?"

"My old man's name was Kempinelli. I just got rid of a few letters."

Drake threw him a astonished look. "You changed your name from Kempinelli to Kemp, and wondered how he found you?"

"I wasn't trying to hide, Drake. Besides, Millie thought it was a good idea.

Drake hit the steering wheel with an open palm, "Here we go again. Am I supposed to know Millie?"

Rollie's eyes lit up. "My grandma."

Drake stared into the taillights ahead of him. "Anything else I don't know?"

"Not unless you wanna talk about my divorce?"

"Bad marriages don't interest me."

"The way you say it, I feel dirty." Rollie tried to remember if he'd already mentioned Kali to Drake. It didn't register.

"It's all personal stuff," Drake said quietly. "It's cool."

"Gee, now I feel fuzzy, and grateful. This might be a good time to tell me where we're going?"

"We're gonna go see an old friend of mine."

"Swell." Then Rollie thought about it. "How old?"

Drake ignored the remark, "She'll know or can find out where the actors are."

"Is this part of your past I should know about?" Rollie asked.

Drake narrowed his eyes and glared silently at Rollie.

Rollie turned away, watching taillights in front of him. "She's just an old friend, right?"

Drake nodded. "An old friend."

"Is she pretty?" Rollie pushed his luck.

Rollie witnessed Drake's upper lip curl.

Chapter 28

Fabrio learned from his phone call back to New York that Anthony Pataglia had been shot, Richie Pataglia was dead, and Gi Carlo was clinging to life. Anthony was shot twice, once in the upper shoulder, and the second bullet tore through the fleshy part of his stomach. JoAnn told Fabrio the shooter must've thought Richie was Anthony. Fabrio cried after he hung up. He hadn't cried in a long time, and it brought out an emotion he hadn't experienced in many years.

Fabrio's limo pulled up in front of Diz O'Lare's fenced, well-lit, and gated country estate. The fencing was snow white and circled the entire property. A decorative light was crested at the top of each fence post. The towering white gate was chain-driven. The palatial single-story ranch house sat a hundred feet up the circular driveway. Fabrio got out of the limo just as O'Lare ran out of the house. He jumped over the door of his little silver Mercedes convertible, and roared around the circular driveway as the gate opened. He zipped through the gate without slowing down, and whizzed off down the street. Fabrio gestured to follow him and then hopped into the front passenger seat next to Barko.

"How close do you want me to get?" Barko asked as he threw the limo into gear.

"I need to talk to him so if ya have to run him off the road to stop him, do it."

"I can do that."

The limo made a quick U-turn, and sped to pull up behind the Mercedes as it raced down the canyon. O'Lare lived out in a place called Acton, a mile or two off the 14 Freeway. It was the country, and yet only minutes from the Valley. O'Lare stayed off the 14 Freeway and took Soledad Canyon heading back toward town. Fabrio was amazed by the limo's speed.

Fabrio glanced at Barko, "I think he made us."

Barko grinned, "It's okay. He can't outrun me."

O'Lare floored it. So did the limo. O'Lare took the curves at a pace the Mercedes was built for. The limo wasn't built to race but stayed right with him.

Fabrio watched O'Lare raise a cell phone to his ear. "You got cell reception in these hills?"

Barko shook his head, "Nah, but he will in a few miles."

"Let's catch 'em before that."

They could see O'Lare put the cell phone down. He pushed the Mercedes, and Barko had no problem forcing the monster Lincoln engine to catch up. The Mercedes nearly lost control on several curves, and started fishtailing all over the road. The limo had a better driver.

Fabrio was enjoying the chase. Obviously O'Lare didn't know how to handle a sports car. The limo bumped the back of the Mercedes. On the third nudge, the Mercedes went off the road sideways, hit a rock, and came to a smoldering halt. O'Lare tried to unbuckle his seatbelt, but it malfunctioned. When he got it unhooked, Fabrio was standing over him.

O'Lare screamed hysterically, "What the hell do you guys want?"

Fabrio remained calm, "Get out of the car!"

"Fuck off."

Fabrio yanked O'Lare out of the car and slammed him down over the hood. He took out a pair of wire cutters, leaned over O'Lare, to hold him in place, and pulled his hand free.

"What are you doing?" O'Lare whimpered.

Finally Fabrio punched him, and he stopped with the vocals, but his bulging eyes were about to explode from his head.

Fabrio leaned closer. "I'm gonna ask you a couple of questions, and you're gonna give me straight answers."

"What did I do?" O'Lare's eyes darted from the cutters to his fingers.

Fabrio slapped him with an open hand, "Shut up. Tell me about Tawny Brock?"

"What about her?" O'Lare snapped a bit too sarcastically.

"Were you messing' with her at the Santino party?" Fabrio leaned down hard.

"That's none of your business!"

Fabrio punched him deep in the groin. The air gushed from O'Lare's lungs. Fabrio dropped down and placed a knee under O'Lare's ribs, forcing the air from his lungs with his body weight. Fabrio's voice dropped to a whisper. "Everything is my business. I'll ask once more. You don't answer; I'll cut off one of your fingers, and try again."

Fabrio placed the wire cutters over one of O'Lare's fingers.

"Wait. For God's sake, wait a minute. What do you want to know?"

"When was the last time you were with her?" Fabrio asked.

O'Lare stammered. "It was around midnight. We were in the swimming pool, and then we went into one of the cabanas. Later we showered. I went to get us a couple of drinks, but when I returned she was gone."

"Where'd she go?" Fabrio didn't move.

"I saw her later, on the stairs with Rollie Kemp, and then Ben Parker took her upstairs with Arnie Aronjelovich. I think she was in the bedroom with Dylan Taylor, and Andre Garrison too."

Fabrio was listening to the same thing he'd heard from the comedian. "Who was she with when you last saw her?"

"They'll know I told you, man." O'Lare started to tear up.

Fabrio added softly. "They won't care if you're dead!"

O'Lare started to panic, "Oh my God. I, ah, she was with Ben on the floor, no, no, wait. She was with Andre and Dylan. They were doin' some crack. I really don't know. She was with all three. Oh, please, don't cut off my fingers."

"Where was Santino?"

"I don't know. It was a party, it was only a party." The blood drained from his face, his eyes searching Fabrio's face, "Are you Tawny's father?"

"You don't wanna meet her father!" Fabrio whispered.

"My agent just called. Said the cops were lookin' for me. He said Tawny was murdered, but I didn't do it. I swear." Tears swelled and rolled smoothly down O'Lare's cheeks where they spilled onto his shirt.

Fabrio jerked him back to his feet. "So where were ya racing' off to?"

"To warn others. I tried to call, but no one's answering and my cell don't work out here."

"So, you just had some fun with Tawny, right?" Fabrio waited.

O'Lare nodded. "Yeah, she likes to, ah, liked to party."

"Did you offer her a role in your next film?"

"She wouldn't work in anything her old man financed."

Fabrio shook his head. "That's not what I asked you."

Diz O'Lare's voice disappeared. His gaze dropped, his head bobbed up and down. "It's what you do, you know, to keep 'em happy. They all want to work."

Fabrio nodded. "What did you offer?" He put the wire cutters in a pocket.

"It was just conversation, man. We all do it so the girls will come to the parties." O'Lare grinned nervously. "If you tease a girl in the right way, it more or less makes things easier when you get her in bed, ya know?"

"Let me get this straight. You and your buddies lie to all the pretty girls, promise them work so you can get laid?"

"Well, yeah, it's a show-biz thing. We don't mean 'em any harm."

Fabrio nodded as if he accepted what was said. With broken body parts and a rearranged face, Fabrio stopped short of killing him.

Screamed out, O'Lare lay in a heap. "You're going to kill me, aren't you?"

"No, you're more important to me alive. I want to get a message to your buddies. The girls you continually con, feed drugs to, and screw around with -- are someone's daughters. They start out innocent, wanting to be in the movies, or on television, and end up getting spit out when you're through with 'em. When she first came to Hollywood, Tawny was a good kid."

"I'm sorry." Diz was almost incoherent.

"No, you're not. You'll do it again when you heal, unless that ugly face of yours can't be repaired." Fabrio turned, and slowly started back to the limo.

"Are you going to leave me out here?"

"Yeah, I am. Time out here will be good for you, unless you'd rather be dead?"

"No, please." O'Lare mumbled.

"Keep your mouth shut. You tell anyone you saw me and --" Fabrio hesitated, as though he had second thoughts. He looked back at O'Lare and waited.

"I won't! I swear on my mother's grave, I won't tell a soul."

"I almost forgot. Her father wanted me to leave you with something personal."

"Please don't." O'Lare begged.

Fabrio kicked him in the groin. Diz passed out. He wanted to kick him a second time, but realized it wasn't necessary.

Fabrio got back in the limo. Barko handed him a wet towel, and a large soft towel.

"What's our next stop?" Barko asked.

"Let's go visit Rollie Kemp."

Chapter 29

Rollie perked up when he saw where Drake was going. Malibu Colony. Gated, exclusive, where movie stars, and the rich and famous lived. Drake pulled to the brightly lit entrance, punched a few numbers, and the vast wrought-iron gate swung open.

"Must be a good friend if you know that number by heart." Rollie said.

Drake ignored the sarcasm. "On your best behavior, tough guy."

They passed through the main gate. Brick, wood and metal barriers surrounded most of the homes. They drove deep into the colony, dropping down to ocean front mansions where Drake stopped at a decorative, brick pedestal. An intercom was embedded above the mailbox. A spectacular, well-lit home sat behind the unusually designed, copper gate. Rollie noticed a silver Lexus SC, with tinted windows, pass by behind them. Drake rang in. Rollie watched the little sports car disappear around the curved roadway. This was Malibu Colony for crying out loud. Everyone had little sports cars, and Rollie needed to stop being so paranoid every time he saw one.

A sultry voice came through the intercom. "Is that you, Drakey?"

"Yes love, it's me."

"Come on in." The sultry voice announced.

Rollie sat back and watched. Boy he wanted to say something witty but thought better of it. Drake Fargo was getting too serious. It was almost too freaky to watch.

Drake pulled into a circular driveway and parked in front of a one-story villa. Tiny lights lined the brick walkway leading to the front door while spotlights covered the yard.

Rollie couldn't keep it in any longer. "Drakey?"

"Don't be a smartass." Drake had a look. A don't mess with me look. "The girl likes me."

"I didn't know girls like you at all?" Rollie thought he might as well tease Drake while he had the opportunity. He'd never seen Drake behave so mysteriously.

"Well, they do, so get used to it. Oh, and be nice. This is a first-class lady, and she knows everybody. Not to mention, she likes to help me from time to time."

"I can be sweet."

Drake punched Rollie's arm. "Get out of the car!"

When the front door opened, Rollie recognized Erinn Wylan immediately. Not only from the Santino party and television, but from the silver screen too. Erinn, in her mid-thirties, was statuesque. She stood over six feet tall and was utterly drop-dead gorgeous. Rollie noticed her legs first. Great legs. The body was slender, and tanned. She wore her long blond hair in a ponytail, drawing more attention to impeccable features and a face that needed little makeup. Her powder-blue eyes spoke volumes about her feelings for Drake. She gushed out and kissed Drake. Not a peck, but a full-mouth kiss. Rollie was more than impressed.

Erinn whispered in a purring tone, "It's good to see you." She ran a hand over his cheek, her eyes studying his.

"You too." He turned back to Rollie. "This is Rollie Kemp, my associate."

Rollie felt uncomfortable when Erinn studied him from head to toe. "You have a good look, Rollie Kemp. Are you a nice guy?"

"Always,"

"I've seen you in a few things, haven't I?" Erinn asked.

"Yeah, a little here, and there. I keep trying."

She dropped her eyes, briefly. "Don't we all." Then she suddenly brightened up. "Well, it's a good thing you met Drake, and have something real to do. I sort of use my ex-husband's money to keep things going until I become the star I've been chasing for years. If that should never happen," she waved both hands in a circle, indicating the house, car, and all her belongings – "I imagine I'll be okay."

"Yeah," Rollie nodded, "Drake does the same for me."

Drake gave him a look, his jaw muscles bulging. The expression told Rollie to shut up, and he did. Back a year or so, Rollie remembered reading how Erinn Wylan, divorced movie mogul Ted Wylan. The report stated she got an oceanfront home in Malibu as part of the settlement, but it didn't go into detail about the house. One glance at the mansion and Rollie understood what a Hollywood divorce from the right man could do for you.

The Pacific Ocean was a stone-throw away, curving right into the middle of her backyard. Rollie realized he could put his entire house in Erinn's garage. The coastline was dotted with lights, a few boats rocked with the tide, and waves crashed gently onto the shore. Rollie thought about the pain, and suffering a divorce like this must've brought. It amazed him how people survived such a terrible ordeal.

Erinn gestured for them to follow her inside, and she led the way. Both men watched Erinn walk. She had a sensual confident stride, crossing one foot over the other as models do on the boardwalk.

"Come on inside. Ellie should have our drinks ready out on the terrace." She talked over her shoulder knowing full well they were both watching her moves.

The house was right out of Architectural Digest. A checkerboard of black and white marble covered the floor. The walls had archways built in, with tiny lights shining down over irreplaceable pieces of art. Abstract paintings hung distinctly throughout, with a large Thomas Kinkade original over the fireplace. Rich leather furniture surrounded a sitting area, while plush cushioned pieces created a circle before the fireplace. A lit glass cabinet contained blown-glass figurines, and various sea-creatures. The marble floors, outlined by tiny lights built into the wall, had several exquisite area rugs placed perfectly in all the right places. A giant fish tank lined one wall, and matched the fishpond waterfall in the foyer, filled with a variety of colorful little vermin dashing nervously in every direction. The den was larger than most houses, and out on the terrace, overlooking an infinity swimming pool, sat the picturesque Pacific Ocean. Even at night, the towering nightlights created magic on the crashing whitecaps. A table had been set up beneath a white canopy. Drinks were poured, and hors d'oeuvres of every kind waited to be eaten. The house matched Erinn's beauty. It was the perfect companion, and a must for every Hollywood divorcee.

"I've missed your calls, you naughty boy. What has kept you away this time?" Erinn didn't take her eyes off Drake.

"I wasn't sure you still wanted me around." Drake said.

"You owe me a dinner, big boy?" Erinn purred while her eyes roamed over him.

Rollie tuned them out. He was on the outside looking in, so he nibbled on all the tasty little things that caught his fancy. The glob of raw meat looked inviting, as did the itty-bitty black seed-looking things. Caviar and steak tartar -- he tasted both and practically drooled over the crackers. The flavors from the ground filet Mignon, Dijon Mustard, Worcestershire sauce, onions, and capers tickled his tongue. He felt the Cognac burn his throat with all the euphoria it meant. Rollie could see the Black Sea materialize before his eyes the moment the delectable Beluga Imperial Malossol caviar touched his taste buds.. Nothing in the world could match the savory treat. Kali had introduced him to Beluga, but when he realized it cost over a hundred bucks per ounce, he avoided buying more. The identifying tease on his palate, however, never left the roll on the tongue. He amused himself as he watched Drake flirt, and Erinn tease. They were an aging Ken and Barbie couple. After they played catch-up, and cooed until nausea surfaced, they finally got around to the purpose of the visit.

"I'm on a case," Drake tried to get to the point, "but how's dinner weekend after next? I'll find a place you've never been. How's that sound?"

Rollie listened and took posture as a piece of furniture.

"Like a real challenge." Erinn smiled.

A maid, Rollie presumed was Ellie, came out and served drinks. She immediately vanished.

Erinn glanced at Rollie, and then Drake. "Now, you didn't come here to pay your debt."

"I have a problem, and need your help." Drake confessed.

"What took you so long to ask?" She settled back. "This must be important."

"It is. A young actress named Tawny Brock was murdered at the Santino party."

"I knew Tawny. We met at several parties." Erinn's smile disappeared. "What do you want me to do?"

Drake told her about the party, the actors they were watching, their escape from The Rainbow House, and who Tawny actually was. Erinn took it all in stride, as though nothing said could possibly surprise her. Rollie loved her nonchalance.

When Drake finished, Erinn brushed a few strands of hair back, retied the ponytail, sipped her wine, and finally spoke. "So, big boy, you came to me for help?"

"Of course." Drake matched her gaze. "No one digs up more dirt than you."

Chapter 30

As he drove into the airport parking structure, John Rader heard one plane after another – take off or land. On the floor below roof parking, a pencil-thin cop stopped him. His LAPD tag read Arvada. Rader and his partner Mustio flashed their badges. Arvada read their names, and logged them in on the clipboard he carried. Arvada was just a kid, and plenty nervous. Rader surmised it was the kid's first murder scene. His skin was smooth, with sprouts of peach fuzz on his chin. Arvada's gun belt looked heavier than his body weight.

"I'll have to ask you to park down here, detective." Arvada pointed up. "The crime scene is up on the rooftop."

The immediate area was clogged with vehicles. Rader gestured with a hand. "Where would you like me to park?" He frowned at Arvada.

Arvada pointed down to a row of police cars. "At the end, if you don't mind?"

Rader followed Arvada's hand and gave him a nod. Mustio sat up as they rolled down an extremely long isle.

"If you're expecting me to drop you off, forget it." Rader said.

"Why couldn't we double park?"

Rader glanced over. "Cause that nice young man might've pissed his pants, that's why." Rader jerked the car into a confined space and turned the engine off. "Let us try not abuse the fact we're guests here, Frank. We all know LAPD is far superior to us lowly gutter trash, so behave."

"My ass," Mustio fumed. "L.A.P.D is no better than us. I hadn't forgotten one thing I learned when I was a member of the elite LAPD, John, and neither have you."

"Everyone seems to have a hot iron up their ass, Frank. I think we should go find out why."

On the rooftop parking lot, Rader was amazed how many bodies had been called out to investigate one dead body. A forensic team had their van, and the CSI boys had a fancier truck. The Scientific Investigation Division had several wagons, and the corner vehicle waited in the shadows. Half a dozen unmarked detective cars were mingled among another half dozen black and whites. The entire roof had been taped off, lights were glowing, and off at the other end of the area Rader saw the Rolls Royce – lit up from a series of portable lights. The trunk lid was up, and the SID photographer was a busy boy, popping pictures of everything visible. Rader and Mustio showed their ID to a female officer. Her nametag identified her as Jackson, black women in her early forties and all business. She took their ID's and used her radio.

"I have two detectives here, John Rader and Frank Mustio." She said.

"Bring 'em over," a male voice barked over the radio.

Jackson returned their ID's. "Follow me."

Jackson led them across the lot, to a table that had been set up under a canopy next to the Rolls. A tall, willowy silver-haired guy came over the shook their hands. Rader glanced at the body and didn't see blood-splatter inside the trunk.

"I'm Commander J.D. Fellows with the Counter Terrorism and Criminal Intelligence Bureau. Glad you could make it. I'd like you to meet Deputy Mike O'Rowrk, Metro Division for organized crime and vice." Fellows called out, "Mike?"

A lean, mean, bodybuilder type black man, turned away from the trunk and gazed over at them. He frowned and then gestured to come on over. J. D. Fellows turned back to Rader and Mustio. "Mike has some questions."

O'Rowrk finished his conversation with other detectives and strolled over. He peeled off latex gloves, and they all shook hands.

"I'm Detective John Rader. My partner, Frank Mustio."

"Mike O'Rowrk. I know about both of you gents, thanks for taking the time to come over." He glanced over his shoulder to the Rolls Royce. "Guy in the trunk got whacked by a pro -- one in the head, and one in the heart. It was done a few days. Lot attendant caught the smell in the wind, and knew right off what it was. Dude usta work at the morgue, so he knows the smell."

"Does the Vic have a name?" Rader asked.

"Yeah, everything's still in his wallet. Name is Ronald Mauten." O'Rowrk turned to make eye contact.

"He recently popped up on our radar when he transferred some serious cash to South America. His latest involvement was with a vic of yours, guy named Louis Baxter."

Rader thought it ironic LAPD wanted help. "Let me guess, you found money and a gun?"

"Looks like two-hundred grand. Ballistics will probably match the piece as the weapon used to take him out."

"So far," Fellows chimed in, "we've got nothing. No prints."

"How can we help you?" Rader said.

O'Rowrk stared silently at Rader. Rader returned the look, unmoved by the attempt to rattle him. Rader watched uneasiness bleeding from O'Rowrk. Obviously LAPD didn't trust sharing with SMPD, and it killed him to include Rader in their confidence. LAPD's Organized Crime Unit didn't trust anyone, and avoided turning things over to the FBI with a passion few understood. Once they glommed on to a case, it was theirs til the end.

"Maybe we should go," Mustio said.

Rader agreed, "Yeah, maybe we should."

The two detectives started to walk off. Fellows gestured 'so what' but O'Rowrk stopped them. "Okay," O'Rowrk said. Rader watched him squirm. He glanced around to make sure they were far enough away from others not to be heard. "We know our Vic worked, indirectly, for the Pataglia brothers. Did union negotiating contracts for them. Nothing unusual there. Then, he connects with this Baxter guy. They were doing exporting and importing, but we don't have a handle on what they were buying or selling. The girl you found at Santino's place was Anthony Pataglia's daughter, and we have reason to believe Louis Baxter crossed lines between the

241

Pataglia's and the Brayden crime families. The girl had an affair with Baxter, and had been seen with him in places she shouldn't have been."

"You're investigating the Pataglia's?" Rader asked.

"Nah, they've been quiet for years. We know their hands are spread all over the place, but we got nothing on them. They look more legitimate than most conglomerates."

Rader waited. This was good, so far. He exchanged a nod toward Mustio. Nothing he heard would help him; except for the fact all three were connected. But who killed them, and why? Baxter was a messenger boy for union money, and the girl was a slut getting even for something her old man did to her. None of it made sense yet.

"At first," O'Rowrk continued, "we thought this was a union thing. Disgruntled members bitching about the lack of compensation stuff gets attention. Someone gets whacked, and things settle out quickly. Baxter played the middle and took money from both sides. It wasn't a smart thing to do, and stuff like this never has a good ending. Death of the girl was a definite message. Someone looking to start a war, or take over territory." O'Rowrk gaze over his shoulder, back to the Rolls Royce. When he turned back, his eyes narrowed. "This hit puts a whole new meaning on the potential significance of what lies ahead."

Rader knew he was being used. Playing dumb always got better results. "I still don't see the dots that connect this mess together?"

"He doesn't know." Fellows said.

O'Rowrk grinned. "Yesterday, someone shot Anthony Pataglia while he enjoyed dinner at his favorite restaurant. The place was packed, and the shooter got away."

"Killed?" Rader asked.

"No, he was lucky." O'Rowrk answered. "His cousin, who happened to look like Anthony Pataglia's twin, was killed with four others. A third man, so far unidentified, was wounded. This last guy carried no ID."

Rader didn't respond. He wanted more and was rewarded for his patience.

"The shooter sprayed bullets throughout the restaurant, but before anyone could go after him, he disappeared. Feds rushed in and assumed the killer had a car waiting. They brilliantly ascertained it was the only way he got away. The Feds got nothing and the Pataglia group aren't talking."

"So who benefits from all this?" Rader was relaxed, trying not to push.

"Pataglia and his family have been operating under the radar for years. Runs his business like a Fortune 500 company. Like I said, there's nothing on the family business. He pays his taxes, accounts for millions of dollars, and no one's been able to penetrate his operation. To the outsider, he's as legitimate as they come. The Brayden crime family in Philly has been trying to move in for years. A few days ago, one of their underbosses, Mark Lipesky, disappeared. The Bureau has a thick file on Lipesky. His son, Drew is a hothead. Dangerous little shit. The Bureau's put a watch for him, and when we got that, we knew all this crap fell under one roof."

"Didn't you say Louis Baxter worked both sides?" Rader asked.

"Yeah, he did." O'Rowrk answered.

"So which side took him out?" Rader pushed.

O'Rowrk exchanged looks with Fellows. Both got tight-lipped.

"What's missing?" Mustio asked.

O'Rowrk cleared his throat. "We know Baxter kept records. We also know he kept notes, for his own protection, and that he was skimming pension funds. He had a ledger."

"And you know this how?" Rader interrupted.

"We had a guy inside. Pataglia received info he shouldn't have, and the other side wants it back. Pataglia refused, his daughter was a loose cannon, and so they silence her – to draw Anthony Pataglia out. The guy in the Rolls worked for Pataglia, and he knew about Baxter's skim. We think this guy was working with Baxter, and If that's true, he too was playing both sides. The other scenario is, all three were worked, and when they were no longer important, got taken out."

"So if you got it all figured out, what's holding you back?' Mustio wanted to know.

"Baxter's place got thrashed, and the ledger is missing." Fellows answered quickly.

"What about the guy you have inside? He must know where the ledger is." Rader said.

"Our guy has disappeared. We're assuming he was found, and taken out." O'Rowrk answered.

"By which side?' Rader didn't like any of this.

"We don't know." O'Rowrk was frustrated. "Both sides will send people. Right now the pension fund is missing millions, a union contract up in the air, whatever is being imported and exported is missing, and there's at least eight dead that we know about. Helluva lot of questions that need answers." Then he got around to asking Rader the one question that brought them to the airport. "What did you guys get from Baxter's condo?'

Rader felt the chill from the ocean breeze cut into his bones. So far O'Rowrk hadn't told him anything that would help close his case. Fact was, all LAPD had done was helped convolute the whole damned thing. "There wasn't much to take. A mysterious intruder beat us to his house. We found it tossed, and got nothing there. The beach condo was buttoned up tight. We found pictures that tied him to the girl, money, drugs, a few weapons, and some serious sex toys. We also found his wife had moved down to Newport to stay with their daughter." Rader shrugged. "That's it."

"No files, ledgers, or books?" O'Rowrk asked with a tone of impatience.

Rader glanced at Mustio. Mustio gestured with both hands he knew nothing more. "So, why were we asked to come down here tonight?"

"You know John, that's a good question." O'Rowrk said as he handed Rader his card. "Call me if you think of anything else." They shook hands. "Oh, I guess you already know this, but I'll throw it out anyway. If these guys think you have their ledger, count on them paying you a visit. I don't know if the entire SMPD force is big enough to stop 'em."

Rader nodded. "That's when I'll call you, Mike, and you can bring in the Calvary to rescue us."

"Let's hope that call doesn't come in too late." O'Rowrk spit out, walking away in a huff. Fellows waited until Rader and Mustio shook his hand, and walked off. Anticipation gnawed at him. Rader hoped there were no dirty cops on the SMPD force. Most of the detective unit at SMPD knew about the files and ledgers they retrieved from Baxter's beach condo, and Rader prayed none of his comrades would sell him out for a few bucks.

Chapter 31

Rollie opened the door to their office, and Drake almost walked over him when the key stuck. Drake wasted no time digging out a silver case from a closet. He moved to Rollie's desk and attempted to open it.

Rollie came up behind him and watched. "I don't like it when you get quiet like this, Drake." Rollie saw Drake's fingers working over the latch. He couldn't get it open, angrily jerked the case and slammed it on the desk. The latches popped open. Drake glared down at the ledger Rollie found in Baxter's house. He thumbed through the pages with such fury, Rollie became concerned he would tear the pages. "The pages are paper, Drake, not plastic."

"When were you gonna tell me about this?" Drake's voice boomed.

"I wanted to look it over first. I told ya, didn't I?" Rollie was defensive.

"In some pecking order, yeah." Drake put his hands over the desk and leaned heavily on them. "Inside this ledger, there are lots of little marks. What does all that crap mean?"

"Baxter was stealing a ton of money from the pension fund. We don't know anything about what he was supporting yet, but we do know he was paying Tawny for info about her father. She hated my uncle."

"So do a lot of other people," Drake spat out, still fuming.

It always amused Rollie when they argued. Drake was a pouter when he didn't get his way. He read over the ledger and was still in the dark. Rollie knew Drake hated to ask questions about anything, especially things he couldn't figure out for himself. It blew over almost as fast as it started. Rollie felt comfortable investigating on his own. Drake would fume, but inside, Rollie could tell, he was proud of Rollie. "Lots of cash was moved around, sent out, retrieved, and invested. I'm not sure who got what, or who paid funds back to the pension plan, but from what I can see my uncle wasn't involved in any of it. All I can gather is a ton of money is missing. What he bought with it is the mystery."

Drake retrieved a small zippered athletic bag from the back room, removed two handguns, several clips of ammo, and finally a couple of windbreakers. He put one of the jackets on and handed the other to Rollie.

"Put it on."

Rollie eyed the unsightly jacket with distaste. A dark brown that wasn't pleasant to the eye, and small orange stripes that ran around the collar, sleeves and waistband. "You gotta be kidding?" Rollie held it up, frowning.

"My latest life-saving toys." Drake said proudly. "Put it on."

"It's hideous."

247

"It's bulletproof."

"A guy shoots you with a high-powered handgun with enough velocity, or worse, a rifle, and you're gonna need more than a little jacket to stop the bullet." Rollie stated.

"I have an old friend who usta work for Honeywell. He made 'em for me."

Rollie put on the jacket. "What is it, a new version of Kevlar?"

Drake loaded the handguns and passed one over to Rollie with several clips. "They're made with a combination of Goldflex, Dyneema threads, a Crisat plate surrounded in titanium, ceramic, and polyethylene." Drake put several clips in the jacket pockets, and then placed a gun into his shoulder holster.

"So you're saying I don't have to worry about getting' shot if I wear this?"

Drake stared at him. "No, that's not what I'm sayin'. You take one in the head, the jacket's not gonna help. He's created a steel-laminated screen mesh that makes it as bullet resistant as anything on the market." Drake was getting testy again.

Rollie pushed his button. "I heard the Interceptor is the best vest on the market."

Drake shouted. "This is fifteen times stronger than the Interceptor, and it's already saved my life twice."

Rollie zipped and unzipped the jacket. "It's still revolting."

Drake ignored him. "We're splitting up for a while. I want you to stay here."

"Where you going?"

"I need to talk with Rader, and if I'm alone he might open up. I know you guys are buddies, but I might stand a better chance of learning something on a professional level. If your relatives are as bad as you say, they won't stop until they get answers. If the actors are innocent, or get in the way, we'll lose our clients and our payday."

"What if they're guilty?' Rollie asked.

"Then we're shit outta luck." Drake snapped.

Rollie looked around the desolate office. "What am I supposed to do while you're gone?"

"Call around, and see if you can find out where these clowns went. I want you to call everyone you know, even some of those dummies who hate you."

Rollie watched Drake zip up his jacket. "So why are you wearing the jacket, Drake? Last time I was at the police station, it didn't appear to be a dangerous place."

"I don't know who killed the girl, Rollie, but if they believe we're in the way, they won't hesitate to take us down. There's more to this deal than meets the eye. I'll be back in a couple of hours."

Before Rollie could protest, Drake was out the door. Rollie moved to his desk, opened the bottom drawer, and put his gun in. He kicked the drawer shut with his foot. About to take the jacket off, thought about it for a second, and kept it on. He started calling people. How the hell did he go from a fun-loving character to a hardnosed detective? Most of the time it was fun, and he did tire of tapping into his investments and savings in-between jobs. He connected with total strangers after several calls. Everyone he called stated the same thing, as though their speech had been rehearsed. Not one had seen Ben Parker or Andre Garrison for days. Even Shelly Bufko, his accountant blew him off. If anyone knew the actors whereabouts, the entertainment industry as a whole weren't talking. Rollie had become an outsider. Want info or favors, and there's nothing in it for your friends, it was unbelievable how fast people became deaf and dumb. He called a stuntman buddy, Chuy Burnett and got Chuy's father instead. The old man was enthusiastic but offered little help. He didn't even know where his son was.

Chuy's father reminded Rollie of his Pop. He couldn't see Tony Kempinelli taking orders from a guy like Drake, or anyone else for that matter. Pop was a putz, a womanizing wife beater. He never gave a rat's ass about his family. He made a colossal mistake, and it got him killed. Pop thought he was a tough guy, crossed the line and they sent someone a whole lot tougher. His memories of good old dad were constant battles with his mother, and both of them getting slapped around. If the old man drank too much, he got belligerent and took it out on everyone. His mother, may she rest in peace, always stood up to him. Even when Pop punched her, she'd get up, wipe the blood from her nose, and defiantly pick up the phone with a threat to call her brother – Anthony Pataglia. Uncle Anthony was someone to avoid. Being a wise guy wasn't on Rollie's agenda. As a kid, all he could think about was getting as far away from his family as possible.

Rollie's mind danced over the guardian of deaf actions, the horrific past he'd managed to conceal. He remembered the day his old man came home covered in blood. His eyes were bloodshot, teary, a black half-dollar beneath the left eye, and lips that trembled out of control. Rollie was twelve years old but could still see panic in his father's eyes, and the blood, lots of blood on his father's shirt. Ma took Pops down into the basement where they believed Rollie wouldn't hear. Rollie heard it all as he sat at the top of the stairs. His old man was supposed to pick a bag up from a bookie, and drop it off at loan shark's office. When he walked into the alley, two guys appeared behind him. Pop said they came out of nowhere, and he defended himself. Rollie heard him cough, and throw up.

His mother whispered angrily, "What did you do, Tony?"

"Whaddya think I did, Anjelica? Two guys jump ya, there ain't no time to ask them if they like blondes. It was them, or me."

His mother gasped. "What did you do to them?"

"The first guy had a knife, Anjelica. I had no choice. I took it away and stuck him with it. He died quickly."

His mother breathed laboriously. "And the other?"

"He had a gun. I didn't recognize them. They were strangers. Guns make noise, so I stuck him with the knife. I took his gun. It's in my pocket. I kept stabbing the guy. Things went to hell in a basket when that man wouldn't die. He grabbed me Anjelica, shook me good, and wouldn't let go. He looked me straight in the eye, and whispered that he worked for Lips. Guy says Lips sent them to pick me up. There was a change of plans, and the drop had to be moved."

"You killed two men who worked for my brother same as you?" Ma whispered loudly.

"Yeah, I killed them both." Tony's pathetic whisper was the worst statement Rollie had ever heard. "I wanted to help the guy, Anjelica. He looked me straight in the eye and asked why I did it, and then he died. Guess I stabbed him too many times."

"What did you do with the bag?" His mother became all business.

"I still got it. I came straight home."

"Then let's get you cleaned up. I'll burn the shirt while you change."

Tony started crying. "What should I do?"

Ma slapped his face and silenced him. Her voice quivered. "You take the bag and go directly over to Anthony's house. You say you were late getting to the loan shark, and thought it best to get right back to him 'cause you didn't want trouble."

"What if someone saw me?" Pop whined.

"You'd already be dead if they did. I can't stand to look at you. Clean yourself up and get out of here."

Two days later, Rollie's dad was dead. Uncle Anthony, even though he strongly suspected Anjelica had helped cover up what Tony did, had enough compassion to move his sister, and little Rollie to Charleston, where they settled down with Uncle Charlie. Uncle Charlie may have been a real uncle, or another former mobster friend of the family, but Rollie wasn't sure either way. It didn't matter. He treated them okay, and when Rollie's ma died from cancer, Uncle Charlie did his best to take care of him. Millie Jefferson also stepped in with unending support and essentially became his grandmother. Uncle Charlie taught Rollie how to fight, throw a mean jab, hit first, ask questions later, and how to pick locks. Charlie had a knack for breaking into things -- stores, banks, safes, and things that got people sent to prison. When Charlie told him about his stay in Federal Prison, how he shared a cell with a suspected serial killer that did it. Rollie lost interest in the family business and became a clown at school. He took being silly to a new level, and all his school mates kept suggesting Rollie would make an excellent attorney. Uncle Charlie said he'd fix things with his old man's enemies, but Rollie had other plans – to get as far away from New York as possible.

Rollie looked around the office, and knew his life was much better than living with family in New York. He never went back, and didn't plan on ever talking to Anthony Pataglia after their last conversation. Anthony called to ask a favor. Rollie said no. Anthony said he was family, and Rollie reminded Anthony that was the reason he changed his name. Anthony called him a loser. Rollie could still feel the anguish in his ears when Anthony yelled, "Don't ever call for help, kid." Uncle or no uncle, Rollie pushed them out of his life, and was damned proud of himself for standing up to him. For a long time, the only thing that troubled Rollie was the feeling of being an oversized round peg that would never find the perfect fit in a square hole. When Drake came along, all that changed.

The phone ring startled him. Rollie stared down at the receiver as it rang a second time. Finally, he snatched it up.

"Yeah?"

"Rollie?" The voice was from a hysterical man.

"That's me, who's this?" Rollie tried to identify the voice.

"There's somebody comin' for you." He was gasping for air.

"Who is this?"

"I had to tell 'em." The guy started sobbing. "I said you had Andre and Ben."

The hair on Rollie's arms stood at attention. "Skeeter? Is that you, Skeeter?" Damn it to hell, couldn't he trust anyone?

"He beat the hell out of me, Rollie."

Skeeter Woods was a stuntman Rollie had befriended years ago. He remembered seeing Skeeter at the party, and in the morning when he and Drake were leaving with Ben and Andre.

"What did you tell him?" Rollie asked.

"I'm sorry, man. I thought he was going to kill me. I didn't give him your name, bro, I just told him two PIs took the guys away from the party." Skeeter continued to sob.

"Why is he coming for me if he doesn't know anything about me?"

"I gave him your address, dude."

The phone went dead, and the lights throughout the office disappeared into an uncanny blackness. Someone had cut the power.

Chapter 32

The computer chirped when the power took a dump. Shadows filled the office, and Rollie scrambled for his gun. Where the hell did he put it? Orange hues, from the streetlights, bled through the windows. Neighbor's homes glistened in the background. Passing cars cast off a rumble from the pavement, and somewhere a lone dog barked. This wasn't a typical Hollywood power failure -- someone had cut the lines. His mind scrambled. A stranger had come to kill him. Pandemonium ruled. In the dark, he squinted to the front of the office, and then back. What the hell was he looking for, visitors or shadows? Under duress it's hard to know how your ears will function. Rollie heard every sound, every creek from the hardwood floor, and the relentless pounding in his chest. A passionate heart thumped against his chest, looking for a way out. Rollie wanted to run, but it was too late.

The house fell into an eerie, shadow-filled maze, and every inch created images of danger. Flickers of nightlife drifted through the windows. He moved to the back of the house, peering through the windows. He saw nothing. Turning around, the back door flew opened. A blinding flashlight strobe took away his sight, and a fist crunched into his jaw. Rollie swung his arm at the light, knocking the flashlight, and his attacker's gun to the floor. The flashlight shattered. He heard the gun slide off and bumped into silence on the carpet. A second fist whacked Rollie's shoulder, sending him up against the wall. He couldn't see a thing. A footstep on a creaky board and Rollie jabbed with a right. He waited a brief second, and then rocked back and threw a left. He connected. He heard a body stumble, and that gave him enough time to scramble after the elusive gun that was now on the floor. The back door closed with a resounding thud. Rollie froze. A hand grabbed his ankle. Rollie kicked and received a blow to his leg. Rollie punched back, hitting a fleshy cheekbone, and then he moved to his left. He felt a surge of wind fly by his head. It just missed. His assailant took another vicious swing. It also missed. Rollie inched away, his hand frantically rummaging for the gun without luck.

Rollie crawled into the shadows, straining his eyes to adjust in the dark. He felt around, looking for his desk. Equilibrium disappeared in the dark. Just when he needed stability, it evaded him. Footsteps scraped the floor, only inches away, and moved with the precision of a large, lethal cat. Rollie lowered himself to the floor and inched toward the front door. He could feel every loose fiber in the carpet rub against his nose. He blinked rapidly, trying to focus in the dark. It didn't work. All he saw were shadows of things he thought were moving. Two shoes came close, just as his hand found the handle of the man's piece on the floor. He froze as the shoes he heard moved off and disappeared from his vision.

"Where are they?" a male voice whispered.

A voice Rollie didn't recognize. Whoever it was, he was right there. Rollie could hear him breathing. A lone bead of sweat ran down his back.

"I didn't come here to hurt you," the voice whispered. "I just want the two actors."

Bullshit, Rollie thought. He held his breath and inched backward. It was the first time he smelled carpet up close and personal, and hoped to live long enough for it to be his last. The guy was between him, and the back door. His only way out was through the front, and that the door had unquestionably been locked earlier. The front door was always locked, wasn't it? Either way, it was the only way out.

The figure moved in the shadows. "You're making this difficult, you little shit! Just tell me where they are?"

This guy worked for his uncle. Now he knew, they'd whack him if he got in the way -- he was no longer family.

"You're not the one important to me," the guy said. "I'll ask your partner right before I kill 'im." More silence. "You know what that means, Rollie?" Rollie didn't answer. "You're like any other outsider. You're expendable." The guy was snarling.

Rollie reached into the desk drawer. Empty. The damn drawer was empty! Keys! A check of the next drawer found his gun. Had he put a bullet in the chamber? Probably not! He grabbed it anyway. Now he had two guns, and no damn keys to get out. The need for keys was overwhelming. It would be his fate, the damned door was locked. He found the keys on top of the desk. His fingers crawled over to the key ring. Yep, they were the right keys. He tucked one weapon in the jacket and inched toward the front door.

The figure turned around. Rollie ducked just before the beam from a second flashlight flashed by. Did the guy see him? The need to act quickly was upon him. He crawled on his belly, soundlessly, a fish out of the water. A flashlight beam swept past Rollie and then he hurriedly got to his knees. The man turned his back to him, searching the floor for his gun. Rollie could see the guy was epic, looking in the opposite direction. Rollie jumped up and ran like hell toward the front door. His chest heaved wildly. His lungs burned as he raced in the dark. He hit the couch and flipped over. He got up and slammed head first into a filing cabinet. Flesh hitting metal created a thump, like a hand slapping a ripe watermelon. Two muffled shots rang out. Damn! The guy had a second gun with a silencer. The shots just missed Rollie's head. Numbness swallowed him. Rollie had never shot at anyone, but now was time to give it a try. Time. No time left. He forced himself to his knees, then his feet. Pain gushed through his head. A warm liquid ran down his cheeks. Blood. He pulled the chamber back. A shell slipped into the channel. He released the safety, and then ran across the room, zigzagging like a helpless rabbit in front of a hungry coyote. He bumped into every piece of furniture in the office.

Just keep running!

Another shot rang out. Splat.

Rollie tripped over a wastebasket as he fired off his first gunshot. He heard the bullet rip through a metal cabinet. The guy laughed. It was humiliating. Rollie rounded the corner of a desk. Another splat sound was fired at him, only this time the bullet hit him right in the chest. The velocity and energy of the bullet knocked him backward. Intense pain. He rolled to his knees by the front door and dug out the keys. In total darkness, he unlocked the door and discharged several shots at the guy. The guy shot back. Rollie was in the middle of a bad dream, a one-sided duel in a fake western movie. Rollie saw an apparition, aimed, and fired. Something fell off a desk and shattered, followed by a heavy thump – a body hitting the floor. Rollie jerked open the door, and flew out. A twinge pierced his left shoulder, and his chest hurt like hell.

Rollie ran a block, darted into a side yard, and dove behind a clump of thorny bushes. Tiny pinpricks produced more pain as something unknown penetrated his skin. He just made another poor decision.

When Rollie caught his breath, he found his cell phone and called Drake. "Someone just tried to kill me."

"Where are you?" Drake asked

"In an alley, hiding behind some cactus or something." Rollie was gasping.

"How'd he try to kill you?"

"He shot at me." Rollie yelled, and then realized he should be quiet.

"Did you shoot back?"

"I shot our cabinets."

"You what?"

Rollie explained. "I tripped over the stupid couch, hit my head, and shot our cabinets!"

"My God, Rollie, you all right?"

"No!" Rollie felt his chest where the bullet had hit him. "Your jacket. It works. It saved my life." God, he hated to admit that.

"Just tell me? Did you shoot the bastard?" Drake was now yelling with excitement.

"Yeah, I think I hit him."

"Then why'd you run?"

"'Cause the guy is a good shot and has flashlights."

Drake hesitated. "He has flashlights?"

"Yeah, and did I mention he tried to kill me."

"Rollie?"

"Ah, gees, Drake, lots of bullets were fired. I probably shot the wall or my desk, but I heard something hit the floor."

"Maybe you got lucky. Stay where you are. I'll be right there."

"Okay."

"One more thing, Rollie."

"What?"

"What do the bushes you're hiding behind look like?"

Chapter 33

Rader sat alone in the vacant RHD room. He hated loose pieces and everything about the case stunk. Angrily he thumbed through a file folder, searching for clues when Captain McBride materialize out of nowhere. Rader looked up and didn't like the darkness in the Captain's eyes.

"It's time to go home, John." McBride said.

Rader looked at his watch. It was after midnight. "The ledger makes no sense."

"Can I see you in my office, detective?"

"Sure, Captain."

Rader got up and followed McBride down the hallway. The moment they entered McBride's office, he closed the door and gestured Rader to sit. He rounded his desk, sank into his chair, and cracked open a bottle of Jack Daniels. He poured them both a drink.

"I've been on the phone all day, John. The FBI wants our files, and so does the Organized Crime Unit from the Metro Division. Our Mayor has talked with LA's Mayor, and they've talked with the Counter Terrorism and Criminal Intelligence Bureau. Arrests should have taken place by now, except we have no suspects, and, therefore, no case. We got ourselves mixed up in a pissing contest between crime families. We have three dead on the west coast, three that we know of, and a dozen dead or wounded in New York. The Feds lost sight of the Lipesky kid in Philly, and his old man has disappeared from the face of the earth. They're assuming he's dead. They know, and now we know, the Lipesky kid is a time bomb. It's amazing people like this are loose, and arrests can't be made." He air-tipped his glass before taking a sip. "You have anything that will help us keep the case, detective?"

The whiskey warmed Rader's throat. He played with a pen, tapping it over the side of his little notebook. "No, I don't. We've gone through the ledger found at Baxter's condo, but it's written in code. We know money's been moved out of the country, laundered, and transferred back. The banks won't cooperate, the damned funds are spread all over the world and then some is transferred back to the originating bank. The only clue we have is the union pension fund received an amount close to half of what was taken in the first place. No illegal activities we can verify 'cause we don't know who took it, what it was used for, or who sent some of it back. We got nothing from the Santino house. The few leads the talent agencies provided led nowhere. Industry people traveled all the time. They didn't have chaperones. Even if they did few if any, would know where they went." Rader hadn't felt this way in years. The usual suspects didn't exist.

"I need something, John, or we turn the ledger over to the Feds by the weekend. If we can't figure out what to do with it, perhaps their people can"

"I agree, Captain. We're drawing blanks. Did anyone get anything out of New York?"

"The same. Anthony Pataglia was shot twice, neither bullet life threatening. The Feds believe the bullets that took Richie Pataglia were meant for Anthony. The two men looked like twins. Pataglia and his men checked out of the hospital. They're being treated privately, out of sight, and off radar. The Feds don't know where they are. Their surveillance experts lost them."

Rader sipped. "How the hell can they lose a guy like him?"

"Exactly my question."

"What about the guy they found in the trunk?" Rader waited to hear what the Captain knew, and wondered if it differed from what he'd learned.

"O'Rowrk, their organized crime guy said the money and files found in that Rolls Royce were planted. Meant to mislead. The vic fucked up. O'Rowrk has no idea what he did, or so he says. They know about the missing pension funds, but the attorney representing the unions won't meet or talk to them or us. Now ask out loud, why would a crime family drop that much stolen money at a crime scene? The pension fund has admitted they need the money back, but based on the bank deposits we're not even sure it belongs to them. If union leaders put the hit out, they too want the money back. We need to get a warrant, scrutinize the pension fund records, and see who had access to the accounts. We know both Baxter and Mauten were involved with moving funds, but we're missing the connection – the why. On top of all this, the two men were always at odds with each other. Why would they suddenly start working together?" McBride hesitated. "Basically, we have nothing."

Rader put the pen and notebook in his pocket. "Tawny Pataglia was killed to draw Anthony Pataglia from his hiding place."

"If the Feds are watching everyone, who wants Pataglia out?" McBride summarized.

"The Brayden crime family wants his assets, but no one can connect them. Maybe the Feds can piece this together? Maybe what we don't know is because it's happening in another state, and may never get a west coast connection?" Rader shrugged out of frustration.

The Captain leaned back in his chair. "Have you or your partner talked with any of your old buddies at LAPD?"

"No, it's been too crazy around here."

"Perhaps it's time to make a few calls? It would help if we knew names connected to the unions, the ones behind the scenes. We need to know about that other list, the movers, shakers, and the silent ones we know nothing about."

Rader retrieved his notebook and made notes. Earlier in the day he heard heat was coming from the Governor's office on down, and the pipeline was growing. Studio executives were nervous. They didn't want their little town turned upside down, nor did they need cops digging into intensely private matters. The union heads were tight lipped. The press, because of the killings, and the labor contract that had recently fallen apart was blaming everyone. Leaks had surfaced in the press about how organized crime still controlled the unions. The whole thing was preposterous, and it had to be squashed. Rader didn't care about agency dickering. All he cared about was someone to lay blame on. Anyone would do.

"Both sides have people in the studios and unions." Rader said out loud.

"Yeah, another coincidence. What do you always say?"

"There are no coincidences." Rader finished his drink.

"Right. So let's find out where all the players are. Maybe it will help close this thing." McBride emptied his glass. "Anything else?"

Rader didn't look up. "Lipesky's ordered the hit on Pataglia's daughter to accelerate their taking over Pataglia's holdings. I think they're killing anyone who gets in their way."

"If that's true, then Pataglia's coming to town."

Rader closed his notebook. "Now that they've fucked up trying to kill him, we can count on it."

"What if they killed the girl for something else?"

"Only way to explain that would be to know what else they're doing." Rader shook his head. "They've been fighting for years, Captain, we're just not seeing it."

A hush fell between them.

Suddenly Rader perked. "How did we miss something so obvious?"

"Miss what?" McBride didn't understand.

Rader got up and started pacing. "What if they did?"

"What if they did?" McBride waited for him. "I can hear the gears grinding, John."

"Since nothing makes sense. What if this whole mess is to settle an old vendetta? We need to go back, look at the Pataglia's, Brayden's, and Lipesky's history. What did Anthony Pataglia do to them? If we can figure that out, we'll know who's after him, and maybe a way to stop them." Rader was getting excited.

McBride poured both another drink. Rader knew Pataglia had become a recluse, and for years -- hadn't been seen in public. Fact was good old Anthony was a vanishing act that ran a tight, and mostly legitimate business, empire. The FBI had moved him to the back burner. Anthony Pataglia had turned his entire business structure legit, and the other families didn't like it. His dirty little secrets had been buried, and now someone was trying to change that. The loss of a family member's life was a justified death. Few people knew they happened, and the loss never seemed to intrude on the public sector. No one cared what mobsters did in-house -- until now.

"I hope you're wrong," Captain McBride said to himself.

"It's just another marble in the basket, Captain. When you think about it, it makes sense -- doesn't it?"

"If you're right, the hit man, who missed in New York, will come here to finish it."

"Yeah he will. When we find the connection, we'll find the killer." Rader said.

Chapter 34

Drake nearly ran over Rollie when he pulled into the driveway where Rollie was hiding. He watched the reaction from Drake and felt like a coward for the first time in his life. He didn't like the feeling. Rollie jumped into the car, and Drake raced off toward their office.

Rollie was still breathing hard. "Why are you going back to the office?"

Drake's jaw tightened, "'Cause I can't wait to get my hands on the shooter."

"He has one of those laser things on his gun, and he has flashlights."

"Flashlights! Well, dang, why didn't you say so? Maybe we should head to Mexico, and find a place to hide?"

Rollie took a withering look out the window. "You're being sarcastic."

"You think?"

"He shot at me, Drake."

"Yeah, so you said."

"Hey! It's the first time anyone ever shot at me."

Drake raised one eyebrow, "He missed, didn't he?"

"No." Rollie could still feel the sting from his chest where the bullet hit.

"I don't see any blood."

"He got me right here in the chest," he pointed at his breastbone, "and it hurts like hell. Right here!" Rollie slammed a finger into the burned spot on the jacket. "See?"

"Are you still alive?" Drake asked without looking at him.

"What kind of question is that?"

"He missed. Next time, if he wants you dead, you'll be dead!"

"Next time?" Where was fun in getting shot at? The intensity in Drake look concerned him. Fargo genuinely wanted to get his hands on the shooter. Maybe he had a death wish?

"Next time," Drake mumbled to himself, "you can count on it... unless we get him first."

"Gee, this is swell." Rollie wanted to go back to school, and complete studying law.

Drake jerked the car over the curb onto the sidewalk. He got out before the car stopped, drew his gun, and raced up the stairs into the office. Rollie, gun in hand stayed right behind him. While Rollie searched for his backbone, and some courage, Drake turned the lights on, and dashed through the office toward the back door. Pearl-sized drops of blood dotted the floor, creating a path out the back door, and down the steps. Rollie glanced down at the blood trail, and felt his chest where the bullet might have penetrated if not for the bulletproof jacket.

"Looks as if you got him," Drake said as he inspected the drops.

Rollie nodded, turned from the droplets and looked around the office. Furniture was over turned. One filing cabinet drawer was open with several bullet holes in the front panel, and more lodged in the surrounding walls.

The phone rang, and both men pivoted, aiming their guns at the tiny electronic device. It rang again. With his gun Drake pointed at the phone and Rollie picked it up.

On the third ring, Rollie answered, "Yeah?"

The voice was an eerie whisper. "I'm not through with you yet."

"Me either, but next time I'll make sure to shoot straighter."

"Pray you're right!" The voice wheezed.

The line was disconnected.

Drake waited... "What'd he say?"

Rollie looked at the phone, then up at Drake. "Said he wasn't through."

"Good! That works for me."

Drake was taunting him on purpose. He wanted under his skin, and Rollie had to fight back. If he allowed this to get to him, he had little chance of ever being a real man. Still ...

"That's cause he's not coming for you!" Rollie regained composure.

"You're forgetting there's two of us. He doesn't know one of us is a very good shot."

"Yeah, you're right, but he probably knows you usually leave your weapon in the car."

"Very funny, kid. Now before, you get yourself all worked up in a snit, just remember I--"

The phone rang. Both men looked down at it. Rollie slowly picked it up.

"Yeah?"

"Rollie?" It was Kali. She was crying.

"I can't talk to you right now, Kali."

Rollie tried to avoid Drake's glare. His partner sadly shook his head. Rollie realized he needed to get away from Kali. It wasn't right to maintain an oppressed relationship as they had going.

Blubbering incoherently she finally stammered. "Are you all right?"

Rollie grew suspect. "How'd you know where to find me?"

"I need to see you, Rollie. I miss you."

"It's time to let go, Kali. It's been years. Move on, and find another guy."

"I can't." Kali's grieving turned to loud sobs.

"Why?"

"'Cause I still love you. I made a mistake, Rollie. Don't make me pay for the rest of my life. The girl that did that wasn't me."

"I gotta go, Kali. This is not a good time. Call me next week."

"Okay." Her voice sounded tired and vulnerable.

Rollie hung up.

"Who was that?" Drake asked.

"My ex-wife."

Drake started to argue, gestured at Rollie with a hand floating in mid-air, and simultaneously shook his head. "How'd she know you worked here, or for that matter, how'd she know you'd be here this late?"

"You sayin' she might be involved?"

"It's a big coincidence. You tell me?" Drake's jaw muscles worked overtime.

They both studied the floor. Rollie tossed Kali around in his mind. She took advantage of him before, so why wouldn't she give it another whirl? He wouldn't put anything past her.

"She couldn't do it alone. She's weak, not violent."

Drake pointed at the bullet holes, and blood. "You said a guy was here, right?"

"Yeah, but --"

The phone rang again. This time Drake snatched up the receiver. "Now listen, you asshole..."

"Are you boys still looking for those runaway actors?" The velvet voice was female.

Nervously, Rollie mouthed "who is it"?

Annoyed, Drake turned his back, "Did they call, Erinn?"

Rollie intentionally walked around and sat in front of Drake.

Drake frowned as he grabbed for a pen. "They tell you where they are?" He set the pen down and glanced at his watch. "Twenty minutes." He looked at Rollie, "We're on our way."

Drake hung up and grabbed his keys. He opened the bottom draw of the desk, retrieved several clips for his gun, and two pair of handcuffs.

"What did she say?" Rollie waited.

"Ben Parker called her. Not that it'll do any good, but lock the back door, and reset the alarm."

Drake headed for the front door. Rollie stayed back at the desk.

"You think he did anything here?"

Drake turned, waiting. "We'll deal with it later. Let's go."

Rollie looked around the room and ran his fingers over the bullet holes. His jaw bulged from grinding down. Something wasn't right -- a gut feeling. His eyes searched around, but all he saw was the mess he created, and the bullet holes. He grabbed a couple of clips for his gun. "You gonna tell me what she said?"

"I've told her for years not to say anything important over the phone. I'm surprised she said Ben's name."

Rollie frowned. "So you run off to meet her every time she has something to say?"

"Yeah, every time."

"No, wonder your feet are so big."

Chapter 35

Fabrio made a few calls, got directions, and drove down into the bowls of Culver City where he met Dr. Bernard Wardar at the 24-hour clinic on Venice Boulevard. At 3 in the morning, traffic was nonexistent. Fabrio worried the cops might pull him over because of the late hour, and he'd have to explain why he was bleeding from a bullet hole. Then he'd have to tell them how he got shot, but luckily he didn't pass another vehicle on the way.

Dr. Wardar was a odd duck from another country. Fabrio couldn't tell one foreigner from another and didn't ask. The Doc was part of the family, and obviously took care when attention was needed. The Doc met Fabrio in the alley behind the clinic and gently ushered him through the back door into a small room at the rear of the clinic. The Doc peeled Fabrio's shirt off and took a long serious look at the gunshot wound in the fleshy part of the shoulder. Pain sizzled through Fabrio's body. A bunch of little race cars were on their way to victory, or in this case,

273

toward his heart. Fabrio was sure the persistent bullet was destined to stop his heart from beating.

"Looks worse than it is." Dr. Wardar said after examining the wound.

Fabrio winced, "I can feel the bullet in there moving."

"No, you can't. It went through and came out cleanly. The pressure you applied has stopped the bleeding. It does, however, look as though you have the pain of a thousand teeth."

"I have things to do." Fabrio said lowly.

"If you can function in agony, I can close the wound up, and you will have no other problems."

"You gonna use stitches?" Fabrio couldn't hide his concern.

"Yes, but you might tear them if you plan to be active. Glue works better."

Fabrio's eyes opened wide, "You gotta be kiddin' me?"

The Doc shook his head, "I do not know kidding."

"So what do you want me to do?"

"Choose?" The Doc said.

"Do whatever will hold the best. I'll deal with the pain." Fabrio couldn't hurt any worse.

"As you wish. Take off your shirt. While I do this, your body will suffer excruciating pain. Will that work for you, or do you need something?

Fabrio looked directly into his eyes, "Like I said, do what you have to do. I'll deal."

"Good, look at the wall please?"

Fabrio striped off his shirt and watched the doctor work from a small table. He wondered how this small, meticulous man ever got involved with guys like him. He could see this guy running any emergency room in the country. He had that look, the one that says 'I know what I'm doing so don't question it'-- and you didn't question. He worked quickly, addressing the problem head on. He stopped the minimal bleeding. It burned like hell, but Fabrio learned as a teenage boy not to respond to distress. If a bigger, much stronger boy punched him, he would never show fear or admit being hurt. Regardless of how hard a guy punched or how much he agonized from the blow, he'd never show it. If you did, the other guy was sure to beat you good. No, it was the look you gave 'em that made a difference, and put the fear of God back down their spine. Fabrio had the look, and knew how to use it. It caught the bullies off guard. He made lots of guys suffer because of his glare and their uncertainty

The doctor pulled the skin together on one side with tweezers, covered the wound with antibiotic ointment, strange appearing goo, and covered it with a gel. He left it clamped, and moved around to the other side where he repeated the action. The guy had class. Never once did he look Fabrio in the eye. Methodical, lost in his work, he was the kind of guy Fabrio respected. Fabrio thought about all the guys he popped, just when they thought they had him. When Mr. Pataglia came along, and liked what he saw, it was like being adopted, and loved for the first time in his life. Respect was what it was all about. Anthony Pataglia liked him right off, gave him respect, taught him honesty, and trust, and brought him in as if he were the old man's son. Anyone who did that for Fabrio earned his loyalty. He was family, and family came first. He owed the man his life, and would die protecting it. The shoulder felt numb. The pain brought tears to his eyes, yet he didn't move. The doc earned his points.

When he was finished, the doctor covered both sides with a compressive dressing, gauze, and then wrapped the shoulder with an ace bandage. He stood back to admire his work, and nodded. "You're good to go."

Fabrio looked at the shoulder, then into the doctor's dark brown eyes. "Will it hold up?"

"Oh yes. I believe it could withstand a punch or two. If you totally abuse it, it might open again. If it does, call me." He handed Fabrio a small container. "Take a couple of these every three or four hours as needed."

Fabrio held up the container, trying to read the label.

"Antibiotics." The Doctor filled in the blank. "They won't affect your mobility."

Outside, in the car, Fabrio flipped opened his cellphone and hit speed-dial.

A raspy voice responded, "Fabby?"

"Gi Carlo. Are you okay?"

"It was a big one, but it went through the belly and out the other side without killin' me. Too close for comfort that's for sure."

"How's Mr. Pataglia doin'?." Fabrio was afraid to ask. The man was like the father he never had.

"He wants you to catch the next flight to Miami."

"What are you talking about, Gi Carlo? I'm on top of things..."

"Too much heat out there and in the city. We're all down in the Keys. Let me know what flight you're on, and we'll pick you up."

"The actors are ..." But once again Fabrio got cut off.

"They left the country. Apparently, Drego Santino went with them. When things cool off, they'll be back." Gi

Carlo started coughing, and Fabrio closed his eyes. He could feel the pain Gi Carlo had.

"You don't sound good, Gi Carlo."

"Don't argue with me Fabby, my body will heal. Just get on a plane and get down here."

Gi Carlo hung up. Fabrio snapped the phone shut and almost broke the case. His jaw tightened. He was in the middle of something and hated to stop for any reason. Fabrio felt close as if he had a few more days the situation would be resolved, and issues closed. He didn't have a choice, not if Pataglia asked him to come back. There was, however, one more thing that could be done, and he was the only one who could do it.

Fabrio thought for a moment and then shook his head. He was silently answering his own questions. He couldn't call in a favor. He had to do this alone. Pieces weren't adding up. The body count was growing, and he was being asked to withdraw. Why? It was times like this, he wished he was smarter. Too many loose ends. Why would someone ordered a hit on Pataglia? Who ordered the hit was the bigger question? Was it Moe Brayden or Drew Lipsky? Or, did they suddenly have a new player trying to grab the reins? The Pataglia family had many enemies, and now someone had stepped over the line. At the moment, it didn't make sense. The Lipsky kid was as good as dead and didn't have the firepower. Brayden had the tools but knew he'd have to take out everyone, and that hadn't happened. It was too sloppy.

Fabrio called the airline, made his reservations on the last flight out and set out to end part of what he was sent out to California to do. Now he felt cheated or worse – like wearing the remains of a coward on his sleeve. He was being asked to turn his back on a mission, abandon all he had done and quit. Well, he'd reluctantly go to Miami, but not before he made one last trip.

The Watcher, on the other hand, had returned to her apartment where she took a long hot bath and planned her next move. Her cell phone rang once. It was a signal. She sat up and quickly climbed from the tub. Hastily, she wrapped her hair in a towel and slipped into her bathrobe. She hurried to her computer and booted it up. One ring on her cell meant an email was coming, giving her new instructions. The screen lit up, and Yahoo opened her home page. She scrolled through and opened her email account. She opened the only message and expanded the screen. The message read: Do what you do best and then get out of town on that vacation you said you were taking. No more excuses. I'll be waiting. She glared at the screen and then erased the message. She clicked on SCUZZ. A program designed to remove every shred of history from her hard drive and leave the computer clean, as if she just purchased it. After the beep, she turned off the computer and got dressed. She packed a bag, loaded her gun and hustled from the apartment.

Rader closed his briefcase and called his wife.

"I'm on my way. You need anything before I get home?"

"Well," his wife purred, "we're alone, and I was thinking about a desert."

"Where would you like to go?" Rader asked as a smile started to spread over his face.

"I was thinking the bedroom would be nice."

"Why do I hear a but in there?" Rader asked as he sat on the side of his desk.

"We'll what if we got creative?"

"So far so good," Rader said.

"Would you be angry if we did something mischievous?"

"I can't think of a reason why I'd be upset, can you?"

"Well, Mr. Policeman, what if when you get home you get undressed, really undressed."

"Sounds as if I'll be naked." Rader said trying to hide his excitement.

"Then you will take the blanket from the foot of the bed and meet me in the garage."

"What will you be wearing?" Rader asked.

"Wearing?" His wife asked in a whisper. "I'll have the other blanket and the car keys."

"Are we leaving the garage?" Rader asked as his attention shifted gears into a concerned thought.

"It wouldn't be any fun if we didn't. I think you should hurry."

The line disconnected. Rader hung up the phone, grabbed his jacket and raced to the doorway. The phone rang again before he could get out of the room. He dashed back and snagged the receiver.

"What did you forget sweetheart?"

"Well, darling," Captain McBride's voice snapped back at him. I just got a call from Organized Crime."

"Sorry Captain. What's up?"

"Seems as though all the crime families performed a disappearing act. Moe Brayden slipped his tail and vanished. The Lipsky kid had become invisible, and the entire Pataglia organization is off radar. Our Organized Task Force has no idea where they are."

"That will change when we pick up those two actors," Rader added quickly, trying to hang up and take flight.

"That won't be any time soon. Word on the street is they flew on a private jet to Parris and were lost in traffic. The team overseas believes they were driven out of France to only God knows where."

"What are you trying to tell me, Captain?" Rader asked a little too harshly.

"We're dead in the water until someone decides to resurface. Even then, it will all but impossible to make an arrest with what we have. Go home. We'll talk tomorrow."

Rader hung up and made a note to call Rollie and Drake in the morning. Perhaps they could help rekindle a trail that had gone fowl. Rollie had baggage he never talked about, and Drake was a book of knowledge. Drake Fargo forgot more than most men had learned about organized crime.

Drake took a shortcut west on Wilshire, north on Bundy and west again on Sunset. As he drove through the Palisades, Rollie was working at the pieces of their puzzle.

"Maybe Tawny was killed by Baxter?" Rollie asked.

Drake shook his head. "Why would he do that?"

"To remove the attention he was about to get from the pension fund." Rollie answered.

"And then they found out and killed him?" Drake asked as he thought it over.

"Makes sense doesn't it?" Rollie asked. "I mean, obviously the guy was up to his neck in cow paddies, so creating a diversion seems to be a reasonable thing to do."

"So that's it then?" Drake asked.

"What if it is?" Rollie quizzed.

"What if it isn't?" Drake asked.

"There you go again, spoiling all the logic." Rollie glanced out into the darkness.

"I think we should still talk to the actors, and Erinn will know where they are."

Rollie shook his head. The more he thought about it the more sense it made. "Somehow it makes more sense if Baxter did it. The actors are plenty dumb, and probably committed lots of rubbish but did they commit murder? Based on what we know, I don't think so. No, the actors had nothing to do with it."

Drake shot him a look. "So I should bill the studio for the work done, and we start looking for another case?"

"Sound good to me, I mean the guy is dead, and if we stop looking, the mob will leave us alone, right?"

"If you say so," Drake said turning his attention back to the road.

A CAR WITHOUT HEADLIGHTS hit them broadside. Glass flew everywhere. Drake lost control, and their SUV veered off the road, rolled several times down a deserted embankment and then hit a telephone pole with such veracity is snapped in two. The top piece of the pole landed over the SUV, crushing the cabin.

Rollie felt the warm liquid running down his face. He glanced over at Drake and found him unconscious. He could smell gasoline and saw the smoke coming from the engine compartment. He scrambled to free his body and found he was pinned in. He couldn't reach the seatbelt release, and wasn't sure he had feelings in his legs.

A slow panic started to settle in his gut. He thought about all the unfinished business, and all the things he wanted to do. He thought about grandma Millie, and that he'd never get to say goodbye. Kali's image appeared as though she was watching him die, and she cried. He loved her, and he hated her. She was, unintentionally, his soul mate. He glanced out, but his vision was blurred from the blood that covered his face. He ran from a crime family he hated and in a twisted way they came back to make a statement. You can never run away or quit a crime family, even if they despise you. His vision started to deteriorate, as though a cloud formation was waiting to take him away. Rollie closed his eyes and listened as the sound of traffic drifted off.

OTHER BOOKS

BY

WILLIAM BYRON HILLMAN

Zebra's Rock and Me
Ghosts and Phantoms Part I The Beginning
The Hard Way
Ghosts and Phantoms Part II
Veronique and Murray
April
Let's Sue 'Em
Quigley's Christmas Adventure
Prematurely Terminated
Bed Rap (February 2013)

AS A FILMMAKER

Quigley
The Adventures of Ragtime
Double Exposure
The Man From Clover Grove
Lovelines
The Photographer
Mr. Toy
Ragin Cajun
Prepping Quigley's Christmas Adventure

AUTHOR'S NOTE

The character Rollie Kemp was created and crafted around a CIA/FBI agent named John. I knew John for years while he was undercover and served opening. He was a great friend of the family and would have done anything for my children. His gift to them will never be forgotten. He passed a few years back, but his outlandish personality was so unique I wanted him to live on as long as I can create stories around him. He had a great sense of humor and maintain his love of life until taking his last breath. He helped hundreds, arrested many and told an unending list of stories that I came around to believe after meeting some of his comrades.

ABOUT THE AUTHOR

William Byron Hillman is an actor, filmmaker, novelist and public speaker.

William Byron Hillman is the published author of ten novels

Bill is also an actor with many films and television credits. He did a two-year stint on "Days of our Lives," appeared in films like Ice Station Zebra, has been a motivational speaker at college campuses nationwide, sold many screenplays and produced, directed and wrote a series of well known movies. As an actor/filmmaker/novelist, Bill has a global following.

Bill currently lives in South Carolina with his wife and 16 paws where he is putting the finishing touches on Bad Rap, Rollie Kemp's fourth thriller.

Author Web Site: http://www.williamhillman.com
Author's Amazon Page:
http://www.amazon.com/author/williamhillman
Author's Blog: http://williambyronhillman.blogspot.com

PREVIEW NEW BOOK

PREVIEW PROLOGUE

GHOSTS AND PHANTOMS II
Terminate Him

Rollie Kemp and Drake Fargo were still alive. Both had survived what should have been a fatal accident. He'd waited long enough.

It had been five months since he ordered everyone to pull back. He had a loathing for failure, and it gnawed constantly in his gut, reminding him of her mistake. She had never failed before, and he knew he should have had her chopped into little pieces and dumped into the ocean as shark food. Any man who failed him would be dead, so why had he spared her? The New York fiasco wasn't her fault. She didn't know that Richie Pataglia looked like Anthony's twin, and it was his fault for not telling her.

He didn't know why he was in hiding. No one knew he was the designer of trying to take out the Pataglia family. It was better, however, to be safe than sorry. Two months in Vancouver and three in San

Francisco gave everyone the impression he was dead. He had to make a play, and he had to get even. The deal was too powerful not to work. In the next year of operation, he'd be making tens of millions of dollars. Time to show the families how to do business in the current climate. The Pataglia's had gone too legit. Their time was up.

She called herself The Watcher. He knew where she was, what she wore and whom she hung out with. He knew her favorite restaurants and clubs and where she exercised. She tossed men around like they were in garbage bags and had no personal friends. She was all about business, trying to make up for her mistakes. He was tired of having her followed.

She had a pedigree for success, and right off, on her biggest job he'd given her, she screwed it up. The bitch should be dead. She owed him and begged for another chance. He relented. They spent a week in Hawaii together. She wasn't the best he'd ever had. He knew she was faking it, but the effort she put into the scam made it fun. She knew he'd have her followed, when he sent her away. She had the guts to do a job right under his nose to prove The Watcher was as good as advertised. Her extraordinary flamboyance is what made her attractive and why she was still alive. Even in failure she carried confidence, and he liked that. A beautiful woman who snuffed life with no more thought than stepping on a bug was impressive.

He stood on the edge of the pool and glared down at the ocean. San Francisco was cold year round. Once in a while the weather let up, and the sun would bake mid day only to tease for a mild evening that never came. What they got instead was crisp icy air that spread over everything in sight the moment the sun set. The blanket of unconscious, cold-blooded arctic wind, cut through the skin and demanded bones of the body to suffer for daring to enjoy. He pulled the jacket together and zipped it up to his neck. That's why most sporting goods stores in the area sold down-insulated jackets year round.

It was time. Five months were long enough to wait. No one would be expecting a second visit, not Rollie Kemp or the Pataglia's. If she failed him again, well, he didn't want to think about that. She was a pro, an ambitious girl who knew the business she was in. Failure wasn't an option.

Inside, he peeled off the thick winter jacket and hung it up. It was ironic trying to enjoy a summer evening in the middle of June when San Francisco obviously paid little attention to the calendar. He opened a briefcase and removed one of several prepaid cell phones. He powered the phone up as he moved to the small desk against the wall. He checked the calendar to make sure it was a Thursday. Rollie Kemp and Drake Fargo were creatures of habit. They had dinner every other Thursday at the same dumpy seafood restaurant in Westwood. He wouldn't put it past them to ordered the same thing on every visit. He punched in a number.

"Yeah, it's me. Are they at the restaurant yet?"

The voice on the other end was a man with a raspy sound. "They just arrived."

"What about our friend?"

"She's at the gym trying to work off the drinks she had with that tennis instructor she likes to tease."

"How much did she have to drink?"

The raspy voice hesitated. "Not sure."

"Let's try a different question. Does she look drunk?"

"No," The raspy voice answered, "but she's a drinker who can put the stuff away. Apparently she can still walk and drive."

"Where are the Pataglia's?"

"Still in the Florida Keys."

"Okay."

"Does okay mean what I think it does?" The raspy voice asked.

"Yeah, let's do this."

The Watcher was in the middle of an exercise class. Her hair was red with yellow, purple and dark blue strands hangin over her shoulders. She wore thick black-framed glasses that changed her facial appearance dramatically. The Watcher did the same exercises as the other twenty women in the room and hated every movement. Most were out of breath and covered in sweat. The Watcher didn't sweat and wasn't out of breath. She did the routine faster and better than the instructor even with a few drinks in her system. The buzz was minor. Having that fourth Scotch and water put her one over the limit and why she turned Mr. Handsome down. He was tempting but too cute for her tastes. She liked rough men, guys who enjoyed pushing women around, and he wasn't one of them. Her cell phone rang, and everyone looked at her purse. It stopped ringing after two rings. A frown settled on her face as her lips curled in a singularly unpleasant position. It was a call she wasn't expecting and had hoped wouldn't come anytime soon. She knew that was wishful thinking. They promised to come back and collect. She owed them, and they never forgot a debt. No one else had the number to that cell phone, so there was no doubt who was calling her. It was time to pay for her mistake, and the only way to stay alive was to honor whatever was asked of her.

Casually she left the aerobics class, grabbed a towel and headed into the dressing room. She checked all toilet stalls to make sure no one was there, and then made the call. She glanced at her reflection in the mirror and smiled. She looked like hell, exactly how she wanted to appear.

"I don't like to wait." His voice was sharp.

"Sorry, I was in an exercise class."

"Are you drunk?" Obviously he had someone watching.

"No," she answered. Damn them, they were still watching her every move. He knew where she was around the clock.

"It's time," he said softly.

"You want me to call you back?" She brushed her hair back and then reached into her purse for lipstick. As she applied it, she listened.

"No, I want you to get in your car and do what you did five months and four days ago. The only difference is your second effort will have different results. You'll need to get out of your car and make sure this time."

The Watcher over-coated her lips and quickly wiped them clean with a paper towel. Her mind started to race. The last time she ran Rollie Kemp and Drake Fargo off the road they survived. She didn't stick around because there were too many cars and witnesses around.

"When?" She asked.

"Tonight. They're having dinner right off Wilshire in Westwood. The place is called Fishy Stuff and More. You know where it is?"

"I know where it is." She kept her emotions in check.

"Good, how far away are you?"

"Twenty minutes." She answered while her mind danced with issues. She was driving her favorite Mercedes convertible. It was a good thing she hadn't registered it yet. She always bought her cars from private parties, and always paid cash. Damn, the car was unique and distinctive, and now it had to go. She glanced back to the mirror and gestured with a shrug that her look was okay and easy to change later. No one would know whom she was even if they got a good look at her.

"Do you need to know what they're eating?" His sarcastic ring was burning.

"What I need to know is where they are going?" She was under his thumb and knew it.

"Malibu. This is Thursday. They have dinner every Thursday, and then they go home. Real creatures of habit they are. Should be easy this time."

"Nothing is easy." She almost laughed. The guy on the other end of the line probably killed or had killed a dozen or more men. He knew how dangerous it was, and even if she disagreed with him there was nothing she could do. "Are they at the restaurant now?"

"They just arrived, so you have time. Behind the dumpster in the back of the restaurant is a box, gas can and canvas bag. Torch the wreckage."

"Why don't I just shoot them?" Her voice sounded cold and methodical.

"Because that's not how we did it last time." He snapped.

"Can I ask you something?" She tried not to purr. He wasn't like most of the guys she dated. He wasn't into purring.

"Make it quick."

"Why don't your guys just take 'em out?"

"That's what I paid you to do. I own you lady and the only way your debts will get settled are after I verify Rollie Kemp is dead. You understand me?"

"I understand."

"Don't try to run on me." He said it with laughter on his tongue.

"You trying to scare me?" She asked while remaining calm.

"No, but we've been watching you. Right now you're in a restroom. You're wearing black tights, a neon yellow skin-tight top and cute little pink tennis shoes."

The Watcher glanced around the room, her eyes drifting back to the mirror to verify they had someone in the gym watching her. The chill she felt inching down her spine was a reminder of whom she was dealing with.

"I never run, and you know that. Both men were lucky last time."

"Yeah, maybe so, but not this time right?"

"I'll make sure."

"Terminate him."

"I'm on my way."

He hung up on her. She threw the phone in her bag and walked out of the restroom.

She drove a few blocks and pulled into a grocery story parking lot. She parked on the side where no one was and striped out of the gym clothes. She put on an all black sweat suit, changed wigs, one with long red hair, and glassed with dark lenses. In the trunk, she kept a package of towels and cleaner. She put on a pair of thin black leather gloves and spent a few minutes wiping the car down. She sprayed the doors, handles, trunk and edges and then moved inside the vehicle where she sprayed and wiped everything in site. She was sweating, and she hated to perspire. Two things could go wrong.

Wiping the car down eliminated one of them but she still had to hit their car and still be able to drive away. That was tricky. If she hit them too hard, she'd do too much damage and might not be able to drive away. Getting stuck at the scene would not be good. If she made it, she'd torch the Mercedes closer to her apartment.

The fourth drink was still hanging around, and she hated to be buzzed while working. She got back behind the wheel and thought about Rollie Kemp. Damn him. Why didn't he die the first time she ran him off the road? She had never done a job the same way before and hated the idea of repeating the same act that failed the first time.

She drove west on Santa Monica Boulevard, cut over Venice to Wilshire and drove by the restaurant. She was more than aware that having four drinks could alter her actions. She assumed her blood alcohol level was off the charts even though she felt sharp. She stayed right at the speed limit and even passed a cop without raising a flag.

The Watcher pulled onto the side street next to the restaurant and parked. Behind the seafood diner she found the dumpster right where he said it would be, only a vagrant was standing inside the bin in search of God knows what. She stayed in the shadows and decided to look inside to make sure Rollie was still there. He was sitting with another man in a corner booth, chatting and stuffing their faces. From the looks of things, they were taking their final bites and would be leaving soon. They waved off refills of their drinks and gestured to the waitress for the check.

When The Watcher returned to the dumpster, the street person was out of the bin and exploring the box and bag left for her.

As the tattered man examined the gas can, she came up behind him. He heard footsteps and spun around to confront her. The Watcher paused. The man was late thirties or older, and obviously had been on the street a long time. He was alert to sounds and that made him dangerous. His face was covered with a ragged beard, and he hadn't had a haircut in months. His eyes darted nervously while his hands gathered his trophies and drew them closer. His clothes were filthy, and his body had a stagnant odor that was repulsive.

When she stepped forward, he pulled out a knife and waved it at her. She put up her hands indicating she didn't want trouble. The bum pointed the knife at her.

"Mine! I got here first, so back off."

"What if what you have there is my stuff?" The Watcher asked while her eyes checked behind him. Her peripheral vision said they were alone.

"You have proof?" The bum asked still pointing the knife at her.

She didn't have time to mess with this idiot. She moved to her left, kept her eyes on the knife and watched how fast he reacted. The guy was quicker than she thought he would be.

"I left it here earlier," The Watcher said while moving back to her right.

The bum followed her movement and shook his head. "Mine, finders keepers."

"Then I'm going to have to take it away from you."

He waved the knife at her, and that was his mistake. She lunged forward, grabbed his wrist and in one twisting movement brought his arm up and then down. The blade plunged into his belly. His hand jerked away from the knife and reached for her. That was his last mistake. The Watcher danced behind him in a blur and snapped his neck. His body crumbled to the ground. She straightened up, looked around and then pulled his body behind the dumpster. She grabbed the bag, box, and gas can in one swift movement and ran back to her car.

The moment she pulled to the corner, Rollie and his partner Drake Fargo drove by, and turned north on Bundy. She casually pulled out and followed. Rollie sat in the passenger seat while his hulking partner drove. Drake Fargo appeared to be bigger than the car and acutely uncomfortable. She drove by them when they turned west on Sunset, and sped up so she could reach the canyon before they did. She would wait in the same dark driveway as before, right across from the drop off. She pulled off Sunset and backed into the driveway. The Watcher checked the gasoline, the rags and her lighter. This time, she would make sure both died as they should have five months ago. Damn that fourth drink.

PREVIEW CHAPTER 1

Drake Fargo looked like Goliath behind the steering wheel of his brand new Sport Utility vehicle, and Rollie Kemp was amused every time Drake made an effort to adjust the seat back. At six feet eight and just a little south of three hundred pounds, Drake wasn't comfortable in any car. His size sixteen shoes, or so he said kept hitting the wrong pedal, and the trip was herky-jerky for the duration.

"You know what you look like?" Rollie asked half chuckling over the words.

"I don't want to hear any of your smart-ass comments, Rollie. Can't you see I'm driving here and need to concentrate?"

"Ah, so this and stop and go jerking us around stuff is because you're protecting the new car?" Rollie laughed.

Drake tossed a warning look at Rollie. Rollie ignored the look because he didn't know how to do shut up. He loved to tease Drake and had been doing so since they met the day Rollie got fired from his first acting role in a major studio film. The director encouraged him to deliver a good punch, so Rollie broke his nose. When it came time for Rollie to pretend to hit the star, the director, and everyone else on the set knew the actor would be afraid of Rollie, so the guy ducked the wrong way and bam! Rollie broke his nose too, and then the guy insisted they fire Rollie. He finished the job but couldn't find another job anywhere in town as an actor. Drake happened to be on the set that day and witnessed Rollie's lack of anger management. When the day ended, and Rollie was told not to come back, Drake offered him a job. Rollie laughed at the idea of being a private detective, but he kept running into Drake. After a spell, they went out to dinner, and Rollie discovered the job offer was genuine. It was a crazy idea, so ridiculous Rollie took him up on it, and they became a extraordinary team. They worked on several cases, but the last one was a dandy.

"Drake, when we get down to Pacific Coast Highway, let's stop at that weird little grocery store and I'll buy us some of that freeze dried fish?"

"I hate fish," Drake answered and continued to struggle with getting comfortable.

"You keep driving as you are and I'll give up eating for a week," Rollie said. "You don't hate fish either. Last time you ate the whole package.

"You didn't say it was Salmon." Drake said still adjusting the seat to different positions.

"I hate to tell you this, Drake, but Salmon is fish."

"I hate this car. Never should've bought it."

"So take it back and get a bigger one." For five, months, Rollie listened to Drake's complaints about how small the car was. Three days after taking delivery he loathed it, and every day since he voiced his displeasure. "I have a great idea. Maybe you should cut back on steroids, and start eating healthy like me."

Drake took one hand off the wheel in a threatening gesture. "You know what I want to do right now?"

"I can't imagine," Rollie said, "but I'm sure you going to tell me, right?"

Drake waved his fist out of frustration. Rollie leaned against the door and enjoyed watching Drake huff and puff because he bought a car that was too small for his massive body. Drake had no fat on his body. It wasn't from being overweight that made all cars small; it was his massive frame and even larger shoe size. "I want to pull over and kick some sense into that empty head of yours."

The car slowed down and then sped up at Drake maneuvered the curves.

"So pull over. We'll exchange a few punches. I'll wear your oversized body down, and we can work up an appetite. Let's do it."

Drake watched Rollie sit forward in anticipation of actually getting out and exchanging blows with him. Rollie never lost his motto, punch first and ask questions later. "You're crazy, Rollie. Sit back. We're not stopping."

"Aw gee," Rollie sat back. "One of these days..."

"I'm going to kill you, but until then why don't you shut up and let me concentrate on the road? I hate winding through this at night."

"Your list of hating things is growing," Rollie laughed.

"I'm warming you Rollie, I'm gonna smack you in the head."

"Oh wow, I'm scared now tough guy."

They were traveling west on Sunset Boulevard, through a canyon area between Brentwood and Pacific Palisades when they came around a curve in the road and got hit, broadsided. The car that hit them came out of nowhere. Glass from the driver's door shattered, spraying tiny fragments everywhere. Control vanished, sending the sports utility vehicle out-of-control. They hit the curb sideways and went airborne sailing down into a ravine. The ground raced by as the strapping machine hit the ground and started rolling over and over down the hillside. Car parts were ejected. Windows broke out, and Rollie Kemp held on to his seatbelt as he watched Drake Fargo, his partner, bounce viciously against the steering wheel and the interior vehicle walls. A plethora of circular blood droplets splattered everywhere. The chunk of metal resembling what was left of the sleek mechanical wonder, teetered, and then rolled one last time coming to rest up-side-down in a thundering clash with the rock-covered hillside.

The heat from the engine was intense. Rollie felt a trickle of sweat running down the middle of his back. He heard footsteps and strained to see who was coming but his vision had changed to a slow-motion mode as the person walked half-way down the hillside.

"Drake, someone's coming," Rollie whispered.

He couldn't see whom it was. His vision blurred from a warm liquid that stung his eyes. Then he saw a blurred image of the person holding a large jar with a rag protruding out the top.

"What the hell is he doing Drake?" Rollie turned to his partner and shook him.

A lighter was ignited, and the cloth set on fire.

"Oh my God, c'mon Drake, we gotta get out of here." Rollie scrambled to get free. The seat belt had him pinned in. Drake Fargo, his partner was unconscious behind the steering wheel. "Get out," Rollie screamed in an almost inaudible whisper. He tried to shout, but nothing came out of his mouth. He looked out as the jar rose and was hurled right at him. "No!" He whispered.

Panic swallowed him. The jar with a burning rag slammed against the wreckage and burst into flames. His skin started melting. This was it. He was going to die. He struggled to no avail. Flames grew. Rubber burned, and there was no way out. He turned to Drake as the older man opened his eyes.

"Goodbye Rollie," Drake said calmly, nodded once and closed his eyes.

Rollie heard a car engine start up and take off.

Rollie opened his eyes with a start, waking from the nightmare. He emitted a muffled scream, turned his head and found the face of Drake Fargo inches away from his nose. All he could smell was garlic from the seafood dinner they had just eaten. He remembered Drake had ordered some shrimp soaked in garlic-laden noodles spread over a thick steak. The way he ordered his dinner was laughable. He said it because it sounded good. A gourmet eater he wasn't. Rollie tried to sit up but quickly discovered he was pinned to the ground. He jerked his head right and then left. Drake's sporty vehicle was burning just over a small slope in the hillside above his left shoulder. A burning tire on the SUV burst, sending debris over them. The heat from the fierce blaze burned at his skin. He heard a siren, in the distance, growing, coming closer. Drake was covered in blood. Rollie looked down at what he could see of his body, and he also had red splatter all over his torso. Up at the top of the hillside people were gathering, looking down at the fire. They obviously couldn't see Rollie or Drake, and Rollie couldn't free his hands to wave at them. It took forever to realize they weren't coming to help. The crowd didn't want to help, they were more interested in watching his car melt into a heap of unrecognizable metal. He tried to focus, but he had no memory to focus on. Was he dead? Was this all a dream? Think dammit! Seafood dinner, pretty waitress with fantastic legs, sweet tasting red wine that Drake ordered without looking at the menu, and garlic, lots of garlic. Rollie could still taste the shrimp and mussels rolled in a noodle garlic sauce. The steak was so tender he could slice it with a spoon. He flinched, recalling the flying glass that showered over his whole body when they got hit. It was deliberate and that he was sure of. Someone had tried to kill them again, in the same place as last time. His eyes traveled over to his partner, Drake Fargo. He was a legendary private eye with a reputation of being tough as nails. The side he didn't show was the one he had with Rollie, a brotherly love that no one knew existed.

"Drake, are you dead?" Rollie asked in trepidation.

"No," Drake mumbled and opened one eye. He stared at Rollie.

"Can you get off me?" Rollie asked in a voice just above the volume of a whisper.

"Negative," Drake's response was weak. "I can't move and not sure I should try."

"Guess you'll have to buy another car," Rollie whispered.

"I was too big for that one anyway," Drake coughed.

"Did you pull me out?" Rollie couldn't remember how he got out of the car.

"You pulled me out and nearly broke my feet jerking on me, don't you remember?" Drake added as he took a deep breath and his entire body shook.

"I told you your feet were too big." Rollie strained to see over the knoll, but all he could see was the top of the hillside where everyone was gathering.

A cop car followed by a second one screeched to a halt. An ambulance roared in behind the cops, and suddenly a group came scrambling down the hillside. Two fire trucks arrived behind them. Men were running dragging hoses were down the hillside. Rollie tried to call out, but his open mouth emitted a near-silent garble.

"We're over here." Rollie tried to scream, but it came out a whisper.

"Is that as loud as you can yell?" Drake asked in an equally weak voice.

"You think you can do better, you scream," Rollie spat out sarcastically.

"I can't breathe," Drake mumbled, gasping for air. "I think one of my lungs has collapsed."

"That's a lame excuse if I ever heard one."

Rollie tried to get up again, but Drake Fargo, all six-feet eight of him had Rollie pinned to the ground. Rollie tried to push two hundred seventy pounds of dead weight off his body without luck. He couldn't budge the thickset man, and it hurt like hell trying.

They were laughing about the case they had just stopped working. The case wasn't solved. It just ended strangely. When there were doubts about a case, they'd go out and share a meal at their favorite Seafood restaurant. It wasn't a celebration. It was facing the fact it ended abruptly and intensely creepy. All the players they were investigating vanished. They had other unusual cases, so this wasn't actually a deal they would lose sleep over. It resembled another case, the former actor one, where the actor shot himself, accused a neighbor of doing the deed and then accidentally put a bullet in his leg showing his girlfriend how it was done the first time. That case ended quickly when the actor got arrested after making a false police report and the whole case was dropped. It was part of what being a private detective was all about. Some cases involved sick people wanting to hurt others, and some were just stupid. He watched the firemen spray down the burning wreckage. They were professionals standing a few feet away and didn't even look their way. How did that commercial go, something about professional grade? Yeah, that was it. The firemen were professional grade firefighters. More cops showed up, and they were all over the hillside with flashlights. Why were the professional grade hero's looking over there? He and Drake were just to their left. Any idiot could see they weren't in the burning car or around the various parts to the wreckage. Were they blind? Then a bright flash of light slammed into his eyes and blinded him.

Rollie tried to blink away from glaring light, but someone was holding his eyelid open. He tried to yell and then felt a tube in his throat.

"Mr. Kemp?" A voice came from behind the light.

Rollie mumbled a sound from deep in his throat, as though he could answer the guy.

"You were in an accident, and now you're at the hospital. We're taking you into surgery, but rest assure you're in good hands."

What? Whose good hands? Who was this guy? Wait. Rollie blinked. They were on the move, pushing his bed down a white hallway. The walls sped by making him dizzy. He had questions. Who would give them permission to operate without his approval was the first one?

The heart monitor beeped, a suction device hissed, and something was pumping air that made an horrible sound. Rollie opened his eyes slowly. His body felt disconnected. He couldn't feel his arms or legs and strained to see if they were still there. They were. He glanced around finding his bed surrounded by a curtain. He heard voices down the hall, and then someone a lot closer than he liked, coughed. His tongue felt immense, his mouth dry. He couldn't move but could sense someone sitting next to the bed. It was painful, but he slowly maneuvered his head to the side and found Kali, his ex-wife, all curled up in a chair. She looked like hell, and yet his heart skipped a beat. He didn't know why he continued to love her, why he cared. While he studied in law school, she partied. She got hooked on drugs, drank too much and slept with every guy she met. Then, when life took an ugly turn, she'd crawl back to Rollie for help. Why he continued to support her, was beyond him. In spite of the roughness around the edges, she was still beautiful. She opened her eyes, and her smile forced him to take a deep breath.

"Hi," she had the sexiest voice he had ever heard.

"How did you know I was here?" Talking hurt his throat.

"I heard about the accident on the news and called Detective Rader."

"How long have you been here?" Rollie was afraid to ask.

"Two days. I had to sign for your surgery." Kali's voice remained a soft whisper.

"How could you sign? You're my ex-wife."

"I lied. They said you needed surgery that you might die, and I couldn't lose you that way, Rollie. I still love you."

Kali got up and kissed his forehead.

"You still using?" Rollie asked. He knew the answer, but he wanted to hear if she would lie to him again.

"A little," she brushed her hair back, tucking loose ends behind her ear. She looked tired, wore no makeup and still exposed a regal beauty. Her eyes were an unusual shade of blue and her oblong face was near perfect. She had high cheekbones, sculptured lips that begged to be kissed, and golden hair that naturally carried various platinum and brown streaks throughout. She could have earned a living as one of the highest paid models in the world. Instead, she gave up.

"You okay?" Rollie studied her face. Tears swell around the edges of her eyes.

"I have to go." She ducked beneath the curtain and walked out of the room.

"Kali?" Rollie called after her, but she didn't stop.

Rollie closed his eyes, sucked in a deep breath that hurt like hell and drifted off.

The curtain jerked back making an awful sound, and a nurse entered his private area.

Rollie opened his eyes, expecting to see Kali, but frowned when he realized the new visitor was a nurse.

"You're awake?" Her voice was warm and velvety. "I'm Cindy, your day nurse."

"Did you see the woman who just left?" Rollie asked.

"No one has been in here for the last six hours," Cindy answered all business.

Rollie nodded, running his tongue around his mouth where the tubes were. She bent over, and he looked into her eyes, pretty blue-green eyes and with brown dots. She smiled.

"My partner?" Rollie spoke over his swollen tongue.

"Out of his second surgery, and while it will take some time, he will recover." She took his temperature, put some small do-dad on his finger and connected a blood pressure machine to his arm. She stepped back to watch the reading.

"How is Drake?" Rollie was sorry he said anything. His throat was raw. He watched the nurse perform her duties. She was extremely professional and impressive. She moved around the bed, made some notes in a hanging chart and then fluffed his pillow.

"I know talking hurts so I'll try to answer all your questions quickly." She smiled again. She wasn't a beautiful woman, but her smile and those incredible eyes were particularly appealing. "Mr. Fargo had four broken ribs, a punctured lung, concussion, dislocated shoulder and severely bruised kidneys. Like you, he had some internal bleeding that luckily got stopped. He is going to be in a lot of pain. His burns are not as severe as yours and will heal without scarring.

"Burns? I have burns?"

"That will hurt, but heal."

"What about the rest of me?" Rollie asked.

"It's a long story." The smiled again. "Would you like to discuss it with the doctor?"

"It hurts to talk, so the less said the better. Is there a short version?

"Seventy nine stitches, bruised kidney's, bleeding in your colon, and you lost your spleen. On the bright side, there were miraculously no major bones broken other than your nose, which will probably hurt more than the stitched wounds. Overall you're a very lucky man to be alive. Your hands were badly burned, but once again, they will heal nicely. They will bring your friend up as soon as he's out of recovery." She checked Rollie over one more time and turned to leave.

"Can I live without a spleen?" Rollie asked.

"You can." She answered.

"Thank you," Rollie mumbled.

"You're welcome, but I think you should thank the doctor when he makes his rounds a little later. I'll be back to check on you in a while. If you need anything, just push the button." She gave him one more smile, closed the curtain and left.

"Great," Rollie garbled.

"You could be dead," a deep voice added, "so don't act like an ungrateful pig."

Rollie looked up as the curtain opened revealing detective John Rader.

"Thought you weren't going to talk to me again?" Rollie studied the detectives face for a reaction but nothing surfaced.

Rader pulled the curtain closed and moved over to Rollie's side where he sank into the only chair in the room. He shook his head as if an extraordinarily sad moment had passed between them. "Someone out there really doesn't like you." Rader glanced over all the bandages and tubes running into Rollie.

"You drove all the way over here to tell me that?" Rollie asked.

"Did you know two guys burned to death in a terrible accident off Sunset the other night?"

"How did the two guys die?" Rollie quizzed.

"The news reported the accident as just another careless mess on a torturous span of roadway."

"What's up, John?" Rollie turned his head as far as it would go and found his old friend. He remembered

308

going through the police academy with Rader and how Rader was only one or two guys who came to visit Rollie after the drunk hit his car. That accident spoiled Rollie from graduating from the academy and becoming a cop. He laughed quietly at the current situation he was living through now.

"We're pretty sure it was a hit, or maybe I should call it a planned accident. Whoever it was waited to hear about the results, and we didn't want to disappoint them. When they figure out you and Drake are still alive, you should be well enough to protect yourself."

"That's comforting," Rollie said as his mind started racing. He assumed it was the same guy who tried to kill him, the one he somehow shot along with the walls and filing cabinets in his office.

"You think you two gentlemen could find it in your heart to take a vacation and get out of the way for a couple of weeks?" Rader said in a suggestive tone.

"I don't get it," Rollie said while watching Rader. The guy was a good cop, but he didn't hide his concern worth a damn.

"Five months ago it looked as though all the crime families were going to war. You survived a strange accident, but when the Pataglia's nearly got wiped out every cop in the country braced for the worst. Nothing happened. Whoever started it pulled back, but now, with you accident, we think it's all about to start again."

"If they want me dead, they'll find me." Rollie closed his eyes. He ran from a crime family, and the slight change in his name from Kempanelli to Kemp was meant to send a message. He wasn't interested in going back, and now they were coming after him. What the hell did his old man do? Or was it something his Uncle Charlie did?

309

"Our friends at organized crime believe the Pataglia shooting and failed attempt on his life has changed the landscape. Retribution is a bitch, but sometimes even a sick mind can re-think his position because the path he's on is too life-threatening. It's not really that amazing to understand survival is king. Right now things are sizzling. The wrong move could start a war no one wants."

"So what, you think they all just packed up and left town and now they're back?" Rollie struggled to get a good look at Rader. The pain in his neck was intense.

"I'll keep some men on your room for a few days, just in case they do come back."

Rollie felt sick. His stomach churned. "I'm not that important."

"You are what they think you are, and now we know." Rader got up.

"Know what?" Rollie asked.

"You're in the way. Tell Drake I stopped by." Rader pulled the curtain back.

"I get mad, John, not scared." Rollie chewed down on the inside of his cheek.

"Yeah, I know all about your temper. Punch first and ask questions later. Not a good plan when the other guy has a gun." Rader glanced back at his friend. "I can keep you dead for a week or so, but after that you're on your own. Take Drake and go visit your grandmother."

"I can't bring her into this mess," Rollie said trying to sit up.

"That's the whole point. If you don't go see her, you know she'll be out here the minute she hears about the accident."

"You wouldn't dare..." Rollie's voice dropped into a growl.

Rader stood at the curtain looking back and making Rollie feel inadequate.

"Like I said, getting away is a good thing. You have a week. When Millie gets on a train and races out here, it won't be my fault. If something happens to her, I hope your shoulders are a lot wider than you think they are."

Rader turned and walked off pulling the curtain closed behind him.

"Come back here, Rader, you hear me? Rader? Rader?" His voice fell on deaf ears. Great, he had a week to heal up enough to get out of town. Drake would never go for it, unless he was so out of it pain would invalidate his reluctance. This wasn't over, not until it was a minute past midnight on a day their ultimatum expired.

www.ingramcontent.com/pod-product-compliance
Lightning Source LLC
Chambersburg PA
CBHW060521180626
46817CB00002B/447